THE END OF HIS JOURNEY

A MYSTERY

Susan Hanafee

ISBN 978-1-66782-042-2 (Print)
ISBN 978-1-66782-043-9 (eBook)

The haunting scene on the cover was taken by my friend, Rob Barke, an Englishman whose photographs I discovered as part of the *Cloud Appreciation Society* on Facebook. His work is amazing and inspiring. He is truly an artist with a lens. And a good guy who loves animals, especially dogs.

I am also indebted to George (Bo) Hamrick and Jack Hanafee who served as my weapons advisors for the book, fully aware that I am not a gun enthusiast. And grateful to editors Colleen O'Brien and Marcy Shortuse and other friends who volunteered to read my novel and offer valued opinions.

Finally, special thanks, as always, to my partner Ian Rogerson who brings me great joy and happiness and doesn't complain that I prefer pounding out stories on my computer to flying around the world.

"Based on the investigation conducted, this case will be closed as unfounded, as the elements of a crime do not exist."

– Sheriff's Office criminal investigation report May 15, 2001.

PROLOGUE

September 23, 2000

911. What's your emergency?
Hello?

This is 911. Sir, do you need police, fire or ambulance?

Ambulance. Jesus…man…he fucking shot himself in the head.

What's the address?

What's the address!? We have a gunshot wound to the head. We need an ambulance now.

OK. What's the address?

15th Street. Seaside Cottage.

What's the phone number?

What is it? Maybe 011…something. I don't know.

How'd he get shot in the head?

He put a gun against his head and fucking pulled the trigger.

OK. How old is he?

21, 22, don't know for sure.

Is he conscious and breathing?

He's bleeding out the fucking head. Hurry please.

We're going to send somebody right there. Just stay on the line with me, ok?

He's definitely gasping for air that's for sure. When the hell will someone get here?

They shouldn't be real long, sir. They were dispatched right after you called.

He's gasping for air. Oh fuck. He stopped breathing.

CHAPTER 1

Monday, December 14, 2019

Wes Avery was nursing his first beer at the Tarpon Bar when he found himself fixated on the man with the pale face and a two, maybe three-day stubble six barstools away.

Wes had spent 35 years in the newspaper business in Indiana and never once taken a real vacation. His skin was so pale back then that his fellow reporters used to tease him about having a Vitamin D deficiency. Now, with a tan to show for the few months he'd been in southwest Florida, he was questioning why the fellow at the end of the bar looked so anemic.

Who lives down here and doesn't get nailed by the sun? Wes mused. Was this guy a visitor seeking a cold one on a hot day? Or a local who didn't get out much? When the bartender called the man by name, Wes decided the latter must be true.

"This 'un's number four, Johnny Boy," the bartender said as he sat a drink in front of the man. Clear liquid displaced by ice cubes kissed the rim of the drinker's glass. Anesthetization without olives or a twist.

The man grunted, took a couple of gulps, looked Wes's direction with unseeing eyes and downed the rest. He threw some bills on the bar and stood up, wavering for a few seconds. When he'd steadied himself, he put on a pair of aviator sunglasses and staggered outside.

The hot air from the outside rushed to meet the air-conditioning inside, creating a draft that caused the red and green tinsel hung around the doorway to shimmy.

"You wanna 'nother beer?" the bartender asked Wes whose gaze was being held captive by the now closed door, the passing thought that Christmas was only a couple of weeks away and the haunting appearance of a man who had aroused his reporter's curiosity.

"Yeah. Why not?" Wes turned to the man and flashed a smile. "My name's Wes Avery. I'm the new reporter at *The Island Sun*. Now that I've tasted your Michelob on draft, I figure we'll be spending a lot of time together. Like Bogey said to Claude Rains in *Casablanca* …'Louis, I think this is the beginning of a beautiful friendship.'"

Wes's face reddened at the stupidity of his remark. He didn't even know the guy. Probably wouldn't be able to place his face in a different setting. "But, then, I'm guessin' that your name isn't Louis. Maybe Billy or Bobby?"

The bartender snickered and reached out to shake Wes's hand. "Fred Norman. My mom used to call me Sunshine. Somewhere along the way it got shortened. Folks been callin' me Shine ever since – more than 40 years now."

"Well Shine, happy to know you. Real happy." Wes gripped the bartender's hand for a couple of seconds, wondering why it had taken him so long to visit this establishment, then reached for his glass again.

"What's the story behind this place…this little island in southwest Florida that looks like it got stuck in the 1950s," Wes asked when the bartender returned with a second beer in a frosty glass. It was as good a conversation starter as any. Wes was sure that Shine would end up being a valued informant; a source that in its early stages needed cultivation.

Shine grabbed a paper napkin and stuck it under Wes's drink, which was already starting to sweat. "Not much to tell. Lots of rich people. The occasional celebrity. A few poor folks who've been here for decades and have land but no money. We've been hit by hurricanes a couple of times. Always survived. Just had a bad spell of red tide. Got everyone stirred up about usin' fertilizer."

Wes focused his hazel eyes on Shine's creviced face and shaved head and thought about his voice; it was as mellow as the beer Wes was consuming. Maybe it was his imagination, but it felt like everyone Wes had met since he moved to southwest Florida was fodder for a few paragraphs in his weekly newspaper column. Interesting people who'd lived hard lives and didn't object to being the topic of a few words in print. Shine was probably one of those. Wes would find out soon enough.

"The town shuts down from July through mid-October. 'Cept for the handful of people here year-round, you won't see a dog on these streets in August and September. Some say that's the best time to be here. Others say that's the months when bad things happen."

"Bad things? In this place? Like what? Drug-running? Murders?" Wes chuckled at the irony in his comment.

Several weeks earlier, he'd played a bit part in the arrest of a local realtor who was using the island as a base to sell drugs into Canada. One of the realtor's cohorts had been murdered. Two others tried to escape, but their private plane had crashed somewhere near the border. A local fisherman – a man named Frank Johnson – was involved but working undercover with drug enforcement officials out of Miami. No confirmation but that was the word on the street.

Wes's gal pal, Leslie Elliott, uncovered the criminal activity and had her life threatened in the process. Wes and the island's deputy sheriff, Bruce Webster, helped her bring the realtor to justice.

It was a shocking turn of events for a small community that was known for its fishing and idyllic lifestyle and that seldom dealt with anything more criminal than purloined fishing equipment or a bit of malicious gossip designed to tarnish someone's reputation.

"Sounds like you know about the drug bust," Shine said, dumping the glass used by the pale-faced man into a sink of soapy water. "Mostly the bad stuff here has to do with the feeling that settles over the town after the heat and mosquitoes have sucked the life out of it. Late summer I'm always breakin' up fights in here. And now there's this crazy December heat wave. Global warming shit."

Shine nodded as if to agree with his own assessment, and then turned his attention to a man wearing a gray Tampa Bay Buccaneers cap; baseball style with the bill curved down around his face. He'd slipped onto the seat once occupied by the pale-faced man and was staring expectantly at the bartender. The guy looked familiar, but Wes couldn't place him.

After a few minutes, Wes returned his focus to his half-empty glass. What would his daily intake of beer be now that he'd given up the hard stuff?

He was 59. Sometimes he thought his best years were behind him: given freely to right the wrongs committed by society on the little guy. Every story he'd ever written about problems and heartache in the big city had lined his face and marked his psyche. He was okay with that.

But now unnamed sources and reporter bias ruled the day. The 24-hour news cycle was emphasizing speed over balance and skewing the truth. Cocky TV reporters were using journalism to create personal brands; drawing attention to themselves and not the story.

Colleges were still turning out a new crop of hungry J-school grads every year, making it easier for newspapers to get rid of the old-timers with their higher salaries. Wes, for one, was glad when he was offered a buyout from Gannett. He took their money and told them what they could do with their "piece of shit rag."

Despite everything, he loved the business and was hoping that old-time journalism still thrived on this small island where the weekly newspaper reported on golf cart parades, the proliferation of iguanas and who attended what party, but wasn't afraid to tackle the occasional controversy or criminal intrigue.

After all, the paper was named *The Island Sun* and was intended to shed light on the darkest corners of the community. Or so Wes was told by the publisher Sara Fortune, the woman who hired him. She was smallish with a quirky sense of humor. She once worked for the *Detroit Free Press* and quit to marry a wealthy auto company executive. When he died, she moved south and bought *The Sun*.

"What's the deal with the guy at the end of the bar?" Wes asked when Shine returned to the sink. "He got a problem?"

6

"The guy in the Bucs hat? Don't know him," the bartender responded without glancing up.

"Naw, the one before him. The one that left after drink number four. Your limit or his?"

Shine put down the glass he was drying and gave Wes a skeptical look. Wes wondered if he'd gone too far; asked too many questions too soon.

"John Mason," Shine finally responded. "My limit. He's here almost every day. Talk to him. He'll tell you his story. What he won't tell you is that his life ended some 20 years ago – on September 23, 2000. Finishing off his body with vodka is takin' a little longer than he expected."

"That bad, huh?"

"Yep," Shine said, turning and heading for a second man who'd slipped onto a barstool halfway between Wes and the customer in the Bucs hat.

Wes took that as a sign that the bartender was done handing out information on Johnny Boy – at least for today. He finished his beer, dropped a $20 bill on the bar and gave a nod in Shine's direction. "See you tomorrow."

Wes stepped outside, letting the screened-door slam behind him. The thwack of wood against wood reminded him of his childhood in the Midwest, where kids spent their summers playing hide and seek outside and their families didn't need a video doorbell to feel secure. He hoped this place was as safe. Everyone said it was. But the drug-running events that unfolded shortly after his arrival and a recent surge of golf cart thefts made him wonder.

He started toward his one-bedroom apartment over the bank but changed his mind, heading instead for the newspaper office a block down the main drag. It was housed in the second story of a 1940s-style island building with a rusty metal roof. It didn't advertise its presence, but everyone who lived on the island at one time or another had climbed the 15 steps to pay homage to this haven of old-fashioned journalism. They carried with them a hand-written press release or obituary or wanted to know why their subscription hadn't made it to their northern residence during the summer.

Wes thought about meeting the small staff for the first time and the feeling he had that he was home again. There was nothing artificial about

7

these folks. They talked his lingo, shared his skepticism, had the same off-beat sense of humor. They fit the cliché he'd heard about real newsies since he was a kid: they had ink running through their veins, a sense of righteous indignation close to the surface and a hunger for the truth.

It was after 6 and only Randy Long, the layout man, was still in the office. He worked in cargo shorts and a t-shirt and wore his graying hair in a ponytail. Randy never had much to say, but Wes knew it was all there – all inside Randy's head. Hadn't he touched every story that appeared in *The Sun* for the last 20 years or more?

"Hey Randy. I was having a couple of beers at the Tarpon Bar when I ran into a guy named Mason, John Mason. You know him?"

Randy glanced up from the screen he was working on. Wes couldn't quite read him. According to his fellow workers, few ever could. "Yep," he finally said and fell silent.

Wes pressed on. "You know how you see someone and they burrow into your thoughts and you want to know more about them?"

Randy sighed, stopped what he was doing and looked up at Wes. His faced remained expressionless but it had a sullenness that wasn't there a second earlier. "Ya wanna know about John Mason? I'm tired, man, and don't want the burden of that story on my mind when I go to bed. Tomorrow. I'll give you some answers tomorrow."

"Fair enough," Wes said, suddenly wondering what he was going to have for dinner.

Tuesday morning, December 15

Wes arrived at the newspaper office shortly after 9 to discover a yellowed copy of *The Sun* on his desk. It was dated December 15, 2000. The front-page headline said that the state attorney's office was still waiting for investigation reports in the death of Toby Mason. He needed to thank Randy for making his request a priority but wanted to read the story first.

"The state Attorney General's office has placed the ball back in the court of the county sheriff's office, saying it has not received enough information to join the investigation into the shooting death of a local man in September.

"A sheriff's office spokesperson said it has been four weeks since the request was made concerning the shooting death of 22-year-old Toby Mason in the early morning hours of September 23. The shooting took place at a residence on the Seaside Cottage property at 15th Street and the beach.

"First reports said that Mason was in the kitchen when someone handed him a gun, and Mason placed the muzzle to his own head and fired a shot.

"At this point the case remains open while the sheriff's office determines whether the shooting was a suicide or an accident."

Wes let out a low whistle, scrutinizing Randy who was busy positioning ad layouts for Friday's edition. He must have had a lot of sleepless nights over this incident. Locals, Wes had learned, were a close group. They tolerated the snowbirds but there was a genuine bond among the folks who grew up in this place that masqueraded as paradise but didn't always live up to its image.

He reread the story. Almost three months had passed since the shooting and law enforcement didn't seem all that interested in what happened. His instinct that something was wrong was spurred on by Randy's anger over the incident two decades after the fact.

The Sun's masthead featured a glowing ball with rays reaching out over the outline of an island with palm trees. For each edition, Randy Long would write a cryptic, almost unnoticeable comment in small letters along one of the rays. The one he'd written for the December 15, 2000 edition, like so many Randy penned, had a meaning known only to him.

"I hear the sound of a thousand clowns crying."

CHAPTER 2

I f the small brown moth noticed the six-inch gecko slinking its way, it gave no sign. Snap. The insect's wings spread out on either side of the lizard's mouth; its body trapped by tiny reptilian teeth. Impressive, Wes thought. Like a baseball player snagging a line drive.

Clutching a large cup of iced tea, Wes leaned back on the bench situated in a small oasis of cabbage palms where he and the hungry lizard had sought refuge from the sweltering temperatures. It was mid-morning, and he needed some fresh air before heading back to the office to work on his weekly column.

The surprising December heat wave was proving painful for a northerner like Wes. Either his body would acclimate to the temperatures and humidity that hit the mid-90s before 10 a.m., or he assumed that one day he'd simply melt into a puddle, leaving only a pair of black sunglasses to validate his existence. Everyone told him the heat was historic. It would ease up soon. His unanswered plea was "When?"

The lizard finished the moth, wings and all, bounced up and down in an affirmation of life and thrust forward his ruby throat. *Here I am ladies. Fed and ready to propagate our species.*

Spotting one of his kind, the lizard raced onto the asphalt driveway that separated the small shady area from the neighboring grocery and a potential paramour. It was a reckless move. When he'd gone a foot or so into the white-hot heat, he hesitated. Slowed down. Stopped. He never moved again. He was fried in the pursuit of love.

"Crap," Wes said, his eyes widening as he witnessed the lizard's final movements. He got up, went over to the deceased creature and picked up the tiny body. He could feel the searing pavement through the bottom of his sneakers. Like the moth, the poor lizard didn't know what hit him. Wes placed the lifeless creature in the shade of a red-flowering hibiscus bush. Maybe, by some miracle, he would rally.

"Another one bites the dust," Randy Long said as he walked into the shady area where Wes was reclaiming his seat on the bench.

"They say Georgia asphalt's hot. I'm guessing it's over 140 degrees on this pavement." Wes said, flicking the sweat off his forehead with his forefinger. "But it's not like there aren't thousands of those lizards around."

A breeze came out of nowhere, rustling the vegetation. Wes lifted his head, turning his face to get the full effect. Randy sat down next to him; the two soaking up the moment and seeming to welcome the cooling caress from nature.

"Did you see the article?" Randy asked when the breeze stilled and the heat could be felt again.

"I did. Thanks."

"There's more. I didn't have time to dig 'em all up. We got police documents, photos, the 911 call. Even stuff from a private investigator. Some woman Mason hired. We talked about doin' an anniversary piece several years ago. Couldn't bring ourselves to dredge up those memories. Maybe it's time we did."

"I get it," Wes said. "Young guy dies. Father and community are distraught over the suicide. Guess that doesn't happen here much. But it's been more than 20 years and…."

"You don't get it," Randy interrupted, his face flushing. "The kid didn't blow his brains out on purpose. Some of the old-timers here, like me, think there was more to it, and the officials covered it up. We're all party to the shame of it 'cause we kept our mouths shut. Twenty years later and there are still no answers."

Randy was like an afternoon thunderstorm in Florida. Filled with fury for a few minutes, then still. He stood up and headed for the newspaper office without a goodbye. Wes didn't take the anger in Randy's voice personally. He knew it was the situation that raised Randy's pique.

So, this was the local take on Toby Mason's death: a mystery that hung over the community. He felt it from Shine, too.

Maybe there was a reason he'd asked Shine about the pale-faced drunk at the bar. A friend of Wes's used to talk about the universe and how everything worked on what he called the big plan. Wes always scoffed at the idea that life was anything more than a series of random events. When things like this happened, though, he wondered.

Wes got up and glanced over at the lizard, still lifeless at the base of the bush. "Rest in peace, little buddy," he said as he turned to go to the newspaper office. "Maybe I can help young Toby do the same."

CHAPTER 3

Wes had finished the lead paragraph of his column when the phone rang and the name Leslie Elliott appeared on his screen. It was a call he was always happy to answer. Today, even though her voice seemed calm, what she had to say made Wes uneasy.

"It's me. Frank's here. Jamie Thompson's alive. And, I guess, coming after me."

"Thompson alive?" *Frank there?* Wes couldn't believe what he was hearing. The police were reporting that Jamie Thompson, one of the drug dealers who eluded capture several weeks ago, was not killed in the crash of his small plane as previously thought.

And, now, Frank Johnson, the fisherman who wooed Leslie, then put her life in danger, was back on the island and in Leslie's condo after disappearing for the same several weeks as the drug dealer.

This isn't good. "I'm on my way," Wes said.

He bounded down the stairs to the parking lot and slid onto the front seat of the new Toyota Highlander he'd purchased when he left his job up north. *Oh man the car's hot*, he thought.

He and Leslie had known each other for at least five years. They met when she was handling public relations for a big midwestern utility and he was reporting on the company's actions. Their working relationship was good enough that when Leslie abruptly left her lucrative position and moved south, she let Wes know of her departure. Six months later, Wes moved to Leslie's island and began his new job as a reporter and co-editor of the paper.

He was barely settled in when Leslie dragged him into her investigation of a drug-dealing scheme taking place in a mysterious house not far from where she lived. *Her obsession with that empty house was something else,* Wes mused. His thoughts grew somber when he returned to the possibility that the surviving drug dealer could be planning on harming Leslie.

He stopped his vehicle at the white gate that separated Leslie's condo complex from the island's only main road and punched in the code, tapping impatiently on the steering wheel as he waited for the metal barrier to rumble open.

Once inside, Wes parked the SUV under a guest canopy and sprinted up the short flight of wooden steps to Leslie's first-floor, waterfront condo. He rang the doorbell and would have let himself in, but his entry was blocked by a yellow lab, barking and wiggling all over in obvious anticipation of attention from whoever was at the front door.

Whalen you are some watchdog, Wes thought.

"Dog, shush," Wes could hear Leslie's voice and then her footsteps on the tile floor coming from the direction of the lanai at the back of the condo. She was quickly at the dog's side, grabbing his collar and pulling him back so Wes could squeeze inside.

"Sorry. This guy needs some serious training," Leslie said, laughing.

"You need to introduce him to Harry, the local dog whisperer."

"If he sticks around. He belongs to Frank and, well, you know Frank...."

Wes eyed his friend. For someone who could be in danger, Leslie looked calm. Her short reddish hair framed impossibly smooth skin. Her green eyes were as welcoming as her smile. Her outfit – shorts and a tank top – were distracting. Although Wes tried not to think of Leslie in terms of her womanly assets, he couldn't help but admire her well-toned figure. She may have been in her mid-40s but looked a decade younger.

The two followed Whalen to the lanai where Wes could see Frank Johnson camped out in one of the Adirondack chairs. Despite the heat, he was wearing jeans and a long-sleeved shirt – the attire of local fishermen who didn't want to deal with skin cancer in their later years.

"Wes is here, Frank," Leslie said, stating the obvious.

Frank put down the *National Geographic* he was reading, rose slowly and extended his hand. His gesture appeared more forced than welcoming.

Wes didn't like the guy. There was a wildness about him that made even sensible women like Leslie weak-kneed, and that other men recognized as a dangerous trait. He also didn't care for Frank's new goatee, which Wes thought gave the fellow a sinister look.

He was especially pissed that Frank left Leslie to fend off a dangerous drug dealer while he spirited his family to safety and vanished with a reported millions in rewards for his undercover police work with the DEA.

Why is she even speaking to this asshole? Wes reluctantly shook Frank's hand.

"Thanks, um, for taking such good care of Leslie," Frank said. "I didn't want to leave her but had no choice."

"Yeah, I guess you didn't," Wes said, as he took a seat on a white beach stool and directed his gaze at the blue-green waters of the North Pass. His voice dripped with sarcasm. His disdain for Frank was palpable. "Lucky for you, she can handle herself…most of the time. All the deputy and I had to do was round up the bad guys after she figured out what was…."

"You want iced tea or water?" Leslie interrupted.

Maybe she doesn't like us talking about her like she's not here, Wes mused.

"Naw, I'm fine. This is one heck of a view," he said, making small talk and then turning toward Frank. "So, what's the deal with Jamie Thompson?"

Leslie took a seat, also looking expectantly at Frank, like she was anticipating hearing something new. *Surely, they talked about Jamie before now. Or maybe they were too busy catching up.* He hated the thought.

"It took a while to locate the wreckage. My DEA source says the fire after the crash pretty much burned up everything, including…."

"Jamie had a parachute," Leslie interrupted. "I saw it when we flew down to Key West for lunch that day – before all hell broke loose. If he's alive, that's how he survived." She stood up and walked toward the kitchen counter on which a large bouquet of red roses had been placed. Whalen padded along behind her.

"You think that's what happened? The guy jumped out of the plane, abandoning the other dealer and I'm guessing millions in drugs?" Wes asked. "Why would he do that?"

Frank shook his head. "I radioed him that he was going to be arrested when he landed in Canada. I had to keep my undercover story intact. Not sure why he just didn't put down someplace else."

"So, you warned him, and he survived to put Leslie in danger...again," Wes said, with no attempt to hide his annoyance. "You are some boyfriend."

Leslie and the dog had returned to the lanai. When Wes made the boyfriend comment, she rolled her eyes and sighed. *Not technically a boyfriend*, he thought he heard her mutter.

"What makes you think Jamie's coming here?" Wes asked, directing his question to Leslie.

She handed him the piece of paper and a ring she'd retrieved from the kitchen counter. Whalen looked at her as though expecting a treat for his role in delivering the goods. "Later, boy," she said. "This came with those flowers yesterday."

Wes read the note – IT'S NOT OVER – and felt the acid in his stomach head for his throat.

"The ring is Jamie's," she said. "I'm not afraid. I don't believe he intends to do anything more than scare me." She paused and looked in Frank's direction.

I bet she's glad he's here but would never admit it. Maybe I am too, Wes thought.

"If that's true, why would he send you the ring and the note? Sounds like more than an empty threat. You gonna use Leslie as bait?" Wes asked, turning once more toward Frank and glaring.

Frank shook his head. "The sheriff and I are meeting in his office in about an hour. The DEA – my former partner from Miami – will be there. Leslie won't be in any danger. I promise."

"What can I do?" Wes asked.

"Stay here with her 'til I get back," Frank said.

"Not necessary." Leslie was on her feet; hands on hips. "I'm going to the meeting. It's my life that's at stake."

Frank mumbled something Wes couldn't quite hear. Wes knew the fisherman shared his view that Leslie was sometimes reckless, rushing into situations without first assessing the danger to herself and others. Although today she seemed more subdued than usual. Maybe she was scared.

"If you hear or see anything let me, um, us know, Wes. I'll keep you posted," she said.

Wes rose from the chair and put his hand on Leslie's shoulder. "Just remember, last time it took a village – at least a sheriff's deputy and an old reporter – to protect you from your inquisitive ways. Don't try to handle this on your own, Ms. Elliott."

"I won't Wes. I won't," she said, glancing over at Frank. "Caution is my new middle name."

Frank mumbled a goodbye but stayed put while Leslie and the dog accompanied Wes to the front door.

"Watch that guy," Wes said softly.

CHAPTER 4

On his way back to the office, Wes picked up a pre-packaged ham and cheese sandwich and a bottle of water from the grocery store next door. He was unwrapping his purchase when Randy Long walked by the desk and dropped off a black binder and a manilla folder, without comment.

"Thanks," Wes said, putting his sandwich to one side and reaching for the binder. It smelled musty and had patches of gray mildew on the front and back covers. Some of the pages had worked loose from the three-ring binder and been stuffed back in, including the first page, which had on it the words *Investigation Report*, the case number, the name of the individual who had prepared the report – one Miriam Capstone – and the date of the report. In smaller type were the words: *Death of Toby Mason*.

It looked official but didn't appear to be a police document. The table of contents listed a photographic section. Wes decided to skip the narrative and go straight for the pictures. He wanted a feel for the cottage where the shooting took place, but the eight by 10 color photos of a porch, living room, sitting room and kitchen were a disappointment. Even when he referred back to the sketch of the shooting at the beginning of the section, the photos told him little.

He needed to see the place for himself. Walk through the rooms. Recreate the scene based on what he learned from the documents. But was that even possible? He didn't know if the house still existed. When new people bought property on the island, they often tore down the old structures to replace them with larger, fancier ones.

He set aside the binder and reached for the manilla folder that included more copies of photographs. He assumed these were taken by the investigating officer the night of the shooting.

A copy of Toby Mason's Florida driver's license was among the papers and photos. It listed him as 6 foot tall and was set to expire in a year. It showed an unsmiling young man in his early 20s with short hair and a slender face. Nice looking but not remarkable. He was identified as an organ donor.

Wes shuddered at the next photo. Even though it was a copy – and a bad one at that – it was clear enough. It was the same young man, but his eyes were closed and blackened, his mouth partly open, and he was sporting at least a week's worth of facial hair. He was very much alive in the driver's license photo. When this photo was taken, life had left him hours earlier.

Under this mask of death were the numbers 391-04. Those same identifiers were attached to the next, even more troubling series of pictures that showed the young man's scalp sliced open and peeled back by what must have been a coroner's tool. Wes was grateful the photos weren't in color.

He set the binder and folder aside, took a long drink of water, got up from his desk and put the ham and cheese sandwich in the small office refrigerator. The idea of food made him queasy.

His short trip took him past Randy who was working on the layout for the next edition. "I covered politics up north," Wes said. "What I'm trying to say is that, um, reporting on a cold case shooting is a little out of my line."

Randy stopped what he was doing and looked at Wes with a chilling earnestness. "Lies, cover-ups, unexplained deaths. Isn't that what politics is all about?"

"Hey, I'm supposed to be the cynic here," Wes said. "But I know what you mean. It's about the truth…whatever that is these days."

Wes picked up the material and headed out the door, dropping the package at his apartment before his next stop, the Tarpon Bar. It was close to 2 o'clock and he was sure Johnny Boy would have downed his four-drink limit and left. But he had to see for himself. Afterward he'd call Leslie. Maybe drive out to her condo again. He wanted to hear what Frank and Sheriff Harry Fleck were planning to do to keep her safe.

Soon, but not until this matter with Jamie Thompson was resolved, Wes would be enlisting Leslie's help in finding out about the shooting at Seaside Cottage. He was confident she wouldn't say no.

CHAPTER 5

The night before

Leslie's reaction when she saw Frank and Whalen walking toward her condo after nearly a month of no communication had been one of joy and relief. When they met at the bottom of her lanai steps, he'd wrapped his arms around her and kissed her; his lips familiar, reassuring.

"Damn I missed you," he said, pulling her tighter toward him.

She reveled in his attention. But once they were settled in her place, the dark thoughts that weighed on her during his absence overtook her euphoria.

She was watching Frank down the turkey sandwich she fixed for him; sitting in the Adirondack chair next to him and fidgeting when she asked the question that had tormented her since he disappeared.

"Why'd you do it? Turn me over to a man who said he would kill me and then run away," she asked.

Frank stopped eating and looked at her, hesitating before responding. His blue eyes seemed to be searching her face for reassurance that there was no anger, just curiosity, behind the question. She couldn't be sure what he was thinking.

"Look, Leslie, all the guys involved in the drug business were dangerous. Worse than you can imagine. Except for Gordon Fike. He was a two-bit criminal, just a realtor, who didn't have the guts to shoot you. A man looking to make a quick buck.

"The other guys – the ones that would commit murder without a second thought – were with me or loading up the plane. I told the deputy where you were and that you needed rescuing. I wanted Gordon to be convinced I was on his side for a couple more hours. You did that for me."

"Oh, how nice of me." Leslie shook her head. Yes, she was strong, but that was no excuse for what Frank had done. "You could have given me a warning and some kind of advantage with that creep. Even if he was drunk, he had a gun. Then you were gone. No word. You took them with you and left me behind to fend for myself."

She hoped he didn't get up and try to touch her in some comforting way. For this short while, being angry with him made her feel good.

"Yeah, you're right," he said, staying put. "Even as I was using you, I'd convinced myself that it wouldn't change anything between us. Has it? I mean, you wouldn't have gone with me that night I left the island…would you?"

"I can't be sure," she said. *But probably not.*

"I thought you'd understand that sometimes strong people like us have to put aside our personal interests so right can be done," he said.

"Why are you back, Frank?" she asked.

"To protect you. If that's possible. To be with you, if only for a short time." His eyes softened.

Leslie's could feel her rage slipping away, even though she wanted to hold onto it for a bit longer. She needed it for protection. Frank Johnson was appealing and sexy; a man you could fall in love with but never trust. Never. And she mustn't forget that.

CHAPTER 6

Tuesday, December 15 in the afternoon

When Leslie, Frank and Whalen entered his office, Sheriff Harry Fleck was sitting behind a large metal desk reading a newspaper – readers perched on his bulbous nose. He had the look of a man whose wife just told him he was going to church instead of fishing. He acknowledged Frank with a nod and avoided eye contact with Leslie.

Even though she helped expose a ring of drug dealers on the island, Sheriff Fleck had never warmed up to Leslie and her inquisitive ways. Never said thanks even though her foolishness, as he called it, had brought him 15-minutes of fame and a commendation from the governor. Never gave enough credit to his deputy, Bruce Webster, who, along with Wes, was one of the real heroes in the drug bust.

And here she was again. Causing trouble. Leslie could see those thoughts written all over his round face.

Don McKechnie, the drug enforcement officer out of Miami, was leaning against the wall next to a Mr. Coffee machine that had seen cleaner days, describing to Deputy Webster the highlights of the Monday Night Football game between the Dolphins and the Patriots.

"So, the guy grabs the ball and runs like he's being chased by…oh hey, Frank, Leslie…." He rushed forward to shake Frank's hand. "Damn, that was one hell of a deal you pulled off. Now we have some clean-up to do."

Deputy Webster flashed a smile at the pair, then refocused on the coffeemaker, removing the filter and old grounds and tossing them into the wastebasket.

"It was her," Frank said without hesitation and a nod toward Leslie. "She deserves the credit."

"Sure, sure. Even if she did blow your cover. At least you got away with all that loot, I mean money that you deserved," McKechnie winked and laughed, then fell silent when the others did not join him.

"So, what's the plan?" Sheriff Fleck asked, removing his glasses and leaning forward; his large belly pushing against the desktop. He coughed, cleared his throat and reached for a pen. When he began drumming it on his desk, the sound…tap, tap, tap…seemed familiar to Leslie.

Was it an S.O.S? So appropriate, she thought, *when you have Larry, Curly and Mo – the sheriff, his deputy and the DEA agent – the three stooges in charge, and they have no clue how to deal with Jamie Thompson, drug dealer and murderer.*

"I guess, um, the plan is to use me as bait…again," Leslie said, her eyes scanning the room for affirmation of what she knew to be the truth.

"Now, Leslie, we have no intention of putting you in harm's way," McKechnie said. He ran his hands through his brown hair and squinted at Frank as though anticipating affirmation from his former law enforcement partner.

"It's the only way," Frank responded. His voice was calm even if his message was unsettling to Leslie. She and Frank would have to be exposed for there to be any hope of capturing Jamie.

"I'll get a couple of guys from Miami to help us. Sheriff, you and your deputy can be on standby," McKechnie said, nodding. "Thompson will make his move soon, and we'll be ready."

The three men swarmed Sheriff Fleck's desk and began talking about schedules and surveillance locations. Leslie started to join them but instead stepped back and surveyed the room, listening abstractly to plans she was sure would go awry.

Her eyes focused on the sign above the sheriff's desk: "At this point, I'm convinced some people were put on the planet just to test my anger management skills."

That's you, Harry Fleck, she thought. *Movie-style, good old boy law enforcement type wearing a uniform that must have fit better 15 pounds ago.*

"Isn't it, Whalen?" she said to the dog, reaching down to pat him where he'd conked out on the sheriff's cool tile floor during the meeting. He was startled by Leslie's touch and the mention of his name.

Leslie had no faith in anyone in that room except Frank, and she wasn't all that sure about him. But she had no choice. She couldn't handle this situation on her own and, in a rare moment of choking down her pride, had recognized that fact.

The meeting wrapped up with Agent McKechnie reviewing what would happen in the next couple of days. Leslie and Frank would continue their normal routine. Three or four DEA agents would be strategically placed near her condo, rotating on four-hour shifts. The deputy would be in a patrol car nearby, alternating his watch duties with the sheriff and temporary policemen hired for the job.

She wasn't worried about the others in her life. Her mother, Ruth, who lived in the same condo complex, and Ruth's new boyfriend, Gale Gammon, were on a month-long holiday cruise. Leslie's closest friends, Deb and Scooter Rankin, lived on the other side of the island and barely knew Jamie Thompson. He had no reason to go after them.

She was concerned about herself and Frank. Even with round-the-clock DEA surveillance, they were being pursued by a ruthless man who somehow escaped the plane crash that killed his fellow drug-dealer. A criminal who appeared to want revenge.

What could go wrong? Leslie wondered. *Everything.*

When Frank turned to leave, the deputy grabbed his arm. "Gotta talk," he whispered, pointing toward the hallway. With the door ajar, it was easy to hear the angst in his voice. "Ya gotta see her. Tell her what happened."

Leslie knew the deputy was talking about Janis Johnson, Frank's soon-to-be ex-wife. The two had separated some time ago, and Frank had custody of their teenage son, Stevie, whom he'd taken with him with he fled the island.

Leslie had seen the deputy and Janis together, laughing, kissing. There was something between them, even though Janis publicly still claimed territorial rights to Frank.

"She's pissed. Real pissed," the deputy said, his voice loud enough that Leslie was sure everyone in the sheriff's office could hear. "She wants more than the money you sent her. She wants answers."

"Don't worry," Leslie heard Frank respond. She imagined him flashing the close-mouthed smile that was his trademark at the deputy. "I know you care about her, Bruce. She's lucky to have a good man like you. I'll talk to her. Everything will be okay."

The man from the bar – the stranger in the Buccaneers cap – pulled a Benson & Hedges cigarette from his pocket, lighting it as he sat down on the green bench near the island post office. The gray-haired woman on the other end of the bench directed a withering look his way.

"Is my smoke bothering you?" he asked with exaggerated politeness.

"Yes, it is." She responded with a grimace and a cough.

"Then fuck off and go sit somewhere else."

He ignored the whispered *screw you* that accompanied her departure and fixed his eyes on the building across the street. There they were, both of them, with that stupid dog, leaving what he knew to be the sheriff's office and talking to a man in a tan suit with pronounced sweat marks under his armpits. No doubt a fed.

He wasn't ready to make his move yet but being so close to them gave him immense satisfaction. He had the ubiquitous look of thousands of Florida outdoorsmen and was confident no one would recognize him. He could move about freely until he'd gotten what he came for.

He was stroking his goatee, considering his alternatives, when he saw a quartet of 20-somethings park their golf cart and claim a table at the outdoor restaurant across the street. Pretty young things with shoulder-length hair, bouncy breasts encased in clinging tops and long legs toasted to an appealing light brown by the Florida sun.

He loved that they were giggling. Most women stopped that coy sound when they reached a certain age – unless they found a new love late in life. It was a shame really. He thought the sound irresistible in its expression of youthful naivete. Under different circumstances, he might have approached them with thoughts of hooking up with one or two. Today, he had other plans.

He rose from the bench, tossed his cigarette onto the brick path and strolled across the street to a small, wrought-iron table not far from the quartet of lovelies. When he heard them order ice cream, he told the waitress he'd have an iced coffee and would be happy to pick up the tab for the table "over there."

The waitress with the curly brown hair and a name badge that said Sue shook her head. "We're not that kind of place," she said, scowling.

"I'm just paying it forward, um, Sue, like they talk about on TV. I have sisters their age. I haven't seen them for months. Missing their laughter, especially around the holidays."

"I'll ask," the waitress said, continuing to purse her lips.

He saw the girls look his direction, then giggle again. He flashed a smile, took off his hat to reveal a thick crop of dark hair and give them a better look at his face. They waved him over. Adventuresome young women; willing to see what this good-looking older man had to offer.

"Hey thanks," the one with the pink tank top said as she pulled out the chair next to her. "I'm Sara. This is Joelle, Nicole, Emily."

"Ladies, I'm Jamie, uh, Phillips. Down here to do some fishing. You girls visiting?"

"My parents own a place down here," Emily said. "On the beach. We're on break…."

He bantered with them until he was sure they felt comfortable with him. Joelle touched his arm a couple of times while they were talking. It was an entrée he hated to refuse.

"You girls are a lot of fun. I've got a friend on the island – he's a practical joker – and I owe him big time. Would you be willing to help me out? I'll pay…." He pulled out his billfold and flashed a wad of $100 bills.

Nicole spoke first: "We're up for anything crazy. Isn't that right?" she said, scanning the faces of the others.

"Oh yeah," Joelle chimed in, squeezing Jamie's arm for the third time and lingering there. "Anything. Just tell us what you want us to do."

Jamie flashed a smile Joelle's direction and flexed his arm muscle to acknowledge her touch. "It involves making some noise on the beach tonight. At just the right time."

CHAPTER 7

Wes's late afternoon trip to the Tarpon yielded one beer and no further information on John Mason who, according to Shine, was a no-show that day.

"If he misses a couple of days, I swing by and check on him," Shine said. "Take him a sandwich and some water and sit with him for a while. You drink too much booze you get dehydrated."

As he was leaving the bar, Wes made a mental note of Shine's kindness. *Christmas is coming. He deserves a good tip.*

Back in his kitchen, Wes pulled out a straight-back chair with a wicker seat and sat down at the small table where he normally drank his morning coffee and read *The New York Times*. Before him was the pile of information on the Mason shooting. He scooted closer, reaching for a cigarette in his shirt pocket like he'd done a thousand times before.

"Shit. I don't smoke anymore," he said to the wall in front of him. And for a moment, he felt sad at the loss of comfort that came with the beloved ritual of lighting…inhaling…exhaling…collecting his thoughts.

He was certain there was much he'd missed the first time through the documents; the subtleties that are often overlooked even by seasoned investigators. He didn't claim to be an expert, but he had good instincts. Knew which questions to ask and what details were important.

He didn't need to review the death photos again; maybe later when their shock value had diminished. He flipped through the police reports and stopped at a letter printed on yellow-lined paper. The words *My Thoughts* were scribbled in different ink – an afterthought perhaps – across the top.

I am the grandfather of Toby Mason. In response to the Island Sun article: Police Rule Mason's Shooting a Suicide! I beg to differ with you Sheriff Harry Fleck. Toby did not commit suicide! You should have done your homework. Check Toby's character. His home – friends – teachers – neighbors! Suicide is for the disturbed – unloved – unwanted – insecure – abused by their parents. No secure future!

I am angry – appalled to read that you as an officer of the law conducted a preliminary investigation and came to the conclusion this was a suicide. The mystery of my precious grandson's death still lingers. Only those who were there know what really happened. You need to continue searching for the truth."

The words *My Loving Grandson* were written on the bottom of the page then crossed out.

Wes wasn't sure what to make of the letter. What did Randy Long say? "There was more to it, and the officials covered it up." The grandfather felt the same way although he'd probably heard the story secondhand from his son or daughter. Wes assumed the pale-faced man was no longer married.

And Harry Fleck was the sheriff back then. That was a surprise. He had to be in his early 40s at the time. A husband, a young father perhaps, starting his career in law enforcement and having to deal with a local tragedy like this. Maybe someone he'd known as a child. So sad.

Wes checked the clock over the kitchen sink. 5:21. *Was John Mason home and passed out on his couch. Was he having alcohol-fueled dreams of his dead son? Was the shooting playing in his head like some grainy black and white horror movie with blood visible only at the moment the bullet traveled through Toby's brain?*

Wes picked up his phone and marked an entry on tomorrow's calendar. 11 – Tarpon Bar. JM. He was going to meet the pale-faced man – hopefully before the second drink – get to know him and find out what he was willing to share about his son's death.

He was rereading the grandfather's letter when Leslie called to report on the meeting with the sheriff, the deputy and the DEA Agent McKechnie.

"Unsatisfactory," she said. "Maybe I should get out of town. Go on a cruise like my mother did. But I'm guessing dear old Jamie would just hang around waiting for my return."

"You could stay at my place," Wes offered. "I can sleep on the couch. You could work on your novel."

"Oh, yeah, that. The Murder of Leslie Elliott. It seems to be unfolding right before our very eyes," she said, then laughed. "Thanks for the invite, Wes. But I'm going to see it through to the end here in my little condo… with Frank at my side."

"And Whalen," Wes said.

"Yes. And Whalen the wonder dog."

CHAPTER 8

After 9 p.m., Tuesday, December 15

A woman's screams from the far end of the beach rocketed Leslie out of the Adirondack chair where, mesmerized by the blackness of the Gulf of Mexico, she was trying not to doze off. Frank had been napping in her bedroom, gearing up for what he told her would be an after-midnight vigil. She fretted about waking him. What if the noise was from a group of crazy teenagers? The village was full of them and it wasn't even Christmas yet.

"Are you guys checking that out?" she opened the screen door of her lanai and yelled into the nothingness below.

"McKechnie's on his way," she heard one of the DEA agents say. "Better get back inside, Ms. Elliott."

"What's going on?" Frank was now beside her, pulling a hooded sweatshirt over his head.

"Screams. Outside," she said, her voice reflecting her anxiety.

"It's okay, Frank. McKechnie's checking…." The other DEA agent's reassurance was cut short by the sound of more shouts in the distance. Female voices. Before Leslie could say anything else, Frank was gone, then back with a gun in the waistband of his shorts and heading down the back steps to the beach below.

Leslie assumed it was the same gun he'd shown her the night before – a 1911, which shoots .45 caliber hollow point bullets and is commonly used by the military. She guessed he was reassuring her that he had a weapon and knew how to use it for their protection. Guns made her nervous just like airplanes did. Too much could go wrong.

"Get inside and lock the sliding doors," he yelled before disappearing into the darkness.

A surge of adrenaline carried Leslie to her bedroom where she rushed to the nightstand and pulled out the pepper spray gun she'd bought several months ago.

The weapon wasn't deadly like Frank's but could render an intruder harmless. Or so the Internet ad assured her when she was contemplating spending $399 with tax. "The PepperBall TCP Launcher gives you control over any unforeseen circumstance…." She hoped that was the case. It had a four out of five-star rating and could shoot 150 feet, which was greater than the length of her condo.

She turned off the light in the bedroom, scurried through the living room to the utility closet and switched off the main breaker. The hum of the air conditioner ceased. The digital clock went blank as did the blue light on the Comcast box. The fridge stopped humming, dropping one last batch of cubes before going silent.

She crept through the second bedroom and onto the patio with its potted hibiscus plants and Dessert Rose bush, crouched down and surveyed the parking area. The streetlight, out for months, had not been replaced. Except for a dim glow from the starry sky, it was pitch black.

Pop! Pop! Pop! *Gunshots? Shit.* Lights went on in the complex, and Leslie, as brave as she often pretended to be, felt her throat go dry. "This is for real," she whispered to herself.

Except for the county iguana hunters who drove white pickup trucks and had their work cut out for them in the warmer months, no one ever fired a gun on the island.

Leslie was searching for some clue as to the source of the sounds when she felt pressure on her arm. She tensed, swallowed hard and turned to face the intruder. Had he killed the others and made it through the DEA defenses to get to her?

Her body relaxed. No threat from this one; it was Whalen. His wet nose nuzzled her cheek. His breath smelled like the dog biscuit she'd given him an hour ago. In the crush of events, she'd forgotten he was in the condo. He had to be curious about what his humans were up to now.

"You scared me, buddy," she whispered, then grabbed his big face between her two hands and give him a kiss on the forehead.

Her plan was to sneak out through the front door and lose herself in the foliage around the complex. It would be safer than hiding behind locks that could be shattered with one good body blow. She could return when the DEA agents or Frank called on her cell phone and said everything was okay.

Whalen was a complication. If she left him behind, he was sure to bark his frustration. If she took him along, would he remain still? For that matter, could he serve as an attack dog if needed? She hoped he would be her protector but wasn't sure he had the right stuff. She pondered her options for a minute and decided she had none. He was going with her. She didn't want Jamie killing the dog when his intended target was nowhere to be found.

"Be very quiet," she said.

The two of them padded back to the living room and down the hallway to the front door. She opened the screen slowly to prevent it from squeaking, grabbed the dog's scruff and pulled him through so she could shut it quietly.

Weapon in hand, she climbed down the steps and, once on the cement walkway, dashed for a clump of sea grapes between her building and her mother's. Although she'd complained mightily to the complex manager that the bushes hadn't been trimmed in six months, she was now happy they were overgrown. Whalen stopped to raise his leg and pee on a nearby shrub before joining her in a small opening between two large branches.

She crouched down but after a few minutes her knees began to ache, so she pulled some giant sea grape leaves into a pile and sat down. She prayed this wasn't a breeding ground for no-see-'ums, Florida's version of the Midwest's infamous chiggers.

Within minutes, she felt her head nodding. The warm winds from the Gulf, Whalen's rhythmic panting and her body's letdown after the terror she felt while escaping were acting like a shot of melatonin. *Can't go to sleep, can't go to sleep.* Despite her struggle, her body slowly eased itself to the ground, her head coming to rest on Whalen's soft stomach, her pepper spray gun falling into the sea grape leaves.

She awoke to the sound of voices and saw a flashing red light creeping across the ground in front of her. Whalen was up now, too, and running toward the police car that Leslie recognized as Deputy Bruce Webster's.

"Bruce!" she shouted. She was getting up when a hand clamped across her mouth, and she felt herself being dragged back to the ground.

"Umph!" She hit the packed sand with a jarring force.

"Hello gorgeous. You been missing me?" Jamie's voice emerged from the darkness, soft and terrifying.

She started to speak. "Keep quiet now. Stay still," he warned.

He held her tight; pressing something that Leslie assumed was a gun against her cheek. The two remained motionless, watching as Deputy Webster greeted the dog, then climbed the steps to Leslie's condo and disappeared behind the door.

"Easy," Jamie said as he removed his hand from her mouth and let it drop to her shoulder. "We can relax while these yo-yos try to figure out where you are."

"Like…a bad…cold," Leslie said. Her voice was gravely, uncertain.

"What?"

"You asked if I missed you. My answer is…like a bad cold," Leslie said after clearing her throat.

Jamie laughed, but she felt his body stiffen. "Still the cheeky bitch. If I didn't have a little something lined up for later, we could have an amazing time together."

"Drug dealers and murderers don't do much for my libido," she said as she watched the deputy and the dog emerge from behind her screen door and head down the steps.

At the car, the deputy crouched down to pat Whalen. "Where's Leslie? Huh? Where she'd go, boy?" The dog glanced over at the tall bushes; the deputy didn't get the hint.

She wanted to cry out again and hope that the deputy could move faster than her captor. But this was not the time to do anything stupid. Jamie and his gun were calling the shots, so to speak.

The drug dealer shifted positions, dropping the weapon from Leslie's cheek and maneuvering her so she could see the outline of his face in the darkness. His Buccaneers cap was turned with the bill to the back.

"Who says I'm a murderer?" he whispered.

"What about Raul, the man on the plane?"

"Oh, yeah, him. When Frank called to say we'd be arrested in Canada, I changed course. We ran into heavy storms. We were going down. One parachute, and it was either him or me. Nothing personal."

"You going to shoot me now or later?"

He shook his head and laughed softly. "There have been times when doing away with you seemed like a good idea. But I'm not in the habit of killing good-looking women or anybody for that matter. It's your boyfriend I'm after. I got some questions for him."

He pulled her close and yanked her to her feet. "You and I are going to walk slowly toward the deputy. No sudden moves."

So, I am the bait. But the big fish is Frank, and I'm powerless to help him, Leslie thought as Jamie tightened his grip on her arm.

Deputy Webster was startled to see two figures emerge from the bushes and then shaken when he realized that one of them was Leslie and other, a tall, muscular man behind her must be the fugitive, Jamie Thompson.

"Y'all right?" the deputy shouted in her direction. She was definitely not all right.

Whalen, standing beside him, began whimpering and wagging his tail, but stayed put.

"She's okay. As long as you don't do anything stupid." Jamie brandished his gun for the deputy to see before returning it to Leslie's back. When the three were within a couple of yards of each other, Jamie shoved Leslie in the deputy's direction.

"Get behind me," the deputy said, pushing her back with his right arm.

"Sorry, Bruce," she said. "I don't know how he found me."

"Here's what's going to happen," Jamie said, continuing to point his gun at the two of them. "I don't want this bitch. It's Frank I'm looking for. You call and tell him to meet me by the fallen tree near the sand bar at the North Pass."

He checked his watch. "Make it 11 o'clock. He comes alone, or I'll take out him and whoever is with him and come back for Leslie."

"What ya want him for?" the deputy asked, his voice reflecting his nervousness. He was used to dealing with underage golf cart drivers, not killers.

"Frank and I need to have a conversation. Nothing that would interest you. Come on. Make the call."

The deputy hit the buttons on his cell. "Thompson's here…with Leslie and me," he said, trying to sound as though he was in charge of the situation. He told Frank about the drug dealer's request to meet by the tree, then nodded several times, eyeing Jamie.

"Ya sure you want to do that?" the deputy said. "Okay. Okay. I'll let her know."

He looked hard at Jamie. "Frank's gonna meet ya at the designated location at 11. He'll come alone…like ya requested."

"Listen, honey, I always liked you," Jamie said to Leslie. "And if Frank comes through, you'll be fine. If not…well…let your imagination conjure up something very ugly."

The deputy and Leslie watched Jamie disappear into the bushes. When he could no longer be seen, Leslie leaned against the deputy who put his arm around her. "Oh, Bruce. I'm so scared for Frank. Why did he agree to meet Jamie alone?"

"It sounded like he was expecting him," the deputy said, shaking his head. "I'll let Agent McKechnie know, and he can alert the others."

"Was there something Frank wanted you to tell me?"

"You? Oh no. It was a message for Janis," the deputy said.

CHAPTER 9

Wednesday morning, December 16

Deputy Webster was responding to a 911 call from dispatch when he spotted Leslie taking a walk along Oceanview Drive – the yellow lab in tow. He was surprised that after last night's trauma she had returned to her morning routine. When she said goodnight, she had seemed rattled and wasn't sure she could sleep. Who wouldn't feel that way?

He remembered their first couple of meetings. How he thought she was a busybody and troublemaker. All that had changed. Even if his boss, the sheriff, didn't care for her, he liked her spunkiness and was glad she and Frank were close.

The deputy waved as he passed her, saw Leslie stop and turn to watch as he stepped out of his car in front of a sprawling pink structure several hundred feet from the Gulf. When she shrugged and shook her head as if to say she had no news, he returned the gesture.

Agent McKechnie had assessed the situation when the sheriff, the other agents, the deputy and Leslie all gathered in the condo parking lot the night before. "We have to give Frank and Jamie space. Stay away from the meeting spot like Jamie said. The druggie's no match for our guy. Frank will contact us when he's ready…when everything's taken care of," he had said.

But all those hours had passed. And there was still nothing but maddening silence.

The deputy sighed and pushed the doorbell. It will all work out, he told himself. Soon this will die down, and he could return to his favorite duty

– looking official and waving to residents as he drove his marked vehicle up and down the village streets.

He checked his reflection in the glass panel by the front door. Khaki shirt and pants neatly pressed over a toned but not muscular figure. His hair slicked back but not greasy-looking. He knew he wasn't handsome, but he wanted to be a good representative of law enforcement for the island that he called home.

The homeowner, a nervous-looking woman in her early eighties, opened the door and ushered the deputy into her living room, encouraging him to have a seat and offering him tea, which he declined.

After a few minutes during which it seemed she was composing herself, she began to speak haltingly about the gruesome find she made while doing turtle patrol on the beach. The dispatcher said her call was jumbled, disjointed. But now that the deputy was speaking to her face-to-face, he clearly understood every word she was saying.

"Terrible. Shocking. It…was…a…body. Awful. Just awful," she said and began dabbing her eyes with a tissue.

The deputy reached out to pat her on the back, not caring that some would say his role was not that of a comforter. "I guess ya better show me where it is," he said after a few more respectful questions.

"Oh, I can't." Her mouth dropped open as if she were readying a scream. The deputy assumed she was reliving the horror of the discovery.

"You'll have to go by yourself. Straight out that way," she said, pointing a shaky finger toward the lanai. "You can't miss it."

Deputy Webster thanked the woman, exited through the lanai and stopped at the back of the house where he pulled out his phone and punched in the sheriff's number. Harry Fleck didn't answer so he left a message. "Old lady saw a body in the Gulf when she was walkin' this mornin'. I'm on my way to check it out. Could be Jamie Thompson."

He tried to keep his manner steady, professional. But as he started down the sandy path that wandered through the seagrasses to the beach, the deputy felt apprehensive. He wasn't fearful of seeing a body. He'd seen enough dead or dying – usually victims of heart attacks or old-age ailments. He'd known many of the deceased and some had been casual friends.

But a corpse in the water is often bloated and covered with marks inflicted by the Gulf's aquatic residents. He'd seen photographs and investigated a bluish arm washed up on the beach. But he wasn't eager to experience a waterlogged corpse, even if it was the remains of a criminal.

Above him, seagulls were flying; swooping and rising in intricate patterns. He watched them, intrigued as always by their maneuvers. When they landed in a tight group not far from a mass half submerged in the water, the deputy froze. Dread sucked the breath from his lungs, locked his legs in place.

Gotta do this, he whispered.

He gulped in the warm sea air, steadied himself and continued on until he was standing next to the body. Looking both directions to make sure there was no one else on the beach, he knelt beside it.

It was surprisingly intact with little discoloration, except for a paleness that comes with death. The face and hair were hidden under a reddish glob of seaweed, except for a hole in the forehead from which small flaps of skin spread out into a star shape. A tiny crab was perched on the torso; the crustacean and blue sweatshirt on the body were moving back and forth with the gentle swells of the Gulf.

When a small wave washed the face clean, exposing familiar features, the deputy recoiled as though punched in the gut. "Oh God," he wailed. He scooped up the lifeless figure that had been his friend for more years than he could remember and hugged it to his breast, rocking back and forth.

"Frank, oh Frank. What happened to ya, buddy?"

Leslie was on the return leg of her walk when she saw Agent McKechnie and another DEA officer emerge from their unmarked car and head for the pink stucco home where she'd last seen Deputy Webster. The sheriff's car was also parked on the side of the road.

"Jamie. They've found Jamie!" she said aloud. "Frank must be there." She was running now, heading for the beach path the two men had taken, fueled by the sense that the worst was over. Whalen was frolicking alongside her.

In the distance, she could see four people close to a form on the beach. McKechnie was pacing. The deputy was looking out at the Gulf and occasionally wiping his face with a tan handkerchief. The sheriff had his arms crossed over his pronounced stomach. The other man she also recognized as a DEA agent was on his phone.

Four. Only four and none of them Frank. Where is he?

The sheriff was the first to spot Leslie. He pointed her out to the deputy who began walking briskly her direction. "Stay where ya are," he shouted.

"Is it Jamie?" she yelled.

He didn't answer until he was beside her. "Everything's gonna be okay," he said. In a move that caught Leslie off-guard, he wrapped his arms around her. She remembered later that he smelled of lime aftershave mixed with sweat. He clung to her as if to keep himself from falling. His cheek was soft against hers as he whispered into her ear: "It's Frank."

The face of the handsome fisherman flashed before her: The blue-gray eyes, the dimple in his chin, the sandy hair – tousled as if he'd just stepped off his boat.

When the vision disappeared into the darkness; Leslie went with it.

CHAPTER 10

Noon on Monday, December 21

The news that Frank Johnson, fisherman and hero, was found dead on the beach sent islanders to the village gathering spots to voice their shock and dismay. Wes Avery tweeted updates and wrote a more detailed account for the newspaper's print edition. Even the snowbirds up north for Christmas responded with disbelief on Facebook at the loss of one of their favorite guides.

The Tampa and Miami news outlets picked up the story with comments from Agent McKechnie, who praised Frank as "an undercover warrior in the fight against the drug traffic in southwest Florida." He said law enforcement would not rest until the killer or killers were found.

CNN and Fox News gave it brief mention, using an old photo from Frank's website that showed him with longer hair and identified him as a former policeman.

Janis Johnson issued a statement through an attorney. She claimed she was too distraught at the loss of her husband to say anything except that his death could be laid at the feet of certain individuals – and they knew who they were – who used the fisherman to advance their self-interests. There was no mention that the two hadn't lived together for some time.

With Frank gone, questions lingered about the whereabouts of Jamie Thompson, the prime murder suspect. Wes had tracked down and interviewed the young women who unwittingly helped Jamie with their screams on the beach. He reported that they were tearful and sorry. They thought they were part of a harmless prank and had no idea where Jamie might be.

Thompson had told the deputy that it was Frank he was after, not Leslie. Law enforcement was now acting on the notion that Leslie was safe. Even Deputy Webster was convinced that the drug dealer was long gone – his horrific mission accomplished.

It had been five days since the discovery of Frank's body; Christmas was less than a week away. Leslie wasn't feeling festive. She couldn't remember the last time she'd showered and had only emerged from her condo to take Whalen for brief walks. She missed the fisherman: his kisses, the newly discovered comfort of his body next to her when she slept, his closed-mouth smile.

The question of whether she was in love with Frank was one she couldn't come to terms with even though she revisited it often. She was infatuated with the idea of him – handsome, reckless, mysterious. But if she was brutally honest with herself, she never saw them parenting his teenage son, Stevie, into adulthood and then growing old together. Especially after Frank abandoned her, without a word.

Still, she couldn't figure out how to handle the guilt she was feeling over what she thought was her part in his death.

"You weren't responsible," Wes told her when she finally returned one of his daily phone calls instead of texting him that she was okay. "Frank knew the risk he was taking. He was the one who put you in harm's way."

"I brought him back here."

"Jamie brought him back here, not you," Wes insisted.

It was Jamie. Not me. Jamie. The words rang in her ears – and maybe stung a bit – as she reached for a lightweight jacket and the dog's leash. Whalen who'd been staring woefully her direction for the last 15 minutes jumped up and was at her side before she could say his name.

"Yes, we're going for a walk…a long one. And we're gonna get wet," she said, reaching down and attaching the leash to his collar, then giving him a pat on the head.

A merciful cool front was coming through, dropping temperatures 20 degrees and churning up the Gulf with white-capped waves determined to eat away at the latest beach renourishment project. Leslie had noticed buzzards circling the area and hoped the winds and cold were chasing them away. Beneficial as they were in the clean-up department, they gave her the willies.

She slipped Whalen a dog treat and headed out the front door into a light drizzle that would normally deter her. Today, the mist felt cooling and renewing – a kind of baptism – and a relief from cabin fever.

The pair walked through the side gate of the complex and onto the main road that led to Oceanview Drive, the wind whipping through Leslie's short hair and ruffling the fur around Whalen's collar. When she got to the footpath the public used for beach access, she took a right and followed the sandy trail to an old boardwalk that crossed the area used by nesting gopher turtles.

She tried not to think of Frank or Jamie, instead focusing on her conversation that morning with her daughter, Meredith, who was spending Christmas with Leslie's ex-husband, Scott. It was a change of plans necessitated by the arrival of Jamie's flowers and his threatening note.

Meredith had never met Frank and was very loyal to her father. "Aww, Mom, why don't you get on a plane right now? You can be here for Christmas Eve. You know how you love Christmas Eve. And you could stay with Dad. Since his breakup with that woman, he's been talking about you a lot. We'll pick you up at the airport."

"I'd love to see you, honey, but, um, I'm sure I couldn't get a flight this late." Leslie didn't want to hurt her daughter's feelings but the last thing she needed was to be around her ex. They were cordial, even friendly at times, but both had moved on. "You'll be here for spring break. We'll have a great time."

A sharp tug on the leash brought Leslie back to the moment. Whalen was sniffing the air and straining the leash; trying his best to pull her off the boardwalk into the scrub grass of the turtle territory and toward the remains of a small boat that washed up in 2005 following Hurricane Katrina.

One of the residents nearby had cleaned out the mechanics and left the wooden vessel to become part of the wild landscape. It was hidden from the general public, but Leslie had discovered it during one of her exploratory walks and learned its history from a neighbor.

Over the years, shifting sand and seagrasses had taken root in the deteriorating structure. The result looked like a beach painting with a story to tell. Today, it was of great interest to the dog.

"Damn, Whalen, you're going to break my arm!" Leslie called him to her side, releasing him from the leash so he could run free. He took off like a shot and headed straight for the boat, bounding over the side of it and positioning himself on what was left of the hull; his barking muted by the wind.

She started toward him, then stopped. *What's that smell?* For one of the few times in her life, and certainly since her island friend Deb had called her out for excessive curiosity and foolhardiness, she did not give in to the urge to explore on her own.

Instead, she reached for her cell phone to call the deputy. "Bruce, it's Leslie. I'm on the beach, um, near where you found, um, Frank. The dog's discovered something by the remains of an old boat. Could be a dead bird or turtle or…. I can't look. Bring some Vick's VapoRub."

On a good day, Deputy Bruce Webster could make it to the north end of the island from the sheriff's office in 15 minutes. This morning, the wail of his police siren reached Leslie's ears in less than 10.

Wes was scanning the lunch menu at the Tarpon Bar and keeping an eye out for Johnny Boy when he got the call from Leslie.

"Jamie? Found? Dead or alive?" Wes said, causing Shine the bartender to stop organizing the unopened bottles of whisky on the shelf at the back of the bar and focus on the reporter.

"Yeah. Um-hmm. So, you discovered him?" Pause. "You called the deputy? Good girl!"

Shine had drawn closer to Wes and was making no attempt to hide his interest in the conversation.

"I'm on my way," Wes said, clicking off the phone and glancing at the bartender. "They found the drug dealer. Dead on the beach, um, just like

Frank Johnson. That's all I know. If your friend comes in, put in a good word for me before he has drink number four. I really want to talk to him about his son."

Shine nodded, seemingly grateful that Wes had given him a tidbit he could share with his customers, along with an assignment.

As he hurried to his car, Wes thought about the events of the past months. He felt no sorrow about the three bodies discovered on the island's shoreline – two drug-dealing cousins named Thompson – one before his arrival – and a fisherman whose motives he considered questionable. But he did worry about Leslie's state of mind, and also wondered how all of this would affect the tourist traffic. It couldn't be good.

He pulled his SUV onto the side of the road, joining a line-up of official-looking vehicles, and sprinted for the beach. He was several hundred feet from the boat remains when he spotted Leslie and Whalen standing off to one side under a golf umbrella imprinted with the word "sheriff."

The deputy was by the boat, taking photos and putting up yellow markers. The sheriff, also close by, was talking to the one DEA agent Wes recognized, Don McKechnie, and four other men he didn't know.

"We don't want pictures of a dead body in the paper," the sheriff yelled, putting up his hand as Wes approached.

"I'm here as a, um, friend of the family," Wes said pointing to Leslie. "But I will have questions for you later."

Apparently satisfied that Wes was not going to hinder his investigation, the sheriff turned his back to the reporter and continued chatting with the other men. Wes joined Leslie, mumbled a greeting and said something about it being a "bad scene." He put his arm around her shoulder and gave her a reassuring squeeze.

"I've been standing here trying to figure out what happened. Did Frank wound Jamie and then Jamie shoot Frank? And was Jamie bleeding so badly he crawled to the side of the boat and died before he could get help. The two bodies weren't even close to each other…."

Wes was surprised at how detached Leslie sounded as she offered her theory on what had transpired. Maybe she was done mourning Frank and, of course, would have no sympathy for Jamie.

Wes glanced at the body, which smelled of death and appeared to have been worked over by buzzards. It looked like Jamie had been shot in the back and managed to crawl to the boat. The discolored sand around him was an indication he died from blood loss. His Bucs cap, which Wes recognized from the Tarpon Bar, was caught up in the tall seagrass.

Wes felt a sudden urge to throw up but composed himself and focused on taking pictures of the sheriff and the others in the now driving rain. When he finished, he turned to Leslie: "You ready to get outta here? It's brutal."

She shivered. "There's nothing we can do for Jamie…or…or Frank. It's time to move on."

CHAPTER 11

Tuesday, December 22

By the next day, Leslie's speculation that Jamie shot Frank after the fisherman fatally wounded him was gaining traction around the community. The paper's layout man, Randy Long, was chatting about it with publisher Sara Fortune as Wes was preparing to leave *The Sun* office enroute to the Tarpon Bar.

"The chamber's going to call and ask us to downplay these shootings," Sara said, looking at Wes as though seeking advice. "But I don't see how we can do it. Two deaths. Not something you can overlook...or bury on the back page."

"I hope you got photos we can use," Randy said to Wes.

"Yeah, well, a few. The sheriff wasn't happy about me being there, and it was raining like hell," he said. "There's a partial photo of Thompson with his cousin Peter and a big fish in our archives. I saw it not long ago. But that's about it. I already filed my story this morning, but I'll have updates."

"Looks like the island's rating in the Conde Nast travel recommendations is gonna take a nosedive," Randy said, never cracking a smile.

"Oh you." Sara rolled her eyes and joined Wes in laughing at the layout man's irreverent humor.

When Wes arrived at the Tarpon, the bartender was eager to share the community speculation. "Like the gunfight at the OK Corral...that's what they're sayin'," Shine said.

"Hard to know. We'll have to wait for the police report," Wes responded.

Shine looked impressed, but the truth was that Wes didn't have any idea what he was talking about. He hoped that Deputy Webster would explain the finer details to him when the reports on both deaths were issued.

"Maybe you can give me a heads up," Shine said, grinning.

"I think we can give you something interesting to talk about when the time comes," Wes said. "Now about that grouper sandwich…."

The reporter had worked hard after dropping off Leslie and the dog, both soaking wet, at her condo. He filled up his Twitter, Instagram and Facebook accounts with the news on the island's latest gruesome discovery.

All that done, he was eager to redirect his energy to another story, this one about the life and tragic death of Toby Mason. The first step in unlocking that island mystery was connecting with the young man's alcoholic father.

Wes finished his sandwich and was about to order another beer when the bar's wooden screen door swung open, bringing with it a gust of cool air and the long-awaited pale-faced man.

John Mason was wearing aviator sunglasses and a leather bomber jacket and looked frail. His gait was that of an 80-year-old, although from something Shine had said, Wes didn't think he was even close to that age. Hard times and tortured thoughts can eat away at a man, aging him beyond his years. Wes knew that all too well.

The pale-faced man slid onto his familiar stool and removed his glasses, setting them carefully on the bar. Shine looked at Wes and winked. "Give him a minute," the bartender whispered.

"So, Johnny Boy, do you want the usual or do you wanna start off with something to warm your innards on this cool day…like a bowl of lobster corn chowder and a cup of coffee?" Shine asked with maternal familiarity.

"Chowder and coffee sound good. But first, I'll have my usual, sir. No sense eating on an empty stomach."

The man and the bartender both laughed. Wes took that as his cue to grab his beer and move to the barstool next to Mason. "Chilly out there. And just last week it was hotter than hell," Wes said, draining the last bit of Michelob from his glass.

"Very true. Do I know you, friend?"

"No, I don't believe we've met. I'm Wes Avery. I'm the new reporter at *The Sun*."

"I'm John Mason. Shine here calls me Johnny Boy. I'm no boy anymore but my bartender can call me anything he wants…as long as he keeps my glass full." He winked at Wes and chuckled softly at his own joke.

"I know the feeling," Wes said, signaling that he could use another beer. On a full stomach, he could handle at least five without that familiar buzz that clouded his judgment. He had a way to go.

"How long have you been in town?" Mason asked. His manner was friendly and cultured. A contrast to the standoffish "Crackers" Wes encountered when he first moved to Florida but still liked for their earthy ways and colorful personalities.

"Let's see. Shy a couple of months. But it feels a lot longer," Wes said. "You?"

"A lifetime," Mason said. He took a sip of the drink the bartender put in front of him and made a sound that reflected both his pleasure and his addiction.

"I'm not a native Floridian. Grew up on the east coast. Greenwich, Connecticut. My mother lived not far from Michael Skakel, the Kennedy who killed that young girl. All those years they tried to solve it…." His voice trailed off.

Wes let Mason ramble on with the hope he would begin to feel comfortable confiding in someone he didn't know. That's how it started with these kinds of stories: the source and reporter establishing trust in a little dance that moved slowly at first then, hopefully, picked up speed.

"Yeah, some of those cases take forever to solve. It's surprising, though, how often the truth wins out. I've written lots of stories about that…" Wes stopped. The crime beat was not his specialty. He didn't like the idea of lying to Mason. Despite what conspiracy theorists and Randy Long thought, politics and crime were not synonymous. Most of the time.

Mason was quickly onto drink number two and Shine still hadn't produced the soup and coffee Wes hoped would keep the pale-faced man sober enough for extended conversation.

"Didn't I hear you order something to eat?" he said. "This place can be plenty slow sometimes."

"You know, you're right. Shine, my man, where is that chowder?"

"Coming right up," the bartender said and disappeared into the kitchen, returning with a large bowl, a package of oyster crackers and a cup of coffee.

"So, you've reported on crimes, shootings?" Mason said after taking a few spoonfuls and pushing the rest to one side.

"Yeah, um, a few."

"Well, I've got one for you. My son. He was shot at a party 20 years ago. Right here on this island." Mason reached for glass number three as Wes sent a pleading look Shine's way. *Can't you slow him down?*

"Really? Your son? Would you share your story with me?" Wes was now feeling the need to make his pitch quickly – before Mason experienced that click in his head that switched him to an alternate, alcohol-fueled reality.

"You're interested? Most folks say it's old news and I should move on. Could you ignore that justice had not been served in the death of a loved one? Is there a parent out there that wouldn't pursue the truth to the end?"

"No, I don't think so," Wes said with sincerity. "I don't have any children, but if I did and one of them was, um, killed, I wouldn't rest until I knew what happened."

Mason downed drink number three and put his fist down on the bar with a loud thud. "Exactly."

"This 'un's number four, Johnny Boy," Shine said, repeating the ritual that signaled the approaching end of coherent conversation. The bartender looked apologetically in the reporter's direction.

"Tell you what," Mason said, stopping the glass short of his lips. "You come to my place tomorrow at 10. We'll talk. Share a little Christmas cheer. My friend the bartender will tell you how to get there."

He emptied the glass, put it on the bar with two 20-dollar bills and slipped on his sunglasses. He turned to look once more at Wes. "Tomorrow," he said as he got up from his barstool, steadied himself and walked out the front door, letting it slam behind him.

"You get what you wanted?" Shine asked as he retrieved the pale-faced man's empty glass and the money.

"Not yet. But maybe soon I'll get what Johnny Boy and others want. Answers."

CHAPTER 12

Wednesday, December 23

Leslie was in a pensive mood when Wes picked her up to take her to the waterfront home where John Mason lived.

"Still thinking about the shootings?" Wes asked.

"Well, yes, and I'm also feeling guilty about not flying home to spend Christmas with my daughter and, um, ex-husband. I told you about him. The plastic surgeon."

"Haven't you been through enough lately?"

Leslie laughed. "I guess I'm still a little raw from how our marriage ended last year. He's the kind of guy that will tell you that both of his marriages failed because he made the wrong choices. Nothing to do with his shortcomings. But I think it was better for both of us. And I sincerely hope he's happy."

As they headed down a dirt road lined with Sabal palms and scrub brushes, Leslie abruptly changed the subject. "Tell me again. What are you getting me into today?"

"That's a funny question coming from you," Wes said. "Usually, you're the one getting others into trouble."

She gave him that look. The one that women give men that can be taken several ways.

"Sorry," Wes said. "So, here's the story. John Mason has lived on the island forever he says. He's been into old paintings, antiques, stuff like that. Had a young son...guy in his 20s...who died in 2000. Shot himself in the head. Police ruled it a suicide, then an accident. Mason and the locals think there was more to it. A coverup of some sort. Although I don't think anyone has offered up a motive."

"Hmm. Did you check the clippings?"

"Naturally," he said as he swerved to avoid a flock of Ibis feeding too close to the road. "Read through them. Saw the photos. I feel the need to start, in person, with the father."

"Makes sense," Leslie said as she checked the numbers on the pole by the side of the road. "Here it is. 2501."

The cinder block house, painted a pale yellow, sat near the edge of a channel that led out into the island's south pass. Moored to a series of covered docks were high-end fishing boats, most in the 30-foot range: a Viking, a Yellowfin, a Freeman, a Contender.

"Nice," Leslie said, surveying the fleet and remembering the schooling she'd gotten from Frank about boats. "Do you suppose Mr. Mason has a rental or fishing guide business?"

"Doubt it," Wes said as the two of them emerged from the SUV. "Check out his vehicle."

Parked near the entrance to the house was an old Volvo, faded brown with a few dents and scratches. Hard to tell the year, Leslie thought, but it had enough rust to hint at its advanced age. She looked beyond the car to the front door which sported a hand-painted sign that read, "No drugs sold here. Stay away."

"Guess he isn't part of any local gang," she said in a mocking tone. "They don't usually turn away business."

The words were barely out of her mouth when the door opened and John Mason appeared. He looked surprised to see Leslie but managed a welcoming smile and invited the couple in.

"Merry Christmas," he said. "Thanks for coming."

He was, as Wes had described earlier to Leslie, a smallish man – not more than 140 pounds – with wispy brown hair, a pale, drawn face and light-colored eyes. She thought they were blue, then green, then decided it didn't matter. They were hollow looking; revealing a man emptied by his sorrow, she guessed.

"Coffee?" he asked when they were both inside, and he'd closed the front door.

Wes said yes; Leslie declined. When Mason went to the small kitchen to retrieve two cups, Leslie glanced around the area that functioned as a dining room, kitchen and living area. There were no holiday decorations although there was a plate of sugar cookies decorated with candy canes made of icing on the coffee table in front of them.

On the floor were thick, oriental rugs – dark and out-of-place for a residence in a southern Florida coastal town. They spoke more of old family homes in the Hamptons. The rattan furniture looked to be mid-century with cushions covered in dark prints and stains. Off to one side were stacks of boxes filled with binders, folders and newspapers. The TV set was turned to CNN with the volume off.

It looked to Leslie that Mason had money, maybe not so much now but at one time. Or he'd acquired these items as an antique dealer and held onto them for his own use.

"It's kind of a mess here. Sorry," Mason said after handing Wes a cup of coffee and starting to sit down. "Sure I can't get you anything, um, ma'am? How about a Christmas cookie?"

"Call me Leslie. No thanks. I'm fine."

"You probably noticed the sign on the front door," he said. "Damn kids knock on my door at 3 a.m. looking for drugs. They must have sold stuff from this house years ago, before I started renting it.

"The guy that owns this place...those are his boat slips." He glanced toward the window that overlooked the channel. "Wouldn't want you to think those are mine. I do okay, but I don't have a fleet of boats. I just keep an eye on them for him and his renters."

Leslie listened to his small talk, thinking that Mason seemed nervous and wondering if he would be willing to tell them much of anything, especially with her there.

Suddenly, he got up and walked to a bookcase across the room. He grabbed the photo off the top shelf. It was of a boy about 14, holding a snook he'd thrust toward the camera to make it appear larger than it was.

"Here he is," Mason said, his face breaking into a half-smile. He showed the picture first to Leslie and then Wes. "My boy, Toby. He was like this all the time. Happy. Fun-loving. They said he committed suicide. No way."

Mason's face started to crumple, but he appeared to reach inside himself and drag back his composure. "He was 22. We were going into business together. He was full of life...so full of life."

There was an awkward silence. Leslie wondered when Wes would stop staring at the photograph and begin questioning the man.

"Goddammit, you're going to help me, aren't you?" Mason was suddenly enraged, pacing, like a man ready to explode. "They've buried it for 20 years. They'll try to stop you...."

"Why don't you sit down and tell us the story, from start to finish," Wes said. His voice was calming. "I'll take notes, if that's okay with you. And we'll go from there. We're gonna do our best to help you."

"I think I need a drink," Mason said, looking at a large, half-full bottle of clear liquid by the kitchen sink.

"If you can talk to us first that would be good," Wes said. "We'll all have something when you've finished. A Christmas toast. That sound okay?"

Mason sighed and sat down, propping his cheek in his hand and looking out the window.

"Let's start with the last time you saw your son alive."

Mason leaned back in the chair, folded his hands on his lap and continued looking out the window as if gathering his thoughts. The overhead fan emitted an occasional squeak as it rotated on high speed; Leslie wished Mason would turn it off as the downdraft was making her chilled. Wes reached out and took one of the cookies, gobbled it down and then positioned his notebook on the arm of the oversized rattan furniture waiting to capture the pale-faced man's words.

After what seemed like an eternity to Leslie, Mason began: "It was about a week before he died. He'd come down from his mother's place – about an hour from here – to fish with friends. Had a couple of steaks with him and a six-pack. Wanted to talk about the business we were going into together… and his new car. The one you saw parked out front. It was an adult car, not some souped-up kid ride. He was making payments. Being very responsible.

"We had our disagreements in the past. Typical father and son stuff. But on that day, we had a good time together. Like everything was on the right track for both of us…at last."

Leslie could see tears forming in his eyes and noticed his lower lip quivering. He sighed as if to compose himself and then continued. "That night he called me and said he wouldn't be out late, and he'd be crashing here. He never came home. That was the last time I heard his voice.

"He wasn't a perfect kid. Had problems with drugs at one time. Went through therapy. Took him longer to finish school than either one of us hoped. But I couldn't judge. Hell, I dropped out of high school to make money, spent a month at Yale and got out of there and never looked back. Toby had a degree and wasn't afraid of work. He mentioned a girlfriend. He didn't tell me her name, but I got the idea he liked her a lot."

Mason got up with his coffee cup and looked at the others. Both declined, although Wes reached for another cookie.

"These are pretty good. You get them at the local bakery?"

Leslie didn't watch him but guessed Mason might have sneaked some of the liquid from the large vodka bottle into his coffee. His first gulp when he sat back down was substantial.

"Bakery? Yeah. I go there a couple of times a week."

"This business you were going in together…what was it?" Wes asked.

"Buying and selling. Mostly things on consignment. I did that when I was starting out and living up near Newport. Wealthy people would put their houses on the market, give me the keys. I sold the lot and took my commission."

"They trusted you?" Leslie interjected.

"I came from a family with a good name. Dysfunctional but few knew. I was the son of their bridge partner and the stepson of a prominent nuclear scientist they worked with. All they cared about was that I had a pedigree.

"The two of us had connections here – and Toby had plenty of charm. We figured we could make a killing…." His voice trailed off as he stood and headed for the kitchen again.

Leslie looked at Wes and rolled her eyes as if to ask if he was drinking.

Mason sat down again and put his cup on the nearby table where Leslie could confirm it was no longer coffee but a clear liquid.

He leaned over and grabbed a cardboard box. "Here's everything. Everything that happened the night they killed my boy. I paid for the depositions. Here's a report from a female investigator who helped me out. I've lost track of all these people, but their work is there. You take this. Read it."

Wes leaned toward the box. "Okay if I go through it now?"

"Uh-huh." Mason watched, sipping his drink, as Wes glanced through the papers.

"They'll kill you if you get too close to the truth," he blurted out after 10 minutes had passed.

"What?" Wes had been immersed in the paperwork until Mason spoke.

"They don't want the truth to come out…even after all this time. Soon as word gets out that you're talking to me, you'll start to feel the pressure… from one source or another."

Wes smiled. "We'll just have to keep it quiet. It's our secret until we know the truth."

"Yeah, well, I know the truth and when you finish with that you will too," Mason said, standing up to end the interview and, Leslie thought, to continue drinking without pretense or interference.

CHAPTER 13

Thursday, December 24

Leslie, Wes and Mason agreed to meet on Monday, December 28. Wes assumed that over the Christmas weekend he and Leslie would visit the infamous Seaside Cottage and review the material from John Mason. Today, on Christmas Eve, a small part of him was wondering if he would have to celebrate the holiday alone again or if some kind soul would take him in.

Leslie answered that question with a phone call in the early afternoon. "We've been invited to a spur-of-the-moment Christmas shindig at Deb and Scooter's. BYOB and a dish to share. They've got all the fried fish you can eat. I'll pick you up at 5 and bring a casserole from both of us. Okay?"

Wes felt himself getting emotional. After Faye left him for another man – and good riddance to her – how many Christmases had he spent alone or working the news desk with other pathetic bastards for overtime pay while everyone else went home to their families? Too many. And even though he didn't really know Deb and Scooter that well, he was glad to be with Leslie.

"I'll be out in front with the booze," he said. "Casual?"

"This is Florida. What else," she said.

Wes showered, put on one of his newer tropical shirts – the loose-fitting white one with outlines of blue ferns – long khakis and loafers without socks. He wasn't sure why, but it felt important to look good.

Shine, the bartender, was wearing a red and white Santa hat and servicing a bar overflowing with customers. There were no empty barstools and no familiar faces at the bar so Wes stood back from the crowd until Shine called his name. He assumed the pale-faced man was long gone – if he'd even dropped by that day.

"What can I get you, Wes?"

"A Michelob on draft and a couple of bottles of the house white to go," he yelled over the din.

"Comin' right up," Shine said.

Wes reached in to get his drink, his arm accidentally nudging the chest of an attractive looking woman in her early 50s with long, thick hair. She was wearing a flowing cover-up over a tight-fitting red tank top. She smelled of gardenias and was nursing a glass of red wine.

"Whoa," she said. "You don't know me well enough to get that familiar."

"I am so sorry," he said and flashed a sheepish look her way. Even though he found her appealing, the touch was unintentional and not his style.

"No problem. I'm Bobbie and this is my husband, Jeff." She pointed to a burly man on her other side, who smiled warmly at Wes and reached out to shake hands.

"I'm Wes…Avery…I'm the, um, sort-of new reporter for *The Sun*." He wanted Bobbie and her husband, who looked like a strong guy, to know he wasn't some arbitrary Joe trying to cop a feel in a crowded bar on Christmas Eve.

"Reporter? The guy who's looking into that shooting 20 years ago? John Mason was telling us all about it a couple of hours ago," Bobbie said, turning her full attention to Wes. "You've got some job. Figuring this out after so long."

Wes pictured himself choking on his beer, slamming his hand down on the bar and saying, "Jeez, I thought this was going to be our secret, Johnny Boy?" He did none of those.

"I'm just, um, looking into it. Newspapers like to do anniversary pieces. 20-year stuff," he said, downplaying his interest.

"It's not like we knew the kid all that well. He was a little young to run in our crowd. But people still talk about him. How sweet he was. Nobody believes he committed suicide. Nobody," Bobbie said with Jeff nodding in agreement.

"Something wasn't right about the whole thing," the husband added when she'd finished. "And that area around Seaside Cottage…a couple of years later, a guy shot himself there, in one of the properties next to the big house. I think he was a psychologist. There's a jinx on that place."

Wes wanted to hear more but needed to leave. He downed his beer and thanked Bobbie and her husband: "I'm off to a party, but I'd like to chat with you again in the future to get more background, names of people you think I should talk to."

Bobbie grabbed a napkin and a nearby pen and wrote her name and phone number on it. "Call us anytime. And you're welcome to come for dinner."

"Thanks, I'd like that," Wes said, picking up the napkin and the bottles of wine Shine put before him and leaving a $100 tip for the bartender, as well as his business card for Bobbie. "Merry Christmas to you all."

The banging of the Tarpon Bar's screen door as he left was a comforting sound. He liked the little community for its informality and friendliness… but he found the sinister undercurrent unsettling.

Cars and golf carts filled the sandy, scrub-grass area in front of Deb and Scooter Rankin's island home. After a trip around the block, Leslie ended up parking her SUV a couple of houses down by a multi-million-dollar residence that was unoccupied. Probably only temporarily, she thought.

"Your friends live in a swanky neighborhood," Wes observed, pointing to the mansion that rose out of the sand like a southwest Florida version of the Taj Mahal, complete with a reflecting pool in the front yard that had as its centerpiece a statue of elephants instead of the usual jumping dolphins.

"Their old home on stilts is out of place even though their property was recently remodeled. But it makes no difference to them. And it would take the jaws of life to pry Scooter from that house," Leslie said.

As they walked toward the festivities, they could hear a band playing *Jingle Bell Rock*. Wes did a dance, twirling around with a bottle of wine in each hand. Leslie laughed and shook her head.

"Thought this was going to be a little more intimate. But it looks like you're in for a real island party," she said.

"Why not," Wes said. "The more the merrier...isn't that what they say?"

"Um, it's not a wake, but Deb and Scooter are planning to say a few words about Frank." Leslie searched Wes's face for a reaction that never came. "Anyway, it should be fun...and nice to see everyone."

Deb, Leslie's best friend, was in charge of the Gallery Centre where local artists exhibited and sold their creations during the winter season. Deb was a round-faced woman in her fifties, with no pretense and a way of making everyone around her feel at ease. She was one of the first people Leslie met when she came to the island. She had also introduced Leslie to Frank.

Scooter, Deb's husband of 30-plus years, was a man of few words and a questionable past that included time spent in prison. Somehow their marriage worked and had, surprisingly, gotten better after a recent fire nearly burned down their old home and severely injured Scooter. The house had been repaired – with contributions from churchgoers and a local realtor – and Scooter appeared to be healing nicely.

When they arrived in the Rankin's backyard, Wes headed for a makeshift bar with colorful holiday lights. Leslie put her veggie casserole on a long piece of plywood on sawhorses. The table's green plastic covering was decorated with cutout snowflakes like little kids used to make in grade school. She squeezed her dish between cheese grits and a macaroni salad with peas and bacon.

The island women knew how to pull together something tasty, even with short notice. The entrée for these large social events was often fresh fish reeled in by the men and cooked up at the Tarpon Bar. After eating grouper and snapper caught the same day, Leslie wondered how she could ever stomach the questionable fish served in most restaurants.

She watched Wes shake hands with Scooter and the other men. He seemed like the kind of guy who never knew a stranger and had a genuine interest in others. She liked that quality in him.

"What's in this?" she heard him ask when Scooter handed Wes one of his famous potions. Red and festive.

"Lots of fruit. Strawberries. Pineapple. Coconut," Scooter replied, winking at the man standing next to him.

"Since when did coconuts become a fruit?" Wes asked. "I thought they were tree nuts."

"When you mix them with rum strange things happen," the man next to Scooter observed with a deadpan face that melted into a big grin.

"Well, then, cheers," Wes said. The men standing around the bar raised their glasses with him and took one swig and then another, followed by a chorus of UMMMMMMs.

"Scooter's in his element," Deb said as she walked toward Leslie, wrapped her arms around her and gave her an extended hug. "How you feeling?"

"I'm okay. It was such a tragedy the way it happened. That night when I thought I was going to die, and Frank left me stranded without a word and, well, broke my heart. The return of Jamie and then Frank and then the, um, shootings. Frank and I didn't have a chance to get to know each other in a normal setting."

"He cared about you. A lot. I know that," Deb said. She tossed her waist-long dark hair to one side and scanned the growing crowd. "He might have even liked this party in his honor. But his life was complicated. Sometimes relationships can't stand up to the realities of life. I think that was the case with you two. Bad timing."

Leslie nodded. She had dwelled too long on her dysfunctional relationship with Frank and wanted desperately to move on. "Looks like half the island is here with more on the way?"

"We just put out the word…like they do at Terry's annual street party every year," Deb said. "You can never predict who's gonna show. Even the band volunteered to play for free. There's no better place in the world than this little bit of real estate."

Leslie was prepared to offer her assessment that even with its warts and strange characters, she was in total agreement. Before she could open her mouth, she was distracted by two familiar figures emerging from the crowd.

The first was Deputy Bruce Webster. His brown hair was slicked back even more than usual and his face was clean shaven. He wore an outfit not unlike the one Wes had on – a loose-fitting camp shirt with a tropical flower that started on his shoulder and merged into full blossom around his trim waistline. Even though he looked world weary, Leslie thought him appealing.

Holding his hand was Janis Johnson, a local artist and the woman that Frank Johnson had been in the process of divorcing before he was killed. Janis's Christmas tree earrings hung from earlobe to shoulder to blend in with a dark green dress that showed off her athletic figure.

Leslie and Janis had one unpleasant meeting in their past – a run-in at the Gallery Centre where Janis had threatened Leslie for going out with her "husband." Leslie was not looking for another confrontation, especially since the object of that disagreement was no longer available to either of them.

Even though not much time had passed since the woman's attack, Janis seemed different from what Leslie remembered. The pompadour the artist was sporting when Leslie first saw her was longer; blonde hair now framed her pretty face. A sequined sweater covered the tattoos on her arms. She looked softer, happier, almost normal.

The deputy was the first to see and acknowledge Leslie and Deb. He whispered something to Janis who looked their way and offered a half-smile. Leslie cringed and hoped no one noticed.

"You know Janis, um Johnson, right?" the deputy said, smiling at Leslie.

You know I do, Leslie thought.

"Yes, so sorry for your loss." Leslie was surprised at the words that came out of her mouth. She wondered why she or anyone else should direct their condolences to this woman. Frank had taken over raising Stevie because Janis was not a caring mom, and the two hadn't lived together for some time. But, as happens in a small community where certain niceties are expected, everyone follows the rules of bereavement etiquette.

"Oh, honey, we're so glad you're here. We're all gonna miss Frank," Deb piped in, first patting Janis on the arm, then giving her a quick hug.

"Thank you," Janis said, looking up at the deputy as he put his arm around her shoulder and gave her a squeeze.

"He was a real friend to so many of us," the deputy said. "And he lost his life trying to make our island safer."

Leslie noticed that Janis didn't react to the deputy's comment.

"Can I get you ladies one of those Christmas drinks?"

"Uh-huh," Leslie said. "I'd like one. And could you ask Wes to join me if you see him over there? I need to warn him about Scooter's concoctions."

The deputy wandered off, Deb with him, laughing and talking like the old friends they were. Janis was the first to speak when the two women were alone. "You stand there like Miss Goody-Goody, acting like you had nothing to do with my husband's death. It was all your fault."

"Excuse me?" Leslie instinctively backed up to put herself out of harm's way in case Janis should become physical as she had the first time they met.

"I owe you, big time. You'll pay for this," Janis said, spitting out her words with increasing venom. "You will pay!"

"I take it the little display of sweetness a few minutes ago was for Bruce and Deb's benefit. You know I had nothing to do with Frank's murder," Leslie responded. She couldn't help the smirk on her face.

"He came back to save you."

"And apparently to speak with you."

Janis recoiled. "Who said I spoke with him? I didn't see him. All I know is that he disappeared, took our son with him and sent me some money. Not enough considering the millions they say he had with him."

Leslie moved to diffuse the situation. "Now that you're a widow, you can move on with your life. You appear to have a good relationship with Bruce. He's a great guy," she said.

"We get along." She directed her gaze at the deputy who was walking toward the two women, drinks in both hands.

"Scooter assures me this will set you free," he said. "Oh, and Wes is over there in a chair. Upright for now."

"Maybe I'd better go rescue him," Leslie said with a forced laugh.

"Don't forget what I said." Janis flashed a syrupy smile Leslie's direction.

"Trust me. I won't."

CHAPTER 14

Friday, December 25

The party at Deb and Scooter's ended at about 2 a.m. with Wes and Leslie staying to help clean up. The next morning, Wes decided he was feeling surprisingly good for his late night out and figured he had Leslie to thank for his clear head. After the second drink, she warned him that Scooter's potions were legendary for their ability to disconnect an individual from reality.

"How many is too many?"

"Since you're on your second one, I'm thinking you've already reached your limit," she told him.

He thought back to the time not that long ago when he consumed too many Caipirinhas on a beach in Brazil and felt momentarily blinded by the strong alcohol. Lesson learned. He wanted to be at the top of his game when he and Leslie trekked through the area around Seaside Cottage. He wanted to have his wits about him when he read through the transcripts of the people that were with Toby Mason in his final minutes. He had a lot to absorb over the next three days.

He dressed and headed down the stairs from his second-story apartment to the empty streets of the village. It was Christmas Day and no stores were open. No fresh-brewed coffee or blueberry scones to be found anywhere. The Tarpon Bar was closed. The pale-faced man would be drinking alone, he guessed. He sighed at the thought of John Mason lost in solitude and alcohol.

He decided to go for a quick run, letting his mind wander through the events of last night.

There were 30 minutes or so of what was supposed to be a wake for Frank Johnson. Eight people stepped up to say kind words about the fisherman, including Deputy Webster who Frank saved from drowning years ago. Wes wasn't impressed with their stories. He couldn't get past his recent memories of the guy.

He did notice that the deputy had a "hot" date for the party and was surprised to learn from Leslie that the woman was Frank's wife. He didn't recall seeing her before and couldn't picture her with Bruce. Frank yes. But the deputy? Nice guy. No way.

Wes finished his run through the empty village and headed up the steps to his apartment. After a cup of barely drinkable instant coffee and a quick shower, he was ready for Leslie to pick him up. She volunteered to drive, saying she thought she knew where Seaside Cottage was and suggested they look like a couple spending a day at the beach.

"No sense in arousing anyone's suspicions."

"I can't imagine anyone there linking us to a 20-year-old shooting," Wes responded. But when he climbed in Leslie's SUV he noticed a beach umbrella, towels and a cooler in the back seat.

Women never listen, he thought.

Once on 15th Street, Leslie eyed the cars of holiday beachgoers lining both sides of the road, and gently nudged a stroller out of the way with her bumper to find a parking space. Homeowners near the beach often put obstacles in the public right-of-way to deter visitors from encroaching on what they saw as their private space. Leslie was not to be dissuaded.

"Is this it?" Wes asked expectantly when Leslie finally came to a stop in front of a small cottage with a pale blue door. It looked like a shoebox compared to most of the nearby residences. A screened-in porch fronted the house. Wes guessed the cottage couldn't be more than 900 square feet, if that.

"Hmm, not big enough," he said, answering his own question.

"I think this is the cottage where some woman killed herself several years ago," Leslie said. "But then I heard that although she lived on the island, she was found dead in Miami. Who knows what's true and what isn't?

I've discovered that on this island truth and fiction often walk the beach hand-in-hand."

"And you can't tell one from the other," Wes said, remembering that Jeff at the bar had mentioned a suicide with different details.

Wes looked to the residence across the street, which was having work done on the roof, the windows and two-car garage. A small CAT earth mover with a Christmas wreath on the back was parked near the front door.

"I hope that's not the place we're looking for," he observed. "There'll be nothing left of the original structure when they're done."

"I'm picturing something quainter," Leslie said, pointing to a residence with white siding and a cedar shake roof. "There!"

In front of the house was a barely visible sign that said *Seaside Cottage*. Underneath, an arrow with the word BEACH on it pointed toward a path that led to the Gulf. "That's where we start," she said.

The house looked closed for the holidays. In the back, Wes and Leslie discovered that the hurricane shutters were down, protecting what Wes guessed was a large lanai. The two circled the property, then stopped by the pool at the side of the house.

"I feel kind of creepy trespassing," Leslie said.

"You've never worried about that before," Wes responded, chuckling at the memory of Leslie tramping through the mystery house where drugs were hidden.

"I've reformed…wait, what's that over there?" She pointed to a cottage partly concealed by overgrown bushes, Chinese ferns and live oak trees whose fallen leaves, caught up in the sea breezes, swirled around a shell driveway.

"I think we've found it!" Wes enthused, as he trotted ahead of Leslie and positioned himself by a window in the front.

"It's THE kitchen," he yelled after peering through the opening. "With the same god-awful wallpaper it had in those photographs from 20 years ago. I can't believe it."

Wes was now inside the porch; his voice filled with the excitement of discovery. "The captain's chairs by the window. They're still here. And the bullet hole in the woodwork by the large kitchen window…I wonder if I can find where it was repaired?"

He stopped and waited for Leslie to catch up before reaching for the door to enter the house from the porch. "It's been waiting for us. For you and me. Why else would it be so, um, unchanged after all these years?"

Wes was always a loner. Never liked being assigned with another reporter on a story and never paid much attention to women after his divorce. But he liked Leslie, and the fact they were sharing this adventure together made him feel good. He wanted to tell her but thought better of it.

"Hello. What's going on?" a slender, gray-haired man in khakis and a yellow polo shirt was walking through the patio door, snapping photos of Wes and Leslie with his cell phone.

"Oh hi," Leslie responded, flashing a smile in his direction. "We're hoping to rent something on the island and heard about this guest house, um, or cottage. It's so cute in a nostalgic way. You know anything about it?"

Wes marveled that she could appear so nonchalant after being caught breaking and entering.

"Rental? The owners, the Beldons, are away and won't be back for another month," the man said, lowering his phone and adopting a less accusatory tone. "I don't think they've ever rented this cottage, but I guess I can give you their phone number."

Such a trusting fool, Wes thought. *We could be burglars for all this guy knows…though I guess he does have our photos.*

"That's so kind of you," Leslie said. "I'm looking for something for my daughter when she comes to visit from college…Ohio State. But I'm a little worried about this location. Wasn't there a shooting here a while back."

The man was suddenly eager to share what he had heard.

"In 2000," he enthused. "A young guy at a party. Drugs or alcohol is my guess. I'm sure your daughter would be fine. That was a long time ago.

"I bought the house over there," he continued, pointing to a residence behind a brick wall to the right of Seaside Cottage. "Never had any problems.

The Beldons are new owners, too. They've talked about tearing down this place and building an office and workout room...."

Leslie frowned. "What a shame. We have so few of these little houses left near the beach. You suppose we could go inside?"

The man hesitated. "Don't know...well...I guess it's all right. Don't tell the Beldons I gave you permission."

"The screen door was unlocked. Maybe they don't care if they're planning to demolish it," Wes observed.

The man turned to leave. "Look around. Let me know if you have any other questions. I'll be across the street at my place. Just come through the gate."

Once the man was outside the porch and walking away, Wes tried the blue door that led from the porch to what looked to be a sitting room. It was unlocked.

"There is where it happened. Where Toby Mason lost his life...just as it was starting," he said when Leslie was beside him and the two were standing in the kitchen that had 1970s-style light-green wallpaper with ugly blue flowers, white appliances, linoleum floor and counter tops.

"There were, best guess, more than 30 people here. Most of them in their 20s. Several married couples, a few singles like Toby. The owners were out of town, and one of the couples rented the main house and guest cottage for the weekend and invited their friends to join them. It was about midnight when the party revved up...got out of hand, some recalled. People showed up who weren't invited. The porch was packed. Music was loud. Lots of alcohol. Everyone having a good time.

"There was horsing around in the kitchen...alcohol-fueled testosterone on display...and suddenly there was a gun in the mix. The word was that it belonged to the owners of the house, but how it ended up in the kitchen where there were a lot of people shit-faced or stoned is one of the mysteries. No one claimed ownership. It was a Walther P38.

"A what?" Leslie interrupted. "Like the gun James Bond used?"

"P38 not PPK. I did some research and found out the P38 was mass produced in Germany starting in the mid-1940s, just about the time the Nazis were expanding the country's war-making capacity. It looks like the guns you see in old war movies. Maybe the people at the party thought it wasn't real…that it was some sort of souvenir or even a toy.

"The story is that Toby grabbed the gun, pointed it to his temple and fired. The house emptied out like it was on fire, leaving behind the couples here for the weekend. Someone called 911, fire rescue. By the time the EMTs got here and made sure the gun was secure, Toby was dead…or so far gone there was no saving him."

Outside the wind had picked up, rustling the leaves in the live oak trees that surrounded the cottage and underscoring the drama of Wes's story. Leslie was quiet for a few minutes and then peppered him with questions.

"Was it a suicide? I know Mason claims it wasn't, but he wasn't there. Didn't know his son's state of mind. And did they find out why there was a gun in the kitchen, and who put it there? And why didn't someone try to stop Toby?"

"That's where it gets tricky," Wes said. "For some reason the police didn't spend much time investigating, didn't mark the house off as a crime scene or dig out the bullet until several weeks later. Didn't test anybody but Toby for powder marks. Once everyone at the party made their brief statements to the investigative officers, they were outta here."

He hesitated, then added, "The police said it was a suicide and then ruled it an accidental death and that was that."

Leslie shook her head. "No wonder Mason's been obsessed with this. I would be too. And you got all that information from the files Mason gave you?"

"And there's more."

"Well, I'm all in," she said. "Where do we go from here?"

"We start with Sherriff Harry Fleck," Wes said. "He was on duty that night."

CHAPTER 15

Sunday morning, December 27

Wes wasn't sure who would be at the sheriff's office on Christmas weekend. He was surprised and pleased when he saw Harry Fleck behind his large desk, drinking coffee and leafing through a magazine.

"Sheriff," Wes said, tapping on the door and then entering without an invitation. He walked toward an empty chair. "Okay if I sit down?"

He and Leslie had decided that the reporter should tackle the Harry Fleck interview on his own. Leslie was too much of a flashpoint for the sheriff and should sit out this one.

"You're a taxpayer. Help yourself," the sheriff said, coughing several times and struggling to clear his throat. "We don't have the reports from those shootings yet, if that's what you're here for. Maybe Tuesday. And I have no comment for the newspaper on what happened until I look at the reports."

"I was just out for a walk and, um, saw your lights on," Wes said. "Looks like you got the short end of the stick…having to work Christmas weekend."

Sheriff Fleck chuckled. "I always schedule myself for this time. Bruce, Deputy Webster, gets to handle New Year's Eve when all the drunks are out and teenagers are driving golf carts like they're at the Daytona 500. I'm on call as are a couple of temps we use. But Bruce keeps things under control."

He got up and poured himself a cup of coffee and grabbed a chocolate donut from a nearby plate piled high with pastries. Wes eyed the goodies but didn't feel comfortable helping himself without an offer, which never came.

"Sometimes things get interesting on my watch." The sheriff strolled back to his desk, taking a chunk out of the donut as he sat down.

"This morning, dispatch got a call from a lady who lives down the street from the big hotel. She was awakened at 3 a.m. by a loud noise on the lanai next to her bedroom. Then she saw a light out there. Her husband got up, grabbed a flashlight and went out to investigate. He found a man standing next to the wicker couch, apparently searching for something, using the flashlight on his iPhone.

"When the husband yelled at him, the guy put up his hands and said he was just wanting a place to sleep and thought the house was empty. The husband tells the guy the house isn't empty and that he should move on. Which the guy does.

"Meanwhile, the wife calls us to report an intruder. She guesses it's a wedding guest. The hotel has a lot of them this time of year. Figures the guy was so loaded, he got lost.

"While she's standing in the kitchen talking to dispatch, she looks out the front window and sees the guy returning. The wife starts screaming at her husband that the guy is coming back. She figures he's got a gun and is going to shoot them. But when the guy enters the porch, he puts his hands up and tells the husband he's looking for his tie.

"The husband doesn't interfere, and the guy finally finds his tie under the couch and staggers out the door. By this time, the wife is frantic and yelling at us to send someone over. So, one of our temporaries goes over there to investigate, and it turns out that the guy got the tie but forgot the lavender lace panties someone draped over the back of the couch.

"The woman's furious; says she just had that couch recovered and now there are semen stains on the cushions." The sheriff is laughing, then coughing and laughing again, wiping his eyes as he leans toward a plastic bag on the right side of the desk.

"And here's the evidence," he said, holding up the panties, which looked like they'd been rolled down in a hurry.

Wes was also chuckling. "You plan on doing a DNA test?"

The sheriff laughed. "Would you, if you were me?"

"Probably not," Wes said. "I'd return those panties to the homeowners so they could tell the story at their next dinner party."

"It's not like crazy stuff happens on this island that often, but lately it feels like we've had 30 nights with a full moon," the sheriff said tossing the plastic bag with the panties into the metal tray marked "in" and wiping his eyes with a large white handkerchief.

"Yeah, it does feel that way," Wes said. He let the conversation simmer for a minute as he pondered how to approach the sheriff about the shooting at Seaside Cottage. He finally decided to plunge in.

"So, I ran into John Mason at the Tarpon the other day. Boy, does he have a story to tell…about how his son was shot and how the police thought it was suicide and then an accident, but he thinks it was something else."

The sheriff's face remained emotionless. "It's sad. I feel for John. Everyone knows he's obsessed with his son's death and tearing himself apart searching for what he thinks is the truth. He spent a lot of money on lawyers and a private detective and still doesn't have the answers he paid for."

"Seems like others on the island think that Mason is right," Wes said.

The sheriff shook his head; still displaying no emotion. "This island is full of storytellers. People who take a fact here and a bit of fiction there and wrap it up into a nice little bundle. They tell their story often enough – without knowing what really happened – and they begin to believe it. And then newcomers like you come along and buy into the locals' tall tales. I know what happened that night. I was there."

Wes pictured the kitchen where Toby lost his life and then shuddered when he remembered the coroner's photos of the young man with his head sliced open.

"Was it…suicide?"

"That's what everyone thought at first. It was accidental. Young people with too much alcohol in their systems playing Russian Roulette or something stupid like that."

"What about the gun owner? Doesn't that person bear some responsibility?"

"It was an old weapon. No one knew where it came from. I'm sure the people there were haunted by what happened. Unfortunately, you can't force people to be responsible around guns when there's alcohol involved…or anger." The sheriff shifted in his chair and began tapping his pen on the desk.

"Did you know him; the kid that died?" Wes asked. He was surprised that the normally mysterious Fleck seemed to be opening up about the shooting, but was unsure how long the lawman's cooperation would last.

"Not well. People had good things to say about him. But he was into drugs at one time…and, uh…kids like that are a threat to others in the community. Especially young girls. If I were you, I wouldn't waste my time on this case," Fleck said. He tossed the pen aside, coughed and brushed crumbs off his khaki-colored shirt.

He looked intently at Wes. "It's old news. Someday John Mason's journey is going to end, just like it will for the rest of us. I'm sorry his final days are filled with so much grief and unhappiness involving the death of his son. I try to protect him…from himself…the best that I can."

Wes sat for a minute, not saying anything and wondering what his next question should be. He decided to punt. "Maybe you're right. Thanks for your help, sheriff. And don't forget to let me know when those reports come in about Frank and Jamie. Oh, and one more question. Whatever happened to the others at the party?"

"Scattered. I wouldn't know where to start to track them down," the sheriff said, returning to his cup of coffee and the last bite of donut.

Wes thanked him, exited into the bright sunshine and looked around at the village streets filling up with people wearing shorts, licking sugar cones filled with drippy ice cream. Their thoughts weren't of a decades-old shooting or the recent deaths of an island fisherman and a drug dealer. They were enjoying a day in paradise. Wes was glad for them, even though his own mind was burdened.

Was Sheriff Fleck right in his assessment that this was a sad accident, the culmination of events that included a gun and alcohol and ended up in the loss of a young life? Wes couldn't shake the thought that Randy Long had planted – that there was much more to the story than the sheriff knew or was willing to share.

CHAPTER 16

Leslie had wished Wes luck in his interrogation of the sheriff and decided that with everything that was going on, she needed to go to church and offer up a prayer in Frank's memory and in her defense. She couldn't shake the feeling that everything, including the fisherman's death, was partly her fault. Especially after having to listen to Janis blaming her.

As she entered the church, she wasn't sure she fit the category of true believer. But as a friend of hers once said: *You might as well believe. If you're right, you'll end up in heaven. If you're wrong, what difference will it make?*

She couldn't argue with his perspective. Plus, she liked the people who attended the island church – most of them at least – and enjoyed taking part in their charitable activities.

The church was festive with wreaths and red bows on each window, a hand-made nativity scene at the front altar and a 15-foot-tall Christmas tree decorated with gingerbread figures in costumes from Jesus's time.

Leslie took a seat by Deb Rankin, who became a church regular when members of the congregation came to her and Scooter's financial aid after the fire.

The service, conducted by Pastor Billy Cordray in a white robe with red, green and gold embellishments, included guitars and a solo horn performance by the local high school music director that brought tears to Leslie's eyes.

The only negative, from Leslie's perspective, was the plea from the building committee chair to consider an end-of-the-year donation to the sanctuary renovation project. Leslie was concerned about the $2-million price tag and was pleased when a tall woman whose face was set in an un-Christian-like scowl stood up and challenged the request.

"Why are we doing this? None of us really want it. You are railroading it through. Better to spend the money on the poor," she said.

Some in the congregation gasped at this note of dissention on a holy weekend. Leslie could see others nodding in agreement. The woman, whose name Leslie remembered was Alice Gerkin, added a final comment before sitting down. "And why don't we ring the church bell anymore to start the service…like we used to?"

The building committee chair, a woman who also appeared to be in her sixties, seemed flustered. She glanced at the pastor who rose from his wooden chair near the organ and stepped toward the microphone.

"Thank you, Crystal for your work on the building project. And we appreciate your concerns, Alice, and would be pleased to go over the plan with you or anyone else in more detail. As for the church bell, I'm happy to say that its renovation is a part of this project. The next time you hear it tolling will indeed be glorious news for all of us."

After the service, Leslie and Deb headed for Fellowship Hall where the Sunday refreshment table was laden with sugar-rich delicacies, including a *Happy Birthday Jesus* cake. Deb was eyeing the table even as Leslie was directing her toward a corner of the room where the two could chat.

"Is something bugging you?" Leslie asked. "I wanted to mention it at the party, but it didn't seem like the right time."

"You mean besides Frank?" Deb said, her eyes tearing. "I think about him a lot. Miss him."

"Me too. But something else…not involving…him," Leslie said, feeling herself getting emotional and not wanting to go down that path again.

"You know me well." Deb looked around to make sure no one else was within hearing distance. "The artists at the Gallery are driving me crazy with their petty bickering and back-biting. There's always been cliques and factions – the watercolor people against the oil painters and mixed media artists and so forth. But lately it's gotten worse.

"At the last show, everyone was bugging me to tell them who sold what and who was making the most money. It's become like a competition. And not a friendly one."

Normally, Deb overlooked the squabbles and displays of artistic temperament that occasionally surfaced at the Gallery. But it appeared to Leslie that these latest concerns were producing extra worry lines on her sweet face. "I'm sorry to hear that. Have you spoken to the board?"

"They know how I feel…that everyone should get along and this should be fun like it used to be," she said. "I have to do whatever they want, whether I like it or not, or I'll be gone."

Leslie put her arm around Deb's shoulder and gave her a squeeze. "Now don't go all dramatic on me. I'm sure that in-fighting exists in every organization on the island."

"Honey, I hope you're right and that things will get better. I put on an extra seven pounds worrying about it," she said, patting her ample hips.

Shootings at the beach, trouble at the Gallery Centre, a possible controversy over a church building project. What was happening to paradise? Leslie wondered.

Over Deb's shoulder, Leslie could see one of the newer church members approaching. A bachelor with an easy manner and a shock of reddish hair flecked with white. A nice guy.

"Ladies, is this conversation private?"

"Not anymore, and you are sure welcome to join us, Paul," Deb said. "You know Leslie, don't you?"

Paul Chambers extended his hand. "Not sure we've been formally introduced. Although I do remember seeing you at one of the art exhibits not long ago. I think you were serving champagne."

That was a lifetime ago, Leslie thought, remembering that was the night she'd met Frank Johnson.

"I missed the last couple of shows," Paul continued. "Sorry about that. I've been so busy at the shooting range. I'm a part owner now, and it's taking up all my extra time. Either of you interested in target shooting?"

Leslie thought back to her recent experiences with guns. Both times they'd been pointed at her with no good intent.

"The closest I've come to firing a weapon is the pepper spray gun I bought online. I've never used it," she said, suddenly remembering she hadn't seen it since she hid in the bushes by her condo and was discovered by Jamie. She'd needed to look for it, especially since it was loaded.

"Oh, that's good," Paul said, appearing relieved. "Those things are dangerous. You should drop by sometime and let me demonstrate the proper use of a weapon for self-protection. I'm a firm believer in women carrying guns. But you should never have a gun unless you've been trained to use it correctly."

Leslie was thinking that firing a weapon was one of the last things she wanted to do given the recent events in her life. Still, Paul might have a point.

"In fact, there have been several ladies you might know that have been taking lessons," Paul continued. "The woman that owns the newspaper. Sara Fortune. She's a pistol herself...."

Leslie noticed that Deb had eased herself away from the conversation and was heading for the refreshment table.

"...Susie Koenig. She's one of your local artists. Paints people's dogs and cats. And there's that other woman. Can't think of her name...I'm sure you know her...."

Leslie was watching Deb maneuver around the table, filling her plate with a slice of chocolate torte, then a piece of cherry cheesecake in a gold foil container and a couple of macaroons that looked to be homemade. Leslie was contemplating graciously ditching Paul to join Deb in a sugar rush. *Food is the universal comforter*, she thought.

"...Johnson. Janis Johnson," Paul said.

Leslie's focus went from Deb's plate to Paul's lips.

"Janis Johnson? What about her?"

"She's a regular at the shooting range. Has been for about six months and is a cracker jack shot. I wouldn't want to be staring down the barrel of any weapon Janis Johnson was holding. No siree."

CHAPTER 17

Monday morning, December 28

"What would you say if I told you that Janis Johnson is an expert markswoman?" Leslie said. She was seated in Wes's Highlander; the two headed for their second interview with John Mason.

"Where did you hear that?" Wes asked, checking his cell phone to make sure they weren't running late.

"At church. From one of the men in our congregation who's part owner of a shooting range. Says she's a cracker jack shot."

"Good for her. And your point is?"

Leslie, exasperated that her reporter friend hadn't jumped to the same conclusion she did, said, "My point is that there could be a chance that Janis was involved in the shootings of her husband and Jamie Thompson."

"What!? The attractive woman I saw at the party a killer? Sorry, Leslie, I'm not buying that."

"You don't know Janis." Leslie felt her exasperation with Wes growing. "You were bedazzled by her looks, but she's tough. The deputy told me that Frank wanted to talk to her. Maybe she went to the beach that night to meet Frank, got there early and shot him, then killed Jamie when he showed up."

"Motive, Miss Detective?"

"She hated Frank."

"But didn't you tell me earlier that she wanted money from him? The law is funny about letting people, like spouses, inherit money from their murder victims."

"Not if they don't know she's the killer," Leslie said almost under her breath.

"Now don't be mad at me," Wes said, grinning. "After we finish with Mason, we'll ask Deputy Webster about it...."

Leslie rolled her eyes and folded her arms across her chest in exasperation. "He's not going to tell us anything. He's in love with her. We need to confront her. Catch her off guard."

"Whatever you say," Wes responded.

The two rode in silence the last couple of miles with Leslie wondering why people had trouble believing her theories, particularly since she was often right. Wes was a reporter with crazy ideas of his own. She never doubted him, even when he went hunting for the long-lost brother of the CEO of a midwestern utility last year and ended up in Brazil.

Now, he was balking at the idea that a good-looking woman could commit murder. Apparently, he wasn't a fan of film noir movies from the 1940s where beautiful but treacherous women often knocked off someone they didn't like. Usually a man.

Sometimes males can be so irritating. And blind when it comes to certain kinds of women, Leslie thought.

Wes parked next to Mason's old Volvo. When Leslie got out, she noticed that one of the tires needed air. It seemed that Mason must have kept the car because it reminded him of his son and their plans for the future. Yet, he wasn't inclined to take care of it.

Wes was knocking loudly on the door when Leslie joined him. *Come on Johnny Boy*, Wes was saying under his breath. He banged again, then checked his watch.

"Maybe he's still asleep," Leslie said. "It's only a few minutes after 9, and if he had too much to drink yesterday...."

Wes was off and heading for the back of the house before Leslie could finish her sentence. She followed, walking quickly to keep up with him. Along the way, she noticed old fishing poles and nets propped haphazardly against the concrete cinder block wall of the house, along with aluminum folding chairs with frayed plastic seats, a couple of coolers and what looked like boat parts. Mason didn't seem like a fisherman, but what really did they know about him?

When she rounded the side of the house, Wes was pounding on the back door. "Mason, Mason you home?" When that brought no results, he cupped his hands to his face and peered through one of the windows.

"Shit," he said. "Call 911."

Leslie reached for the phone in her purse and pressed the three digits.

"What is it?" she asked Wes, who had tried the door, found it locked and was lifting a cinder block in preparation for tossing it through one of the windows.

"He's sprawled face down on the floor. There's a broken glass next to him, like he passed out while drinking." With that, Wes heaved the block through one of the panes, shattering it and stepping through. He opened the door for Leslie, then rushed toward the body on the floor.

"Is he breathing?" Leslie said, the phone to her ear. "Yes, um, my name's Leslie Elliott and we found a man passed out at 2501 Egret Road. That's on Anibonie Island. Please send an ambulance."

"Barely," Wes said.

"Yes, he's breathing, sort of, and we can feel a pulse...right?" she said surveying Wes who had several bloody cuts on his arm from the broken window. He nodded. Mason had a pulse.

"No, we don't know what happened. We discovered him on the floor. We had to break in."

Leslie watched Wes hurry to the kitchen. When he returned with a wet paper towel, he gently rolled the pale-faced man onto his back and cradled his head, dabbing the left side of his face with the towel.

"You okay, buddy?" Wes asked. There was no response, only the sound of labored breathing.

"Can I do anything?" Leslie said, after telling the 911 operator she had to go, despite the woman's insistence that she stay on the line.

As he sat there, Mason's head in his lap, Leslie saw Wes looking at the boxes stacked by the television set. It was obvious Mason had not given the reporter all his files during their first meeting.

"Load those in the car," he said, glancing over at the stack.

"What?! Those boxes?"

"Yes, before anyone gets here. If he's bad, this may be the last time we have access to this house and those records," Wes said.

Leslie thought about challenging Wes's command to remove Mason's personal files, then picked up the first box and headed for the car, leaving by the front door. She had just closed the trunk after depositing the fourth container when the ambulance arrived, along with Deputy Webster in his police car.

"In there," she said to the EMTs, pointing toward the front door.

The deputy stayed behind. "Let's talk," he said. He didn't pull out his notebook. Leslie wondered why he bothered to come for what must be a routine ambulance run.

"What are you two doin' here?" he said. He seemed testy, not as friendly as usual. Maybe Frank's death or the trauma of the last few days had shaken him. Leslie suddenly felt uncomfortable. It was almost like their first meeting, when he was investigating a dead animal Leslie reported and was barely civil to her.

"Wes has been taking to John Mason about his son's death, and we were here today for another interview. When Mason didn't answer the front door, we went around to the back and Wes saw him on the floor and smashed a window…"

"Ya broke in?"

"Well, yes, Bruce. Both doors were locked. It's not like Mr. Mason got off the floor and opened the door for us." She was starting to get agitated with the man she thought was her friend.

"Why is it that whenever there's a problem, yer right there," he said. "In the middle."

"Hey, hey. This is me, Leslie."

The deputy hesitated. "Sorry, I'm jus' doin' my job."

Something was wrong with Bruce, just like there had been something upsetting Deb. Leslie could see it on their faces. In Bruce's case maybe it was the loss of his friend, Frank. Or maybe it was more.

"Are you having problems with Janis?" Leslie blurted out. "It's none of my business, but she was definitely wired at the party…when you weren't around."

Bruce sighed heavily. "Janis has a vengeance in her heart toward Frank like I've never seen. She can't stop talkin' about his death. Almost like she's happy and pissed at the same time. God, Leslie, she's manic about it."

"I heard she was handy with a gun," Leslie said.

"We go target shooting. She's better than me."

Leslie watched Bruce pull out his khaki-colored handkerchief to blow his nose. Best not to say anymore, she thought. She'd planted the seed but suspected that Bruce had already gone there, even if reluctantly.

"We should have the autopsy reports any day. Not sure why they're takin' so long."

Leslie reached over and patted the deputy on the back, then looked expectedly at the front door. "I hope Mason's okay."

"And that's another concern," the deputy said softly and without elaboration.

The EMTs emerged with Mason on a stretcher and Wes following close behind.

"Dehydrated is their best guess. Bruised himself pretty bad when he fell," Wes said. "But they think he'll be fine."

Wes reached for his phone and tapped in a number he was reading from a piece of paper he found in an address book on the coffee table.

"This is Wes Avery. Are you the owner of 2501 Egret Road? Okay, well, I'm afraid I had to bust one of your windows to get to your renter, John Mason. We found him on the floor. Ambulance is picking him up and taking him to the hospital. Sorry about the window. Let me know if I owe you for it."

Leslie watched the deputy's face as Wes spoke. She wondered what heavy burdens he was hiding behind his wall of worry.

Wes dropped Leslie at her condo, continuing on to the emergency room at the mainland hospital. He checked in with the nurse, telling her he was a friend of the man who'd been brought in by ambulance from the island. She directed him to a small area with uncomfortable plastic chairs and a large TV screen with the channel set to HGTV.

Emergency rooms were never cheerful and while hospital personnel were usually cordial, the thought of spending endless hours waiting for a report that he might be denied was not pleasant or productive from Wes's viewpoint.

A wiry woman in a wheelchair several feet away was groaning loudly and laughing, as though trying to be good-natured about the pain. Wes found himself feeling sorry for her but helpless to soothe her. She was in the right place. A younger man, his arm in a sling, was bouncing one leg up and down, making Wes antsy.

Two others and Wes. This was a small-town emergency room. He imagined what it must be like in a big city ER and shuddered.

"Mr. Avery," the nurse called him to her counter. "The doctor's willing to speak with you because we have no other contact information for the patient. He'll be out in a minute."

"Thank you." Wes took a seat, and 15 minutes later a portly figure in a white shirt and pants arrived. He mumbled his name. Wes caught the word *doctor* but nothing else.

"Mr. Mason is resting comfortably. We're running tests. We'll keep him here overnight. Do you have any idea what his problem might be?"

"He's a heavy drinker," Wes said. "I don't think he does drugs. We were supposed to meet this morning. When we got to his house, I found him on the floor."

"I see. Perhaps that accounts for the bruising around his ribs, arm and jaw line. Should we call you when he's ready to be released?" the doctor asked.

"Yeah, sure, why not." It was the least he could do for Johnny Boy.

On the way home, Wes remembered the alcoholics he'd worked with during his newspaper career; one in particular – a guy named Ed – was in his 50s when Wes joined the staff. As a young man, he was legendary for being a top-notch reporter. As he aged, he was better known as the newspaper's biggest lush.

One day after lunch, Ed was sitting at his desk with his head resting on a Royal typewriter. When the phone started ringing, Ed kept his head on the typewriter and his eyes closed but reached one hand out and started searching for the source of the noise. When he picked up a nearby ashtray, cigarette butts and ashes fell onto his shoulder. Oblivious to the mess, he put the ashtray to his ear and said, "Hello…hello."

Wes, then a 22-year-old, nearly fell out of his chair laughing. "It's the phone, Ed. Not the ashtray," he shouted at the man.

Today, he would have been more sympathetic to someone hooked on an addictive substance. Like Shine said, alcohol was just as lethal as drugs like cocaine. It just took longer to kill. Once those demons were in someone's system, the future was sadly predictable.

He called Leslie and told her that Mason was going to be okay – for now. When he returned to his apartment, he unloaded the back of his vehicle, making a couple of trips carrying Mason's boxes up the steps. The thought occurred to him that Mason wouldn't be happy when he learned he'd been relieved of his documents. Wes would be truthful and hope it wasn't a problem. After all, they were working together on this mystery.

He had one more call to make before he could delve into the additional paperwork on Toby Mason's death. "Shine? Wes Avery. I wanted you to know we had to take Mason to the emergency room. We found him on the floor. They said he'd be okay…I'll call you when I know more."

The bartender at the Tarpon Bar thanked Wes and also mentioned the Christmas tip. "Let me know if I can help," he offered. Wes was sure he was sincere.

After the call, Wes took the yellow legal pad from the couch where he was sitting to the kitchen table and began making notes.

The people that were invited to the party:

Toby Mason, who shot himself in the head in the kitchen.

Jessi and Sloan Parker, the hosts. She was asleep in the main house and Sloan was in the kitchen when the shooting took place.

Elisa and Abelardo (Abe) Chaves, a Hispanic couple from Miami. Elisa was also in the main house when the shooting took place. Abe was on the porch with other partygoers.

Chip Shelton, who went into the kitchen right before the shooting, saw the gun and made the 911 call. His girlfriend was supposed to attend the party but begged off because she had a cold.

Kika and Broky Lewis. He was a Native American who worked with Parker. He and Kika were on the porch and Broky said he saw Toby shoot himself through the window. Kika left right after the shooting and refused to talk to anyone about it.

An unknown number of 20-somethings, never officially identified, who showed up uninvited and left when the shooting took place.

Was there anyone else? he scribbled.

Wes scrutinized the list. He decided to skip the hosts for now. On to Elisa Chaves who was there with her husband, Abelardo. Even though she was sleeping in the main house when the shooting took place, he decided to start by interviewing her. It was his experience that women were almost always better at remembering details and sharing them. Unless a controlling husband got in the way.

CHAPTER 18

Monday evening

The sheriff said the young people at the party the night of the shooting had scattered to the four winds. It wasn't that far Wes discovered; an Internet search turned up a phone number for an Elisa Chaves who lived in Sarasota.

"Hello," a woman's voice answered. In the background, Wes could hear the sound of water running. Probably washing the dinner dishes.

"Elisa Chaves?"

"Yeah." The woman sounded hesitant, like she was expecting Wes to try to sell her an extended warranty for her car.

"My name's Wes Avery, and I'm a reporter for *The Island Sun*. We're thinking about doing a look back at the shooting involving Toby Mason, and I'd like to speak with you about it."

His opening patter was always friendly and straightforward. Sometimes the person on the other end would hang up, sometimes they'd be happy to chat. He wasn't sure how Elisa would react until he heard a heavy sigh and the words that followed didn't include a "no thanks."

"Like what do you want to know? That was a long time ago."

A foot in the door. "I'm interested in your memories of that evening and any information you might have…that maybe you forgot to share back then. Things like that. I'd really like to speak with you in person.

Silence.

"At whatever time and place works for you," he added, hoping not to lose her. "I'd be willing to let you see your part of the story before it comes out in print…to be 100 percent accurate. I can give you the number of the paper, and they can assure you I'm on the level."

The silence lingered. Wes waited, hoping she would finally feel compelled to fill the void.

"I'm not interested in dragging up those memories," Elisa finally said.

"I totally understand. There are people in this community that feel as you do. Maybe this story will bring them some peace."

"Peace? I doubt that," she said. Her laugh felt more like an expression of irony than of humor.

"Well, I know it still weighs on the young man's father. Um, he's in the hospital…."

"Hospital?"

"A bad fall. I spoke with him right before Christmas about the shooting. He's still wanting to know the truth," Wes said.

She hesitated again and then said okay as if she didn't really mean it. "As long as I get to see anything you plan to put in the paper…before it's published."

Wes hoped his voice didn't reflect the excitement he was feeling. "Sure. Sure. How about tomorrow? You name the time."

"I work from home so tomorrow's okay. Before the kids get home from school. About 1?"

The tone of her voice had lightened. Maybe she was buying into the idea that talking about what happened would be therapeutic.

"My friend, Leslie Elliott, will be with me, if that's okay," Wes said. "She helps me take notes. And, um, your husband? Is he around?"

"Abe? We're not together anymore. He lives in Montana. Builds log homes. I'll give you his number…but I'm pretty sure he won't talk to you. None of them will. I might be the only one that isn't scared."

"Okay. Thanks. See you tomorrow," Wes said, clicking off and wondering why any of the party attendees should be "scared," especially after all this time.

Tuesday, December 29

Wes and Leslie had no trouble finding Elisa Chaves's home. It was a modest, concrete block structure with a garage, a tidy yard and a *for sale by owner* sign near the front sidewalk.

The doorbell was answered immediately by a petite woman in her forties, short blonde hair with dark roots, a white blouse and slim skirt that stopped just above her knees. She was wearing high heels and heavy make-up.

"We need to make this quick," she said without bothering to introduce herself. "I have a showing in about 30 minutes."

Wes winced. He was hoping for an hour or two but would take whatever amount of time he could get.

"What a lovely place," Leslie said as she stepped in the front door and surveyed what looked to be a recently remodeled living room and kitchen combo. "I'm Leslie Elliott. I work with Wes."

It wasn't exactly true, but the introduction served its purpose. Elisa Chaves ushered the two to a tan leather couch and sat down on the edge of a companion chair nearby; fidgeting with the tassel of the pillow that she moved from the back to the side.

"What do you want to know?" she asked.

Wes cleared his throat. Leslie turned on the tape recorder of her iPhone and brought out a small notebook.

"Did you know Toby Mason?"

Elisa shook her head. "Yes, but he was closer to my husband, Abe. He was a nice guy."

"How did you come to be in Seaside Cottage in the first place?"

"Jessi and Sloan Parker invited us for the weekend – me and Abe were newlyweds at the time. Abe and Sloan knew each other since grade school. The Parkers had rented the place for the weekend."

Wes shifted in his seat. She was answering his questions but not embellishing. "The day you arrived. What did you do for the rest of the day?"

"It was a Friday, the 22nd, I think. We might have went to the store that night – to get dinner just for that first night before everybody else got there so that we could find what we wanted to eat."

Elisa ran her fingers through the pillow fringe again. Wes decided she was nervous despite the calm facade she was hoping to portray.

"The next day you got up and who was there?"

Elisa scooted back slightly, resting her back on the chair but still fiddling with the pillow.

"We all knew each other, either from work or school. The Parkers. Me and Abe. Kika and Broky Lewis; he worked with Sloan. Chip Shelton was supposed to bring his new girlfriend – we were all excited to meet her – but she had a cold so didn't show. And Toby.

"The Parkers and us slept in the main house. Everyone else was squeezed into the guest house. All of us spent part of the next day out on the boat, then just hung out, playing cards and stuff in the cottage. Toby was gone for a while, then came back later."

Elisa checked her watch while Wes scanned notes he'd brought with him.

"Was everyone drinking?" Wes asked.

"There was always beer in the cooler when we were on the boat, but I don't remember who was drinking on that day. Most of the guys. I don't think any of them were drunk early on."

"Were you aware at this point while you were out on the boat that there was a gun around?"

"There was always a gun, whether my husband or with Sloan, they'd always carry a gun. They had permits," she said matter-of-factly. "They didn't have them in their pocket or anything, but my husband, um my ex, would always have one in the truck with him and the same with Sloan."

"Who owned the gun in the kitchen? The one Toby used to shoot himself?

"No one knew. That's what my husband said. It just showed up. Like someone found it in a drawer or something."

"Okay. Let's talk about what led up to the shooting," Wes said.

Even after 20 years it seemed to him that Elisa Chaves's memory was holding up. There was drinking. There were guns, including a mystery weapon. A typical group of 20-somethings boating, fishing, drinking, having fun. Wes hoped Elisa would be able to pinpoint where things went terribly wrong.

She sighed and wrinkled her brow as if trying to picture the details. "We were having Subway sandwiches for dinner. Broky Lewis and Chip Shelton were picking them up when Toby returned and had a girl with him. She looked young. He never introduced her…guess he thought we all knew her. Or if he did, I didn't catch her name. We kinda teased him because he hadn't mentioned this girl before.

"After we finished eating, we started playing a card game. It's like if you lose the card game, you end up being the drunker one. At the end of the game, Toby seemed drunker.

"In the middle of the game, Toby tells the girl she needs to leave. She's young, real young, maybe 16 or so. He says he doesn't want her to get into trouble at home. I got the idea that she didn't want her parents to know she was with him. She just took off walking, so I assumed she didn't live too far away.

"She leaves, and I decide to go to the main house and go to bed. It must have been around 10. Jessi Parker says she's going with me. It was kind of spooky being in that place, so I was glad to have some company walking to the main house from the cottage."

Elisa's cell phone rang. "Excuse me. In five minutes? Okay I'm here."

She stood up. Wes could barely hide his disappointment. Just as they were getting to the part of Elisa's story that might be most helpful, he sensed she was going to end the conversation.

"These people that want to look at the house will be here in five minutes," she said. "Can you find something else to do for 15, like sit in the car or something. When they leave, I'll talk to you some more."

"We'll definitely be back," Wes said as he and Leslie headed for the door.

They got into Wes's SUV and rolled down the windows to let a draft flow through the vehicle. It was a perfect day with no clouds and no threat of rain. But Wes's thoughts were dark. It seemed as though Elisa was telling the truth and, at the same time, giving him nothing he could sink his teeth into.

"Is that the first time you heard there was a girl with Toby?" Leslie asked.

Wes nodded, remembering that Mason had said that his son told him about a girlfriend but never mentioned her name.

"Elisa said she was 16 or so. Isn't that jailbait for a 22-year-old?" Leslie said.

"The age of consent in Florida is 18, but I'm not sure why I know that," Wes responded, thinking that Leslie might be onto something. "So, yes, Toby would have been treading on dangerous ground. Unless the parents didn't care or didn't know about it."

"Have you seen any mention of this girl in the documents?"

"Can't say that I have," Wes responded. "But then she wasn't around when the shooting occurred so maybe she's not relevant."

Leslie shook her head. "It feels like if she was there, even for a short time, she might know something. But how can we track her down if no one knows her name?"

Wes shrugged and turned on the car's Sirius radio to the '80s on 8 channel. *Crazy Little Thing Called Love* was playing.

"Do you suppose Toby thought he was in love?" Leslie said when the song finished.

Wes gave her a strange look. "A 22-year-old with a girl of 16? What is love and why is that we pursue it so vehemently without really understanding it? And why does it often leave so quickly…like hunger after you've eaten?"

"Hmm. That's very philosophical of you, Wes. I don't understand it either," she said turning to glance toward Elisa's residence to keep from conjuring up thoughts of Frank. "What I do know is that the couple who was looking at the house is leaving."

"All right," Wes enthused, as he opened the door of the SUV and headed for the house with Leslie close behind.

When they returned to their seats in the living room, Wes launched into his next question. He could feel his excitement growing as they closed in on what he hoped would be important details of the shooting.

"What happened after you went to bed?"

"I got woke up at 2:30 in the morning to Kika Lewis opening the door and saying, 'Get up. Toby just shot himself in the head.' Kika said a lot of people had showed up at the party uninvited. A bunch of them were in the kitchen when this gun turned up. There was horsing around, and the gun went off and it was Toby. He'd shot himself in the head.

"Kika was leaving. She didn't want to stick around. And did I want to go with her? I said no 'cause we lived in Miami and how would I get home? She said Abe was on the porch when the shooting happened. He was working on his paramedic certification, and so he was in the kitchen right away, hoping he could help Toby. We couldn't leave."

She lowered her head into her hands. Wes waited respectfully for her to return from her memories to the present.

"You okay?" he finally asked.

"Yeah. I got dressed and went over to the cottage. Jessi came with me, but she didn't go inside. She just stood outside, crying. I didn't want to look, but I had to. Toby was in a fetal position. That's all I saw. Then I hauled butt outside 'cause the smell was awful."

"Smell?" Leslie said in a small voice.

"I remember reading somewhere that particularly with trauma that results in death, the muscles relax leading to pooping or peeing or both," Wes said, "unless the person had recently gone to the bathroom."

"Yeah, that must have been it," Elisa said. "Well then, um, my memory gets a little crazy. Maybe I was in shock. But it seems it wasn't too long before the sheriff shows up. Maybe Chip had already called 911. I can't say for sure. Not the ambulance yet but the sheriff. And the sheriff sees Toby and tells everyone to get out of the kitchen. I guess because they're messing up the crime scene or whatever, and Abe tells me that Toby's still breathing, and the sheriff is working on him.

"It was maybe ten minutes before the ambulance arrived. But they wouldn't come in until they were sure the gun was gone, even with the sheriff there.

"What happened to the gun?"

Elisa shrugged. "I never saw it."

"So, you and Jessi were outside. Where was everybody else?" Was continued.

"Broky joined us, and he just kept saying, 'What the hell is going on?' And then he was asking if we could give him a ride home because his wife took the car."

Wes checked his notes. "And where was Sloan? He and his wife were the hosts, right?"

"He was in shock, very much in shock," Elisa said. "Almost hyper. Like he didn't know what was going on. He kept yelling, 'Why, Toby? Why?' He might have been the only one saying that, but all of us were thinking it."

"And did he say anything else?"

Elisa shook her head and stood up. "My youngest will be home from school soon, so we can't talk anymore. I'm sorry. You can call me some other time if you want."

Wes swallowed hard. He was prepared to stay there all night if needed. He had more questions. But he could see by the look on her face that Elisa was exhausted from reliving the memory. And if he was honest with himself, he was too.

CHAPTER 19

Tuesday afternoon, December 29

On the way home, Wes and Leslie stopped by the hospital to check on John Mason's condition. They agreed as they walked down the corridor toward his room not to mention their conversation with Elisa Chaves. Best to wait until the pale-faced man was home from the hospital and Wes had spoken with some of the other partygoers.

They found him in a double bedroom. The other patient, closer to the door, was napping and snoring softly. Mason's bed was near a window – the curtain between him and the sleeper pulled halfway for privacy and moving slightly with the draft created by a ceiling fan.

The pale-faced man's head was turned toward the window; he was also resting it seemed. When they approached, his eyes popped open, and he shuddered as though he'd seen something frightening. Wes was taken aback by his expression and wondered if he was going through the DTs after being in the hospital without any alcohol for 24 hours.

"Mr. Mason. Leslie Elliott. How are you feeling?" Leslie asked in a sympathetic voice.

Mason mumbled something and rolled over on his side, turning his back to them. Based on the groan he emitted, Wes assumed he was in a lot of pain.

"Oh God," Leslie whispered. She nudged Wes and tilted her head, indicating the entire left side of Mason's face. It was not slightly bruised as it first appeared in his home but swollen an ugly black and yellowish-green; like the loser in a boxing match with Mike Tyson.

"Seems like you had a bad fall Johnny Boy," Wes said, trying to sound cheerful. "Are they treating you okay here?"

Mason muttered something that Wes couldn't hear. He walked around to the other side of the bed and leaned down, his face close to the banged-up patient. "Do you want water?"

"Geow." The voice was soft at first, the words garbled. Then, fueled by some powerful inner force, he propped himself on one elbow and emitted a cry of pain that ended in two words: "Get out!"

A nurse entering the room rushed to Mason's bedside and gave Wes and Leslie a look that said they should leave.

"Now Mr. Mason," she said kindly "Mustn't exert yourself. Can I get you something?" Her voice was cheerful, even as she glanced over her shoulder and glared at Wes and Leslie. "Please," she whispered.

"What was that all about?" Leslie said as the two of them exited the room.

"Beats me. I'd like to talk to that doctor that said he was resting comfortably, doing fine and would be released soon. He didn't seem fine at all," Wes said, scanning the hallway for someone that looked official.

"Looks like there's a workstation over there," Leslie said, pointing to an area with computers where a portly man in a white jacket and pants was taking a drink out of a coffee cup.

"That's him," Wes said, rushing forward and touching the man on the arm. "I spoke with you yesterday about John Mason, who's in the room down there…106, I think. You said something about him leaving the hospital."

The doctor sat down his cup. "Yes, he was complaining of severe pain in his side, so we did a scan and found he had several broken ribs. He must have hit something sharp when he fell. In his condition, I expect him to be here another day or two, maybe longer."

"He's a drinker, you know. Are you giving him something?"

"His, um, addiction is exacerbating the issues from the fall. We won't release him before he's ready," the doctor said, reaching for a clipboard on a nearby desk.

"Please keep me informed," Wes said.

"Of course," the doctor said, turning his full attention to the papers in his hand.

"Poor guy," Leslie said as they headed out the hospital door. "Why do you think he was so angry? You didn't have anything to do with the fall. You may have saved his life."

Wes sighed. "With drinkers you never know. I knew this wouldn't be an easy story, but I'm eager to move on with the next interview.

"Who's that?"

"Abe Chaves. The young man who wanted to be a paramedic but ended up building houses out west."

CHAPTER 20

Tuesday evening, December 29

Elisa Chaves had written down the phone number of her ex-husband, Abe, and given it to Wes as he was leaving her house. When he dropped off Leslie and headed for his apartment, his adrenaline was pumping. He didn't want to wait until tomorrow to make the call.

He reached into the refrigerator, grabbed a beer and sat down at the kitchen table. He briefly wondered if Leslie would be upset with him for going ahead without her and then decided it would be okay. She understood that a reporter on a mission had a sense of urgency even when dealing with a 20-year-old story.

He couldn't recall having a disagreement with her, even when she was a public relations officer for a utility and their interests were often opposing; he wanting to get information and she not wanting to give it to him. Now that they had joined forces on this story and were living minutes apart, he found himself thinking of her often.

But, moving on, he punched Abe's number into his cell phone.

"Chaves," was the immediate response.

"Abelardo, this is Wes Avery...."

"Yeah, my ex-wife said you'd be contacting me." Chaves's voice was husky with a trace of a Hispanic accent. "Call me Abe."

"Sure thing. She also told me you wouldn't want to talk to me. I hope that isn't the case," Wes said, chuckling as if to ease any tension that might exist regarding the call. "Something about everyone being scared."

"I'll talk unless you ask me somethin' I don't wanna answer," Chaves said. "As far as being scared. I'm out here in Montana. Ain't no one gonna come after me."

"Good, and I'll make every effort to make sure that Elisa isn't put in harm's way," Wes said, recognizing it was a commitment he couldn't keep.

"Fair enough," Chaves said.

"For starters, I have to ask. Who would come after you, and why?"

"Things were said that night. Threats were made...."

"By whom?" Wes interrupted.

"I'd rather not say. People involved are still around."

Wes took another sip of beer. "Okay. You and Sloan Parker still friends?"

"Sloan didn't make any threats if that's what you're drivin' at," Chaves said, his tone defensive.

"No, no, I just wandered if you two saw each other now and then... what with you being in Montana and he's still in...."

"Florida. At least that's where he was when we talked a couple of years ago. We never discussed that evening. I didn't bring it up. He didn't bring it up. It happened. We all felt bad. It was over," Chaves said.

In the background, Wes could hear a TV and other indistinct noises. He was curious to know if Chaves lived alone or had a new family. He hadn't thought to ask Elisa how long the two had been divorced, or if they were just separated. He wanted to know how life had changed for these young people. But he was mindful of the time and fearful of losing Chaves, so he pressed on with questions about that evening.

"When you went into that kitchen after hearing the shot...."

"It was Chip who came out onto the porch yelling that Toby shot himself. It was Chip who called 911."

"Oh, right. So, what happened next?"

Wes could hear Abe sneeze. "Excuse me, got a cold. He, Toby, was on the kitchen floor. I believe he was on his left side and on the ground gaspin' for air.

"And, you know, I wasn't a full-fledged paramedic so maybe I couldn't tell how bad he was, but it seemed to me that even though there was a lot of blood, the wound to his head might be superficial."

"Really?" Wes said, thinking back to the autopsy photos that showed what looked to be a trough cut through Toby's head by a bullet and widened by a coroner's scalpel. "He wasn't that bad?"

"It was a long time ago and the situation was out of control, and we were all shook up or something. My judgment wasn't the best; I'd been drinkin' like everyone else. But I didn't think he was gonna die. I mean there was a puddle of blood. And I remember tellin' Broky and Sloan to get some towels to put around his head. But I thought he had a chance…and that his breathing was labored because he was in shock or somethin'…not because he was gonna die right there.

"Sloan was just, like screaming. 'Why,' just why. And Broky was saying, 'Abe do somethin'.' But there was nothing more I could do. So, when the sheriff showed up, and we talked to him, right away he told us to leave. He said he would take care of Toby 'til the ambulance got there.

"We all went out to the truck, someone's pickup truck, and were standing around it not sayin' anything. And then the EMTs showed up and the first thing they said is, 'Where's the gun?' They didn't know the sheriff was in there with Toby. Someone got the gun, but I can't remember who.

"What happened to the gun?"

"I don't know. I saw it on the floor next to Toby. And I never saw it after that," Chaves said.

Wes hesitated. "Do you know who bought the gun into the kitchen… and handed it to Toby…or whatever happened?"

"I couldn't say. I was on the porch. It was loud and the place was packed. When the gun went off and everyone realized what happened, they disappeared. Like evaporated."

"Abe, do you blame anyone in the kitchen – or at the party – for Toby's death?"

"No, sir, I do not," he said. "Only Toby. Poor guy."

Wes was able to get a promise from Chaves that he would answer more questions as the story developed. He also obtained phone numbers for Chip Shelton, Broky Lewis and his wife, Kika, and Jessi and Sloan Parker. Chaves told him the contact information was more than 10 years old. But it was a starting point.

"Before we hang up…and I thank you for being so open with me…was there a girl with Toby at the party that evening? A young girl about 16? Your ex-wife mentioned her."

"I don't know why she would say that," he said. "Toby was alone."

CHAPTER 21

Wednesday morning, December 30

The sign on the window said *Shoot Like a Girl! Saturdays 2:30 p.m. Ladies only. Concealed Carry License Classes.*

When Leslie entered the door of Mike's One Stop Gun Shop, about a 30-minute drive from the island, she found herself facing a wall of weapons. Twice in recent months she'd been on the business-end of a gun someone else was holding. Nothing would get her to change her mind about guns, especially some misogynistic shooting class. She didn't like them and never would.

"Can I help you ma'am?" The man behind the counter looked to be in his late 20s, short blond hair and glasses perched atop his head. He was wearing a long-sleeved black t-shirt with the word Mike's printed over the left side pocket.

"I'm looking for Paul Chambers? I know him from church."

"Mr. Chambers isn't here at the moment, but I'd be happy to help you. Are you wanting something specific?"

"Information mostly," she said. "Some of my friends have been taking shooting lessons, and I was wondering if that was something I might enjoy."

"Certainly. Most women make great shooters. They are patient, they listen and they don't feel like they have to show innate mastery at the first shot. Do you know what kind of guns they have?"

The man was friendly. Maybe she had misinterpreted the sign. Perhaps it meant that women were better with guns than men. She could endorse that sentiment, even if she didn't know whether it was true or not.

"Not really. One of them said something about a Walther P-something."
It was the only gun name she knew; Wes had mentioned it in connection
with the shooting at Seaside Cottage.

"That's an old one. Our latest data indicates women like the Smith &
Wesson M&P Shield, 9-millimeter. Followed by the Glock 19 Gen 4. We also
have some nice SIG Sauers that some ladies prefer," he said. "By the way, my
name's Matt."

"Matt, I'm Leslie." She didn't really want her name out there. What if
Matt knew Janis well and told her that Leslie had been in the shop?

"I think you could get excited about this Smith & Wesson. It's a sweet
gun; a great little package for women. There are no sharp edges or bulges…
nothing to snag on your clothes," Matt said, reaching inside the glass case in
front of him and pulling out a gun with a M&P logo and the words *9 Shield*
printed on it.

"Try it on," he said, handing her the weapon. "This one retails for $350
but I could probably do a little better than that and also give you a break
on ammunition and shooting lessons. You shouldn't buy a gun unless you're
up for learning how to use it and keeping it from being used against
you. Becoming proficient pertaining to your self-protection needs a personal
commitment. We're here to help with that," he said, smiling.

Leslie tried not to display her feelings of revulsion. She was willing to
use the pepper spray gun, but this was different. The pepper spray gun could
stun or render someone helpless. The purpose behind this *sweet* little Smith &
Wesson was to protect yourself by possibly killing another person.

No thanks, she thought.

"Oh, it feels very light," she said, feigning enthusiasm. "So, I mean,
what kind of bullets would you use in a gun like this. And if you shot someone – like in self-defense – could you, um, kill them with this gun?"

She returned the Smith & Wesson to the counter, being careful to
point it away from Matt and herself. By the look on his face, Leslie knew that
Matt was keenly aware he was dealing with a gun novice; practically a gun
idiot. She hoped he would tolerate her long enough to answer her questions

before moving on to another customer in the crowded store with its busy range.

"9-millimeter bullets. Kill someone? It depends," he said, politely. "A typical bullet like you see in films – one that's nice and rounded – will do the job but penetrates deeply, often through a body. We call that over-penetration when talking self-protection, and that could be dangerous to bystanders."

He moved the gun on the glass counter to align perfectly with the edges. *OCD*, thought Leslie.

He went on. "Now a hollow point, where you have a rounded tip filled with soft plastic, is a different story. When it encounters soft tissue there are pieces that peel back on each side. They do a lot of damage, stay in the body and don't over-penetrate. I recommend rounded bullets for target shooting and hollow points for self-protection."

It didn't seem that Matt was uncomfortable with her questions, so she pressed on. "If I shoot someone in the head, out of self-defense, will it go through the skull or become imbedded in the soft tissue? Uh, let's say we're on a beach."

"If you shoot someone in the head with a round-nose bullet and you're on the beach, you're probably going to be looking for that bullet in the sand," Matt said. "Why do you ask?"

She hoped he didn't think she was planning a murder. "Just curious. I heard about a shooting like that on the coast. And how close would someone have to be to kill that person?"

"Depends on how good a shot you are. The closer the better, not more than 50 yards. And you'd have to be a good shot at that distance."

Leslie decided to go for it. "My friend Janis Johnson comes here for target practice. I was, um, wondering what kind of gun she has."

Matt's face reddened. "I-I know her very well. She, um, is very attractive, well, I mean she's a very good shooter. She comes here a couple of times a week. I believe she has a Glock 19, Gen 4, which she recently purchased from me. She also owns a .22 rifle. It's good out to a hundred yards, especially if you shoot like Janis does. I've seen her do 10 out of 10 on an eight-inch target 100 yards away."

"You're saying she could drop, say, a deer – *or poor Frank* – from a long distance away?"

"I'd say she could hit it at that range, although you wouldn't use a .22 on a deer. It's not powerful enough. To be sure of a clean, immediate kill you might want to use an AR-15 firing 5.56 NATO millimeter ammo at least, or even better, a .300 Blackout.

"That rifle is a semi-automatic, meaning one shot per trigger pull with the next bullet chambered as the bolt returns. The 5.56 bullet is smaller than a 9-millimeter but because the brass cartridge case has more powder it gives you more than 1,000 feet per second more velocity. That's what causes all the damage. The .300 Blackout is a much heavier bullet and hits even harder.

Leslie was in for it. The man liked his subject.

"And let's say there were two deer standing together," he continued. "With the AR-15, the second shot could be fired before the other deer was spooked by the first. The rifle and ammo are good for 500 yards easily. Of course, the AR-15 is very loud unless you use a different cartridge in it or use it with a suppressor…you know, a silencer."

"Wow," Leslie said. Her brain was spinning, but she was also impressed with Matt's detailed knowledge and his willingness to share what she considered to be damning evidence about Janis Johnson's artillery and her gun prowess.

"You know, I'm a writer, and you've brought up some ideas for a novel I'm working on," Leslie continued. "If someone is shot, and you can retrieve the bullet intact, can you use that bullet to tell who did the killing?"

Matt rubbed the side of his face, hesitating as though pondering the question. "It's not easy. When a bullet is fired, scratches are imparted on it by the rifling in the barrel. If you knew which gun was used in a murder and you discovered that another bullet had the same rifling marks, you could deduce that the gun was used in both murders."

"I think I've seen that in the movies," Leslie said and laughed.

Out of the corner of her eye, Leslie could see a woman approaching the front door of the gun shop. A quick second glance confirmed it was Janis Johnson, the very person she didn't want to run into.

"Matt. It's been a pleasure meeting you, but I just realized I have a dental appointment. I'll be back...to...um...check out the M&P," she said, stepping behind a display rack of sale items and bending down as though looking at something. When Janis breezed past her enroute to the shooting range, Leslie stood up and made a beeline for the exit.

CHAPTER 22

Wednesday noon, December 30

Wes was in his office – his column on changes to policies at the local health clinic completed – and was searching the Internet for the names of Broky Lewis and Chip Shelton. He was saving the Parkers for later since they were the hosts for the weekend. He'd tried the numbers Abe Chaves gave him for the two men, but neither was valid.

Both men were important to his research. Broky Lewis because he was supposedly on the porch, yet claimed to see Toby shoot himself. His wife was there, too, but no one indicated she had seen anything, and she left immediately after the shooting.

Chip Shelton was important because he was said to be in the kitchen when the shooting took place. He also was the one who made the 911 call.

When Wes's cell phone rang, he was glad to see it was Leslie calling.

"Guess where I was this morning?" she greeted him with the eagerness she always exhibited when she thought she was onto something. "Shopping for a gun and some information on Janis Johnson."

"That sounds like a non sequitur," Wes said, chuckling.

"I was at Mike's One Stop Gun Shop," she enthused, "and just missed running into Janis there. I think she was on her way to do some target practice."

"And what juicy tidbit did you discover…other than that guns and bullets can kill people?" he asked.

"Well, I would argue that people kill people," Leslie said. "Anyway, I think I'm onto something that I can share with you tomorrow at my place. A New Year's Eve dinner. I will actually cook for you, Mr. Avery."

Wes paused. "Just us?"

"That isn't a frightening concept, is it?" Leslie said. "I can ask Deb and Scooter if you insist. But I really want to get you alone to talk about murders and shootings and ring in the new year with some blood and gore."

Wes was enjoying the playful banter between the two of them. It had been a while since Leslie seemed so light-hearted. "I'll bring the champagne and the details of my interview with Abe Chaves," he said.

"Abe? You spoke to him without me around?" Leslie asked. "I'm dying to hear what he had to say. Maybe that's the wrong word."

"Dying or not dying did come up. He seems to think that Toby could have survived his head wound. Unlikely, but an interesting theory."

"And did he mention the girl? The 16-year-old?"

"He denied that she existed," Wes said. "He suggested that his ex-wife made her up."

"I'd believe her over him."

"Me, too," Wes said. "So, tomorrow? What time?"

"Let's say 5:30. And, to be honest, I may or may not make it to midnight," Leslie said, chuckling. "See you then."

When Wes clicked off, he realized he'd forgotten to give Leslie an update on John Mason and his release from the hospital. The doctor had called to say that the sheriff would pick up Mason when he was ready to leave the hospital, and Wes didn't need to worry, his friend was doing fine. Just a little sore.

Wes wasn't sure what to make of that arrangement and whether he should be bothered by it. He was on Mason's wrong side and didn't know why. When the pale-faced man was home again, he'd pay him a visit, take a bottle of good vodka with him – even if reluctantly – and see if he could straighten things out.

That would be a good time to return the paperwork he took from Mason's living room. Or it might be an even better idea to return it before Mason came home from the hospital. Definitely a better idea, given the current state of their relationship. He hoped the broken window wasn't fixed.

He returned to the task at hand, his fingers traveling over his keyboard in search of Broky Lewis. There was Bruce Lewis, an accountant. He found the story of a man named Brandon Lewis who disappeared in 2010. There was Bracy Lewis, a professor of contemporary literature.

He was disappointed to finally discover the obituary of a Florida man named B. D. Lewis, who drowned while python hunting in the Everglades three years ago. Wes didn't fancy calling up Lewis's widow, Kika, to bring up the shooting that so traumatized her 20 years ago. The man's age, the fact that he was a Native American and the location of his death all pointed to him being the Broky Lewis Wes was seeking.

At least I've got his deposition, he thought as he began rummaging through the papers from Mason's house.

The interview with Lewis, which occurred a year after the death of Toby Mason, was part of a civil suit that John Mason brought on behalf of his son. The suit charged that the family who owned the property was responsible for the presence of the Walther P38 and therefore liable for Toby's death, even though they weren't on the premises at the time of the shooting. Mason was seeking $1 million in damages.

Wes figured it was really a fishing expedition, launched by Mason in hopes of finding out details about the shooting that weren't revealed at the time of his son's death.

The suit hadn't gone anywhere. At least Mason never mentioned it and there was little paperwork on it except for the depositions. Wes wondered if the legal effort had been worth Mason's time and money.

The first 50 pages of Lewis' deposition revealed nothing new and substituted a lot of "I don't remember" comments for facts. Still, Wes read on, focusing on the part where Lewis said he was on the porch with about 15 other people when he glanced in the window and saw Toby point a gun to his head.

"He was looking at it. And I think I looked away and then I looked back and he had it against his head. And he pulled the trigger instantaneously. It was real quick.

"Then I saw everyone empty out of the kitchen except for Sloan and Chip, who were trying to help Toby. And I went inside, and I smelled gunpowder and saw blood all over the place, and I stayed there for a few minutes and then walked outside. I couldn't believe it happened. And Kika is yelling at me that she's outta there…and I need to drive her home now or find a ride later."

"Didn't anyone check the weapon to see if it was loaded?" Lewis was asked.

"If they did, I didn't see it. I didn't see the gun until it was in Toby's hand."

"Did the Parkers, in any way, express concern about the incident?" the attorney conducting the deposition asked Lewis.

"Yes. Especially Jessi. She was standing outside when the ambulance took him away and was saying: "I'm sorry. I'm sorry. I'm sorry.""

Wes paused. He put aside the deposition and stood up to stretch. Reading depositions, looking for little nuggets in all those meaningless questions and answers, was tedious and not always fruitful. So far, that was the case with Broky Lewis's testimony.

"Hey Randy," Wes said as he wandered into the room where the New Year's Eve edition was being put together. "You know anything about guns?"

"I might," the layout man responded. "Like what?"

"Like if you have an old weapon, from around World War II, how do you tell if it's loaded or not without, um, taking it apart?"

"Looking into the Toby Mason shooting?"

"I guess I am. And, well, so far nothing. But there are ideas forming in my addled brain," Wes said.

"My wife's cousin, a real jerk, has a Glock," Randy said as he continued manipulating the photographs on the computer screen in front of him. "He was showing it to me once. And I remember how he told me that the magazine carried six bullets, but he could fix it so the gun had seven. He'd pull the slide back and put the first bullet in the barrel. Then he'd fill that empty space in the magazine and that gave him seven bullets instead of the usual six.

"With him, you always assumed that when he was carrying it was loaded. Gun owners I know don't walk around with empty weapons."

"But the gun that was used in the Toby Mason shooting was a Walther P38," Wes said. "I read someplace that it had a loaded-chamber indicator, a small piece of rod that stuck out of the top when there was a round in the chamber."

"There was no doubt it was loaded," Randy said, looking at Wes through his thick computer glasses. "The kid died."

Wes fumbled in his shirt pocket for the pack of cigarettes that wasn't there. "It feels like I'm back to square one. An accidental shooting. A tragedy. Nothing else to see here folks," he said.

Randy sighed and leaned across the layout table, closer to Wes. "You're not lookin' at this right. Forget about the gun. What happened after the shooting?" he said in a half-whisper.

Wes felt himself getting irritated at this cat-and-mouse game. "Listen, man, if you know the answers, why keep me in suspense?"

"Because 20-year-old hearsay isn't always right," Randy snapped back. "You find out for yourself, and if it matches what I've heard, then maybe we're on the right track."

Wes rolled his eyes at Randy's stubbornness, sighed and returned to his desk. He was glad to see the words "wrapping up" in the deposition. But on page 87, there was a nugget. The questioner asked about the "young girl in the golf cart."

The attorney representing the homeowners in the deposition objected saying that the question "assumes facts not in evidence that there was an underage girl."

There she is again. The mysterious female. Who doesn't want us to know she was there…if she was? And why? Wes mused. *And what part did she play, if any, in Toby Mason's death? Maybe she brought the gun to the party?* It was a question he and Leslie could discuss tomorrow night.

On page 100 he stopped and circled the question, "When you gave this statement to one of the sheriff's deputies after the incident, did you lie to him? Or make anything up? Did you have a motive to lie? And did anybody tell you to lie?

To each question, Lewis answered no.

Wes leaned back in his chair and stared out the window toward the street below. The pieces were not falling into place unless he wanted to believe the conclusions the police reached: accidental shooting, no idea where the gun came from, no mysterious young female, no one trying to cover up anything.

He shook his head. *No Randy, I'm not giving up*, he thought but did not say aloud.

CHAPTER 23

New Year's Eve

Leslie pulled open the lanai sliders to help air out the cooking aromas from corned beef and cabbage, new potatoes and carrots, black-eyed peas and collard greens. All were on the menu in hopes they would bring good luck in the new year.

She contemplated serving pickled herring as an appetizer; a guarantee of prosperity. But she thought better of feeding Wes all those strong flavors when she wasn't sure if his tastes were exotic or simple, or if he was picky like her daughter.

Well, he's getting a home-cooked meal – whether he likes it or not, she thought and then chided herself for agonizing over food with everything else that had happened lately.

At the sound of the sliders opening, the dog got down from a pink chair in the living room where he'd been sleeping and headed onto the lanai, lifting his head and sniffing.

"Are you passing judgment on my cooking, Whalen?" she asked him. "Or just wanting to go outside?" At the mention of his name, the dog turned to look at her but made no move to return to the living room.

"Okay, I get it. Give me a sec, and we'll get out of here," she said.

She was headed for Whalen's leash, when a ding on her phone alerted her to a text from her mother. Ruth was wrapping up the holiday cruise with her boyfriend, a charming man in his late 70s, and would be home soon.

"Happy New Year!"

"Same to you and Gale," Leslie texted.

"Are you spending the evening ALONE?"

"No. Wes Avery coming over for dinner."

"That old reporter?"

"He's not that old and a good guy."

"You can do better."

Leslie responded with an eye-rolling emoji.

"Gale and I are getting married."

"What?!!!!! Great news. So happy for you."

"You can help plan the wedding."

"Sure." Eye-rolling emoji considered but not sent. "Dinner cooking. Got to go."

"Love you," Ruth wrote.

"U2," Leslie responded, adding an emoji with hearts for eyes. "Safe travels."

Gale Gammon was a nice man, and her mother deserved to be happy after such a long and often bitter period as a widow. However, Leslie wasn't sure how excited she was about the wedding ceremony. Her own nuptials to ex-husband Scott had been a debacle. Her mother invited 350 guests to the wedding – most of whom Leslie didn't know – insisted on throwing a lavish engagement party and expected Scott's parents to pay for it.

By the time the wedding date arrived, the mother-of-the-bride and the mother-of-the-groom were barely speaking. Surely, Ruth hadn't forgotten how weddings can go awry. Surely, she wouldn't want to put everyone through a lavish affair when the bride and groom were in their 70s?

Why don't they just get married on the cruise liner by the captain? That way mother could be the center of attention for hundreds of guests, whether she knows them or not, Leslie thought as she headed for the bedroom to change clothes.

She slipped into a short sleeve satiny top with brocade pants – all black. The contrast of the dark color with her reddish hair and alabaster skin was always striking. In the midst of applying lipstick, she wondered why she was going to all this trouble for Wes.

Because he's a friend, and friends are not to be taken for granted, she told herself.

Back in the kitchen, she decanted a bottle of red wine to let it breathe, pouring a glass for herself and heading for the lanai with the dog leash in her hand. She told Wes to be there about 5:30 – half an hour from now. The sun would be setting, giving them an end-of-the-year view of the Gulf and its often-dramatic twilights.

As she and the dog descended the back steps to the strip of beach below, she looked out at the waves breaking softly against the seawall and thought of Frank. The two of them enjoyed this view, sitting on the lanai together, sometimes not even talking; two people who cared about each other and were comfortable with the silence is how Leslie viewed it.

She wondered what kind of relationship he had with Janis. Deb said Frank was a good man, always trying to do the best for his family. Yet, Deputy Webster indicated that Janis "had a vengeance in her heart" toward him.

Walking along the seawall with the dog, sipping her wine, Leslie envisioned the scene in which Frank was murdered by Janis.

It was a moonlit night. Janis had returned Frank's call and they agreed to talk in person. He also told her he was meeting Jamie. The quicker Frank resolved any issues with Janis, especially as they related to their son Stevie, the sooner he could leave the island. Leslie never expected him to stay, and Frank hadn't indicated he would.

Janis was so angry with Frank that she showed up early. They had an argument…about money or their son…and Janis pulled out her gun and shot Frank in the head. People would think Jamie did it, and she'd be off scot-free. When Jamie happened on the scene and saw Janis with a gun in her hand and Frank down, he took off running and she shot him in the back.

That was one theory. *And a good one,* Leslie thought, congratulating herself.

Another was that Janis and Frank had an argument on the beach, and she returned to her vehicle and got her .22 rifle, waited for Jamie to arrive so she could take both of them out and make it appear that one had killed the other.

Leslie wondered if the police would be willing to confiscate Janis's weapons and determine that the bullets came from one of her guns. Matt at the gun shop had suggested that was possible. Deputy Webster would be reluctant to implicate his girlfriend, but how could he ignore the logic of Leslie's theory? Other than Jamie, she was the only one with a motive for killing her DEA fisherman husband.

Leslie thought of Frank leaving with his gun and heading for the beach after she and he heard the screams…she remembered checking the darkened parking lot…the encounter in the bushes with Jamie…his comment that he didn't want to kill Leslie but was using her to set up a conversation with Frank. Talk, not kill.

She stopped, frustrating Whalen who was straining to reach a group of seagulls about 20 feet away. *Wait a minute!* she thought. The parking lot was dark that night. Leslie couldn't see anyone or anything well, which meant Janis couldn't either.

She reached for her phone to check the phase of the moon on December 15. It was a sliver – a tiny fingernail of light. Unless she had a night vision gadget, which seemed a stretch for a casual shooter, even a good one, Janis couldn't have shot Frank between the eyes with her .22 caliber rifle from 1,000 feet away or even half that distance.

The idea that she could pull out her Glock 19 and shoot him in the head from a few feet away was also unlikely. The minute she reached for a weapon; Frank would be all over her.

Damn. If Janis wasn't the killer and Jamie was iffy, who could it be?

Wes arrived exactly on time, carrying two bottles of champagne and a liter of 15-year-old McCallan. He'd given up the hard stuff, but this was a special evening and the pricy Scotch was the perfect choice for climbing off the bandwagon…for one night. He'd have one or two drinks and leave the bottle with Leslie.

"It smells amazing in here," he said as Leslie opened the screen door.

"You're joking," she said. "Even the dog wanted out when I started cooking the cabbage and collard greens."

"I'm a southern boy," Wes said. "Love all that stuff and haven't had it for years."

"How do you feel about Brussel sprouts?" she asked, grinning.

"Overcooked, undercooked or raw. Bring 'em on," he responded.

"My kind of man," she said.

Wes set the Scotch on the kitchen counter and offered the two champagne bottles to Leslie for later.

"Let's hope this year will be better than last," she said as she slipped them into the wine cooler that doubled as a side table in her tiny condo living room.

Wes put a couple of ice cubes in a glass, added a touch of water and then the Scotch and took a sip as he followed Leslie to the lanai. *Damn that's good.* He thought of the pale-faced man, celebrating a dry New Year's Eve in a hospital bed. Alone with his horrifying images, whatever they might be.

"You start," Wes said after they settled into the Adirondack chairs, and he'd grabbed a cracker with a piece of brie.

"I was so excited to tell you about Janis, and how I was certain she shot Frank and then Jamie. But the more I thought about it, the more my theory fell apart," Leslie said, shaking her head. "I'm losing my touch."

"Why was that?" Wes said, eyeing the dog, who was sitting close to the plate of appetizers and licking his lips. "You want cheese, boy?"

The dog whined, snapped the morsel out of Wes' fingers, chewed, swallowed and then turned his focus to Leslie, who waved him off. "Not now," she said, scooting her chair at a 45-degree angle to Wes's.

"There was only a sliver of moon that night. Unless Janis had a night vision scope, I'm not sure she could have put a bullet between Frank's eyes.

She may be good, but she's not Calamity Jane. I mean, who keeps high-powered night vision equipment handy on an island in southwest Florida?"

"I'm trying to envision Sheriff Harry Fleck with military headgear…or his deputy. Maybe the DEA guy would have one," Wes said.

"If they had something, it would probably be an older model and not as powerful as the new ones," Leslie said, getting up and heading for the kitchen. "You want me to bring the Scotch with me?"

"Not if you expect me to be lucid by dinnertime."

"Let's say the law enforcement team – I like to think of them as the three stooges – had night vision paraphernalia, why would any of them shoot Frank?" Leslie asked when she returned to the lanai carrying the bottle of red wine.

"Maybe it was a mistake," Wes said, taking another sip and staring out at the Gulf of Mexico, which was the color of sea glass with reflections of golden clouds throughout. "Look at this sunset. Does it get any better?"

Wes was surprised at how relaxed he felt. It must be the fine, aged whisky. But, also, there was no pressure. He and Leslie were just two people who had a history, sharing drinks on a quiet New Year's Eve. Discussing mayhem and murder.

"I'm hoping we'll know more when the autopsy report arrives. So, what do we now know about the Seaside Cottage shooting?" Leslie asked.

Wes took a sip, grabbed another cracker and began ticking off the mental notes he'd made earlier.

"No one offered any explanation as to why the gun was brought into the kitchen in the first place or where it came from. Or why someone didn't try to stop Toby.

"Abe Chaves also introduced the possibility that Toby was not fatally wounded and that the bullet only grazed his head. At that time, however, Abe was not a fully certified paramedic, and, ultimately, Toby died, making his medical observations suspect.

"Elisa Chaves and Abe had similar stories, except that Elisa insisted that Toby was with an underage girl, and Abe was emphatic that his ex-wife was wrong about there being a much younger female with the group.

"Then there was Randy Long's odd comment about looking into what happened after the shooting, and Elisa's statement that the partygoers were scared to talk, with Abe saying they'd been warned.

"The shooting took place in the kitchen where Abe, Broky Lewis and Sloan Parker tried to help Toby and Chip Shelton called 911. The sheriff showed up, the ambulance came, followed by more police. Everyone went home and that was it.

"And now John Mason, who was so passionate and eager to talk about his son's death, has mysteriously – and angrily – gone silent."

"Are we sure that's the order of the events?" Leslie asked.

"What do you mean?"

"The sheriff – Harry Fleck – showed up before the ambulance. Is that unusual?"

"Maybe he was in the neighborhood when the dispatcher notified the police," Wes said. "Sounds like he did the right thing. Chasing everyone out of there and administering aid to the kid."

"Did Harry say anything about the shooting that might clear up any contradictions?" Leslie asked.

"He suggested it was a lethal combination of youth, alcohol and fire-arms," Wes responded and then fell silent, continuing to sip his drink and stare at the water.

The last bit of bright orange sun had melted into the Gulf. Visible to Wes and Leslie, but miles away and on another beach somewhere, a few fire-works rose and exploded into faint reds and purples with splashes of white. There were always those revelers, mostly kids, who couldn't wait for total darkness.

"You ready to eat?" Leslie said, scooting her chair back to its original location. "It's early, but if I keep drinking, I won't remember how to use a knife and fork."

Wes was also feeling woozy. "I'm ready."

They lingered over the meal, with Wes occasionally slipping Whalen morsels of corned beef under the table. They reminisced about their shared experiences, laughing about politicians they had known, Wes downplaying some of his more liberal thoughts in deference to what he assumed was Leslie's conservative bent.

After dinner they took a blanket, the champagne, two glasses and a handful of dog biscuits to the strip of sand below Leslie's condo. They removed their shoes, sat on the seawall, letting their feet dangle in the warm water below. Next to them, on the blanket, Whalen slept, undisturbed by the distant explosions.

Any thoughts of John Mason and his dead son were now gone from Wes's mind. His focus was on the woman sitting next to him. She was smart, attractive and fun to be with. Easy and comfortable. Unlike any other woman he'd known.

"You warm enough?" he asked as the evening breeze picked up.

"A little chilly. Maybe I should get a sweater," she said.

He looked over at the blanket covered with dog and clumps of sand. "Scoot a little closer to me," he said and was surprised when she did. He put his arm around her.

When the sky to the southwest filled with explosions of magenta, orange and blue from the county fireworks display, he leaned toward her, hesitating to make sure it was okay, then kissed her softly.

Wes awoke the next morning, looked beyond his throbbing head to a champagne glass on the nightstand and realized with a sickening feel in his gut that he was in Leslie's bed. He couldn't remember making love to her. He couldn't remember anything much beyond the kiss. It felt like he'd made a trip to the alcohol-fueled reality that John Mason often frequented.

If anything happened between the two of them, he wouldn't want it fueled by alcohol.

Next to him Leslie cleared her throat. "You awake?" she asked.

"I think so, but I'm not sure," he said, hesitantly. "I'm not sure about much of anything this morning."

"Let me confirm that you had too much to drink and that Whalen and I helped you into bed and decided to sleep with you to make sure you didn't walk out of the lanai and fall into the drink," she said, laughing playfully.

He looked down and could see he was dressed. She was, too. He felt a sense of relief, mixed with a twinge of regret.

CHAPTER 24

Friday, New Year's Day

Wes declined breakfast and thanked Leslie for the evening; grateful that she gave him a hug and kiss on the cheek. It was a sign that he hadn't done anything inappropriate to jeopardize their friendship.

New Year's Day wasn't an opportunity to move the ball forward on anything unless you were a football player or liked parades of flowers. Wes took a shower, drank Alka-Selzer and wandered aimlessly through the pages of Thursday's *New York Times* before finally deciding this was the day he was returning the boxes of papers that belonged to John Mason.

He made copies of the ones he needed to keep. If Mason was going to stay angry, he couldn't legitimately keep any of the documents. He had to proceed without them.

He loaded the boxes into his Highlander and drove to the pale-yellow cinder block home where he last saw Mason sprawled on the living room floor. He pulled out one box and carried it around back. The window Wes smashed to get into the house was not repaired, but was covered with a piece of cardboard held in place by duct tape.

No surprise there, Wes thought.

He removed the cardboard, tossed the box onto the living floor and climbed cautiously through the broken window, careful not to cut himself again on the few shards still clinging to the frame. Once inside, he placed the box by the television set and next to a stack of old newspapers.

There was still broken glass on the floor where Mason had fallen. Wes found a broom and dustpan in a tall cabinet by the kitchen and cleaned up the mess, then tidied up dirty dishes and an ashtray that was filled with half-smoked cigarettes. He was glad the butts didn't look appealing. The cravings were there, but he was hoping not to ever give in again.

Although he wasn't sure why, he also made the bed.

He used the front door to bring in the rest of the boxes, then retaped the broken window and departed by the back door. He hoped no one noticed that it was unlocked.

Instead of leaving the vicinity, he decided to drive beyond Mason's house to the end of a cul-de-sac where the properties were better maintained and looked to be more expensive. He was eager to learn about the more remote parts of the island – and the stories they could tell.

He was finishing his impromptu tour when he caught a glimpse of a white vehicle bouncing down the rutted road, coming his direction. When he realized it was turning into 2501, he pulled his SUV into a nearby driveway and ducked down.

Peering through the lower part of the Highlander's window, he spotted the green and yellow trim that marked the sheriff's vehicle. When it was partially out of sight, Wes exited his car and sought cover in a row of podocarpus bushes not far from Mason's house. From there he could watch Sheriff Fleck emerge from the vehicle, go around to the passenger side and open the door.

It took a few minutes for Mason to emerge. When he did step onto the shell driveway, Wes gasped. The pale-faced man had never looked robust. Today, he appeared to be rapping on death's door.

Sheriff Fleck grasped Mason's arm and escorted him to the front entrance. When the sheriff discovered the door wasn't locked, Wes could hear him admonishing Mason about safety and saw the old man cower in response. *Jeez, take it easy, Harry,* Wes thought, feeling badly that he was the one who'd forgotten to bolt it from the inside.

As the two men disappeared inside the house, Wes returned to his car, slumped down again and waited for the sheriff to depart. Remembering that it was Harry Fleck's weekend off, Wes found himself thinking kind thoughts about the law enforcement official. He could have left Mason in the hospital for another day but instead brought him home. He appeared to be concerned about his well-being, even if his manner was gruff.

Wes noticed the sheriff was empty-handed when he and Mason arrived and found himself worried that there was nothing in the house for the pale-faced man to eat – or drink. When he was sure the sheriff was nowhere in the vicinity, Wes left the neighborhood, racing his Highlander toward the village, thinking that the stores would be closed and wondering what he might have in his apartment for Mason to consume.

He discovered cheese, lunchmeat and bread, cereal and milk – none of which had expired. That would tide Mason over until either he could go to the grocery store or find a friend to do it for him. Maybe Shine the bartender; if Mason didn't want help from Wes.

He took the groceries from his refrigerator and put them in a Publix bag. Then searched his closet, finding the half-full bottle of vodka he'd brought with him when he moved to Florida and stuck it in the bag next to the food. He didn't like the idea of enabling an alcoholic. But forcing Mason to go through the DTs in his condition didn't seem like the humane thing to do either.

Back at 2501, Wes gingerly tapped on the front door. When no one answered, he knocked more forcefully and called out Mason's name.

"Johnny Boy, are you there?"

The door opened a fraction. Before it could close, Wes wedged his foot against it.

"I brought you food and vodka," he said. "Please let me in. I won't hurt you."

Mason opened the door slowly, said nothing and shuffled toward the kitchen, with Wes following.

"Put it there," he said softly, indicating the kitchen counter.

"I was worried about you when I found you on the floor. That's when they took you to the hospital," Wes said.

"I know, and I thank you for helping me – and for bringing this." Mason, who'd been rooting through the bag, pulled out the vodka.

"You should put that stuff, except for the cereal, in the fridge," Wes said as he watched Mason pour the vodka into a glass and drink it down without benefit of ice.

"Guess you might as well sit down," Mason said, pointing to the couch and then pouring himself another vodka. To this one he added ice cubes.

"Yeah, well, I'm not sure what happened and then at the hospital you seemed mad at us…Leslie and me. We were both concerned and surprised."

"I was warned," Mason said, stroking the yellowish-green bruise that covered the side of his face. He sat down on the couch and sighed heavily.

"Warned? About what? By whom?" Wes was incredulous. Who would threaten a harmless old man who was still looking for answers about the death of his son? If anybody should be warned it was Wes, who was opening up a can of worms that had been sealed for two decades.

"I shouldn't say," Mason said, touching his side.

"I thought you fell. Did someone do this to you?"

Mason did not respond.

Wes felt rage erupt throughout his body. "We have to report this to the sheriff. Did you tell him that someone hurt you?"

The pale-faced man looked at Wes, tears forming in his eyes. "You have to forget about my son."

"But the sheriff? What did he say?"

"He said I shouldn't be talking about this…to anyone…for my sake and theirs."

Wes looked at Mason for a few seconds, muttered something about having to go, then stormed out of the house, climbed into his car and reached in his pocket for the cigarette that wasn't there. "Fuck!" he screamed.

He gunned the engine, kicking up dust and crushed shells as he backed out of the driveway and raced onto Egret Road, sailing over the ruts as if the road was flat. He sped through the mostly empty village, barely slowing down at the four-way stops. When he reached the building that housed the sheriff's headquarters, he parked his vehicle and got out, slamming the door behind him.

As he walked across the street, he could feel his heart pounding. His jaw hurt from clenching his teeth. He remembered being this angry only once before. That was when an editor killed a story Wes had written exposing graft in the mayor's office that went to the top. He was a young reporter and the editor said he didn't have enough evidence to back up his claim. Wes exploded verbally and almost lost his job.

Today, he tried to calm himself as he headed for the sheriff's office. *Don't take it out on the deputy if the sheriff isn't there*, he told himself.

Deputy Webster was sitting at the sheriff's large desk watching football on the new TV recently installed above the area where the coffee pot resided. His feet were propped up, and he was leaning back, drinking something that looked like beer.

When Wes threw open the door, the deputy scrambled to remove his feet and move the glass to a less conspicuous location.

"Where's Fleck?" Wes growled.

"Happy New Year to ya," the deputy said. He appeared to relax after realizing that the visitor was Wes and not some other island resident who might be inclined to report the deputy for lax behavior.

"Yeah, sure. Happy New Year, Bruce. Where's your boss?"

"This is his weekend off so I'm guessin' he's home watchin' some movie or somethin' on TV," the deputy said. "Ya got a problem?"

"Yeah, with him," Wes said. "I think he knows who beat up John Mason and threatened him to keep quiet about his son's death. And he's not doing anything about it."

"Hold on," the deputy said, getting up out of his chair and starting to pace. "I know that's a touchy subject with Harry because some people just won't let it go. But he'd never let anyone lay a hand on Mason. Never. I'd swear to that on a stack of bibles. If John told ya that, he was either lying or ya misunderstood him."

Wes thought of the pathetic figure sitting on his couch, tears in his eye, bruises on his face and neck and broken ribs and felt the anger surge through his body again.

"I don't know who the sheriff's protecting or why. But the truth has to come out."

The deputy took his handkerchief out of his back pocket and began wiping his brow. He was clearly upset.

"Back off and let me handle this. You don't wanna get on the wrong side of Harry Fleck. Not now. Seems like he's got a lot on his mind. Please let me handle it, Wes. Please."

Shit, Wes said under his breath. Fleck had been sheriff a long time. The people who elected him and the higher-ups he answered to in Tallahassee didn't seem to have a problem with him. They were not going to switch their allegiance to a reporter for a small-town paper or their sympathies to a man known to many as an alcoholic.

"Okay, Bruce. But if something happens to that old man, Harry Fleck will go down and you with him," Wes said as he turned and stormed out of the office.

CHAPTER 25

Saturday morning, January 2

After Wes left her apartment, Leslie situated herself and the dog on the lanai, made a phone call to her daughter to wish her Happy New Year and to tell her that her grandmother was getting married. Meredith was delighted and offered to be the maid-of-honor. Leslie shuddered at the thought of the two women she loved plotting the perfect nuptials; over-the-top and expensive were the words that came to mind.

She spent the rest of New Year's Day reading *Magpie Murders* and marveling at the author's creativity. Her novel, if it ever got written, would be a mystery, too. But intrigue had been hitting too close to home these days, and Leslie was reluctant to fictionalize the events of the last few months in her own literary efforts.

The other thought that crossed her mind and lingered during the day was the kiss from Wes. It was unexpected but not unwelcome. A display of affection from a male friend on New Year's Eve was acceptable, even if it came with a surprising amount of electricity.

The next morning, she got up early, took the dog for his usual walk past the unfinished house that belonged to Whalen's previous owner, now deceased. Past the path to the beach that Leslie had taken to discover Jamie's corpse. Past the pink house where she'd seen Deputy Webster the day Frank's body was discovered.

This feels like the highway through hell, she told herself, thinking that she needed a different route, one filled with happier memories.

When they returned, she fed Whalen his breakfast kibble, munching on a slice of wheat toast as she headed for the shower. She was meeting her friend Deb at the Gallery Centre about 11 and hoped the two of them could go to lunch afterward. Deb might have picked up information about the Seaside Cottage shooting over the years.

The dog had demonstrated he had a strong bladder, so Leslie wasn't worried about leaving him for the four or five hours it would take to help Deb start setting up for the Centre's Gala, held annually on Friday of the first full week after New Year's.

It was a fundraiser that marked the beginning of a long season of art shows and sales, classes and workshops. The plan was to get everyone on the same page and in a good frame of mind before the season was in full swing.

Deb appeared frazzled when Leslie arrived. "Thank God you're here," she said. "A lot of these biddies are no shows today for this reason or that. I got half a dozen folks but can always use a few more willing hands."

Leslie extended her arms. "Here are two," she said.

Deb had a long list of tasks, that included scrubbing the art class paint spots off the hardwood floors. Chairs and easels had to be put away. And because some art pieces would be raffled off, the metal display stands needed to be unfolded and draped with beige linen. Leslie was picking at a particularly tough burnt umber glob when she saw Deb scurrying toward her.

"One of the artists bringing in her stuff needs help," Deb said. Leslie noticed but discounted the strange expression on Deb's face.

"Sure thing," Leslie said. She was glad to be standing after 40 minutes on her hands and knees.

She trotted out the front door and toward the ramp that led to the street. When she saw a familiar Lincoln Town car parked with its trunk up, she stopped dead in her tracks and pivoted. Deb was waiting for her, blocking the gallery entrance.

"That's Frank's old car. You sent me out there to help Janis Johnson," Leslie steamed. "Screw that. I'm going back to scrubbing floors."

"I don't think so," Deb said. "It's time you two mended fences. This is a small town. You had the same man in common. At least be civil."

Leslie rolled her eyes. "She's treated me like dirt. Why should I be nice to her? Except for the deputy, I doubt she has many friends."

"Exactly," Deb said. "Get rid of all bitterness, rage and anger, brawling and slander, along with every form of malice. Be kind and compassionate to one another, forgiving each other, just as in Christ God forgave you."

Leslie stared at Deb.

"Ephesians 4, verses 31 and 32. Learned that in our Bible study group the other night. I memorized it so I could say those very words to you when you told me to fuck off after I suggested you reach out to Janis."

Leslie's mouth dropped open as she searched for a response. "I-I don't know what to address first," she finally said. "The somewhat shocking news that you and Scooter are going to Bible…."

"I didn't say Scooter was going. Hell will freeze over before that happens. But I'm going and getting to know some of the nice snowbirds in your church."

"Well, that's good," Leslie said. "But Janis…." She turned to look at the woman who'd just dropped a box of yellow papers that were being picked up by the late morning Gulf breezes and scattered across the street.

"Shit," Leslie heard her say and then saw her lower her head and put her hands over her eyes.

"See what I mean," Deb said. "She needs a friend."

"Why the hell does it have to be me?" Leslie trotted down the ramp, a scowl on her face, and was soon collecting the papers, trying to keep them from heading toward the busy four-way intersection nearby. When she'd gathered all of them, she headed back to the Lincoln, steeling herself for what was to come.

"Need some help?" Leslie said. She was careful not to sound artificial or syrupy.

Janis looked up, seemed startled and froze her face into a look of distaste that matched Leslie's earlier expression. "Not from you."

"If not from me, then who?" Leslie responded, looking around as if searching for another pair of hands.

Janis sighed, handed Leslie a heavy box and then piled another on top of that.

"Got it," Leslie said. Trying to pretend the load wasn't too much for her, she took off for the gallery door where Deb was still standing.

"Put it down here," she said, "and get the rest of it."

"Bible study doesn't qualify you to act like God," Leslie said under her breath.

"I heard that," Deb said with a grin.

Leslie passed Janis who was also stopped by Deb. After four trips, the two women ended up together at the entrance.

"See that table over there? Here's a bottle of wine from our last show. I know it's not 5 o'clock, and I can't guarantee this is any good, but I want the two of you to go over and celebrate being loved by a great guy who is no longer with us. Get past this bitterness and see what you can do together to honor his memory. Got it?"

Deb was a formidable woman in size and character. You don't survive a 30-year marriage to a man like Scooter without having the female equivalent of balls, Frank once said about his friend. Leslie remembered his words when she took her seat at the white painted picnic table across from Janis and poured two small glasses of wine.

It was almost noon. After struggling for several months, the weather had managed to achieve the perfect balance of temperature and humidity that makes Florida the place to be in the winter. The same soft wind from the west that had scattered Janis's papers carried with it a hint of jasmine.

"You go first," Leslie said, eager to end the torture as soon as possible.

"To the fuckin' bastard I married," Janis said and emptied the plastic cup. She also appeared to want the lovefest to be over quickly.

"The fuckin' bastard," Leslie repeated and drank about half of her glass.

"Your turn," Janis said, smirking and looking over at Deb who was standing by the gallery entrance with her arms crossed.

Leslie paused. "To the man I thought loved me, but who ditched me when times got tough and it suited his purpose." She'd been thinking that all along. In the mood of the moment, it felt good to hear herself say those words.

"You, too?" Janis said, a look of surprise on her face. "To the fucker who ditched me when times got tough." She held her glass out to Leslie who filled it halfway and then watched Janis empty it again.

"Looks like we're gonna need a bigger bottle," Leslie said as she checked the amount of wine left. Bonding with Janis was not easy.

"To one hell of a lover," Janis said, raising her glass and eyeing Leslie.

Leslie paused, then said softly: "One hell of a lover."

Janis reached for the bottle, put it to her lips, draining it and tossing the empty into the grassy area around the table. "To my son, Stevie. I love him and want him back. Desperately."

"To Stevie," Leslie said.

Before Leslie emptied her glass, Janis put her head on the table and began sobbing. Leslie could feel tears forming in her eyes and her heart softening. She got up, went to the other side of the table and put her arm around the woman who'd been her bitter enemy just minutes ago.

"It's almost noon and I could use something to eat," Leslie said.

Janis raised her head and wiped her eyes with the back of her hands. "Me, too."

Leslie remembered seeing a photograph of a much-younger Janis on a boat with Frank and the Realtor Gordon Fike, who'd recently been arrested for drug dealing on the island. She was beautiful back then and, if Leslie was honest, she would admit that age had not been unkind to her. She was still amazing looking. Moreover, this was a fragile person who should be forgiven and helped, if possible.

When both women stood up, Deb left her post and walked toward them with what looked to be a key in her hand.

"Why don't you continue your discussion about Frank at the Tarpon. Here's the key to the gallery's golf cart. Try not to run over anyone on the way there."

CHAPTER 26

When Wes opened the door to the Tarpon Bar, he was stunned to see John Mason, still bruised, sitting between two attractive females at the bar, talking and laughing as though he was 30 years younger and hadn't recently suffered a beating at the hands of a mystery attacker.

What a quick recovery, he thought.

But even more surprising were the identities of the two woman he was with. The one with her arm draped over his shoulder was Janis Johnson. The other one, laughing and slapping Johnny Boy on the arm, was Leslie.

He wondered if he'd entered the Twilight Zone.

It was obvious none of them was sober. How much alcohol they'd consumed and their level of intoxication was up for debate. How had these three individuals ended up together on these barstools at 1 p.m. on a Saturday afternoon? Wes shook his head.

"Look who's here," Shine the bartender said. At which point the three of them turned, raised their glasses and yelled "Wes!" He would have said it reminded him of a scene from the old TV show *Cheers* if it hadn't been so surreal.

"Join us," Janis said and patted the seat of the barstool next to her. She leaned beyond the pale-faced man so she could see Leslie. "You okay with that?"

"I got no claims on Wes," Leslie said. "And even if I did, I'd be happy to share him with you, sister."

"That's good to hear," Wes murmured sarcastically, taking a sip of the beer Shine placed before him.

"Do you know these ladies?" Johnny Boy asked, looking at Wes. His eyes weren't completely glazed over, so the reporter assumed that John Mason had not reached his four-drink limit. Or maybe the presence of the women had energized him. Wes remembered reading somewhere that Mason, now single, had been married three times.

"Unfortunately, yes. So why are we celebrating?" Wes asked. "We are celebrating, aren't we?"

"The life, loves and times of Frank Johnson, fisherman," Leslie said.

"Drinkin' to the sexy prick," Janis added.

All three took a drink. "To the prick," they said in unison, then laughed heartily.

"How long has this been going on?" Wes asked Shine over the din. He was thinking that this frivolity as it related to the murder of Frank Johnson was in bad taste. At the same time, he understood that the two women shared strong emotions where the fisherman was concerned.

"About an hour, give or take. They descended on Johnny Boy the minute he came through the door. It's like they gave him a shot of adrenaline. I haven't seen him this fired up – ever."

"And how many drinks have the ladies had?"

"Three shots of tequila, maybe four, plus whatever they were drinking before they came here. They keep saying something about being united in the fight against bad boys."

Shine winked, then left Wes for another customer who'd taken a seat at the far end of the bar.

Two nights ago, Leslie was trying to figure out how Janis killed her ex-husband. Today, they are sisters united against a poor dead guy. This is why I'm no longer married, Wes thought as he sipped on his beer and contemplated what his next step should be.

"Anybody had lunch?" he finally asked, looking for a way to tamp down the alcohol-fueled rowdiness that had overtaken the three.

"To lunch," Johnny Boy said, raising his glass.

Obviously not, Wes thought. "I'm starving. What are you guys having?"

They looked at him with blank faces. "I'll have a cheeseburger," Leslie finally said. "And fries."

"Frank would want us to eat fish," Janis said, giggling.

Before they could raise their glasses in a toast to fish, Wes yelled out to Shine that everyone wanted a grouper sandwich and fries – as soon as possible. The bartender disappeared into the kitchen. "Coming right up," he said when he returned.

Wes wolfed down his sandwich, requested another beer and contemplated dragging the women out of the bar and leaving Johnny Boy to fend for himself.

"Should we order another round of tequila?" he heard Leslie ask after picking at her fish sandwich for about 10 minutes. Janis, both elbows on the bar and a French fry hanging out of her mouth, shook her head.

"Naw," she said. "Gotta go help Deb."

"Oh, yeah, Deb," Leslie said, then snorted. "Serves her right she got abandoned."

"And the dog," Wes said.

"The dog? Oh shit, poor Whalen," Leslie said, checking her watch three times as though she couldn't quite read what it said.

Wes stood up. "I'll drive all of you home," he said.

"Are we leaving?" the pale-faced man asked. "Ladies, you're welcome to come home with me."

"I think they'll pass, Johnny Boy," Wes said, assessing that however many drinks Mason had, he wasn't fit to drive. "Maybe some other time."

After corralling them into his SUV, Wes deposited Janis at the Gallery Centre, marching her up to a surprised Deb, who was busy directing volunteers hanging paintings. "I believe this one belongs to you," he said, turning around and leaving without waiting for a response.

The pale-faced man was also an easy drop-off. Wes opened the front door, which wasn't locked, guided Mason to his couch and sat him down. "If you need anything, call me," he said.

Mason grunted something Wes couldn't understand and reached for the TV remote.

Leslie was sitting in the front seat of Wes's Highlander, alternating between repentant and rowdy on the way home. He'd never seen her in this condition. Based on his past experiences with drunks, he didn't consider it endearing. Well, kind of endearing, but not something he wanted to see again from her anytime soon.

When they reached her apartment, he helped her up the steps and inside the door, then guided her to the bedroom where she threw herself across the blue and white striped comforter and was soon snoring loudly.

The dog watched the proceedings, waiting until Wes was back in the living room before whining and glancing toward the screen door.

"Let's go," Wes said, heading for the entryway where Whalen's leash hung from a wooden peg.

Leslie was still asleep when Wes and Whalen returned. It was past 4 and Wes wasn't sure if the dog had been fed, so he poured a generous bowl of brown chunks that advertising itself as perfect for your pet, grabbed a beer from Leslie's refrigerator and settled into one of the chairs on the lanai.

It was shortly after 5 when Wes heard Leslie get up and stagger into the bathroom. He tried to pretend he didn't hear her throwing up. A few minutes past 7 she emerged. Wes was on the lanai drinking another beer and munching on cheese and stale crackers. Whalen was asleep in his favorite chair.

"Hair of the dog," she said. "That's what I feel like. Hair of the shedding dog."

"You deserve to feel that bad," Wes said.

She sat down in the chair next to him, looking at him with those pale green eyes. Apologies were written all over her face.

"So, here's the good news," she said when he didn't react to her pathetic expression. "Janis and I had a moment. Thanks to Deb. Funny thing. Janis thought I had something to do with Frank's death. I told her I thought she'd shot him."

"Let me guess. You discovered you both wanted to kill him but didn't."

Leslie tried to say figuratively three times and gave up. "Yes, we did want to kill him but wouldn't, of course. At least I wouldn't. Janis told me she tried to call Frank that night…like the deputy told her to do. He didn't answer. She never got to speak with him.

"Did I tell you Janis knows a lot about guns?" she added. "She thinks the two of us can figure out who shot Frank once we get the police or autopsy reports or whatever they are."

Wes looked at her skeptically. "You think Harry Fleck is going to give you any information?"

"Not Harry. Bruce. The deputy would do anything for Janis, Wes. She and I are going to solve this."

"What if it was some random guy Jamie brought along. Some drug dealer without a real motive who thought Frank needed to be done away with it," Wes said.

"Hold onto that thought," Leslie said, as she stood up, shakily, and headed for the kitchen where she got a glass of water and a couple of aspirin.

"Hey Whalen, you want dinner?" she called out to the dog on his back in his favorite chair; his four legs splayed out from his body. He sighed, managed to roll over, get down off the chair and head for the kitchen.

"I already fed him," Wes yelled.

Leslie looked down at Whalen who was standing next to his empty bowl. "You little trickster. No second meals for you. We don't want you getting fat."

She returned to the lanai, with a defeated-looking Whalen walking slowly behind her. She set her water on a table, plopped down and started talking.

"I think Jamie came to this island alone. He wasn't really part of the hard-core drug gang. He and his cousin, Peter, were the Canadian transport and distribution guys. Jamie tried to sound scary and, if cornered, he could be tough. But that wasn't him. I think he wanted some of Frank's millions. That's what he came back for."

Wes watched Leslie empty her glass and then look expectantly at him. "Well?" she said.

"I'm not discounting your theory," he said. "In fact, I think it's not bad at all. I'm just still marveling at how two women who loved the same man and hated each other with such passion could bond in a couple of hours over booze."

Leslie grinned. "It's obvious you don't understand how the female mind works."

Wes couldn't argue with that.

CHAPTER 27

Sunday evening, January 3

"This is Chip. You know the drill." Wes had left three messages for Chip Shelton in the last two days with no response. He had no idea where the guy lived or if he'd be willing to talk, but he wasn't giving up.

If the voicemails didn't work, he'd take the next step – paying the Internet service that provides an address and other contact information to go along with a phone number. He wasn't eager to ambush him, but he desperately wanted to hear Shelton's perspective on what happened that night at Seaside Cottage.

In the meantime, he'd reluctantly agreed to play corpse for Leslie and Janis who decided to meet on the beach after dark to see if they could recreate Frank's and Jamie's shootings. He thought it was a hare-brained scheme but also recognized you could never discount Leslie's wild ideas.

It was close to 6 when Wes and Leslie arrived at the spot where she thought Frank's body was found. She admitted she couldn't be sure but remembered the deputy saying he discovered poor Frank on the beach some distance beyond the pink mansion on Oceanview.

"The moon's a waxing crescent," Leslie said as she looked up into the star-filled sky. "It could work."

"And that means?" Wes asked.

"There's not gonna be much natural light," she said. "Like the night Frank died."

Wes pressed the button on his watch to illuminate the dials: 6:12 was the time. He was eager to get on with the reenactment so he could return to his apartment to watch Sunday Night Football and all the hoopla that preceded it. He was a big fan of the longtime commentator, Al Michaels, and had met the guy when both were much younger. "How's Janis going to find us?"

"There's your answer," Leslie said as two figures emerged from the darkness. "Looks like she brought the deputy with her."

Wes was relieved, thinking that with someone from law enforcement there, the evening would be more productive than he anticipated. As the two approached, he noticed the deputy was carrying a rifle or was it a shotgun with a night scope attached? Wes, not being familiar with guns, didn't know the difference.

"Comrades in the fight," Wes joked when the pair arrived at the spot not far from a fallen tree and near the large sand bar that stretched several hundred yards into the Gulf.

"Thanks for coming, Bruce," Leslie added. There was a touch of reproach in her voice; Wes assumed it was directed at his attempt at humor.

"It's been a tough weekend, but Janis needed me. Um, glad you two have, um, are finally friendly," the deputy said.

"Don't get sentimental on us, honey," Janis said. "Let's see what we can figure out. Now that we're all on the same side."

The deputy cleared his throat. "Whoever shot Frank must've ambushed him. No one could get the better of Frank up close unless it was someone he trusted."

"And that wouldn't be Jamie, right, or really anyone," Leslie said as a statement of fact.

"Right, and the gun was in the waistband of his shorts like ya said, Leslie. If yer feelin' threatened, you don't keep yer weapon someplace where ya can't get to it easy."

Wes pointed toward the sand dunes and clumps of seagrass that he thought could be a good hiding place. "If it wasn't someone he knew, then it had to be someone with Jamie – another drug guy who was out there somewhere,"

"Another druggie wouldn't have shot Jamie, would he?" Janis asked. "What would be the point?"

All four nodded.

"What do we know about the bullet that killed Frank?" Wes asked. As he'd told Randy Long at the newspaper, he wasn't a police reporter. But he'd watched enough detective series on TV to assume the bullet was an important detail.

"Never found it," the deputy said.

"And Jamie?" Wes continued.

"A .300 Blackout expanding bullet," the deputy answered.

Leslie gasped. "That's what Matt at the shooting range talked about. How you could kill someone 1,000 feet away...."

"You were at the shooting range and talked to Matt?" Janis asked Leslie.

"I'll tell you about it later. I was, um, just testing some theories."

"How come we're just hearing about this bullet information?" Wes interrupted.

"The sheriff got the report on Friday and locked it up in his desk before I could get a good look at it," the deputy said. "I heard him talkin' to Agent McKechnie about it."

"The DEA guy?" Wes was in full reporter mode now. He was already thinking about how he could obtain a copy, wondering if a FOIA request would be the appropriate mechanism. Sometimes officials had the nerve to ignore reporters who requested documents under the Freedom of Information Act. Sheriff Fleck might be one of those. The only recourse in those cases is to file a lawsuit and force discovery through the courts.

"Bruce, can you sneak it out of his desk?" Leslie asked.

"I-I can try," the deputy responded. "Harry runs the show, ya know. Keeps things to himself. Him lockin' up the shootin' report...well...that's Harry."

"Can we get on with this little play?" Wes said, checking the time on his phone again and thinking that Bruce was once more providing alibis for his boss.

Leslie and Janis's plan involved Wes standing on the beach by himself, wearing a hoodie and pretending to be Frank. The shooter, portrayed by the deputy, would be hidden behind the sand dune to the far left of where Jamie's body was found by the boat.

After providing those instructions, Leslie walked about 30 feet from where Wes was standing and put on a hat not unlike the one Jamie was wearing the night he died. Janis sat down on a large branch of the dead tree that had fallen decades ago, and was now a refuge for crabs, lizards and other beach life, to act as observer.

I can't see a damn thing, Wes thought, wondering how Frank, Jamie and the shooter navigated the beach in the dark.

The wind from the northeast had picked up, along with the surf. The tide was out, leaving an expansive beach.

"Can't see shit without the scope," the deputy's voice emerged from the darkness, confirming what Wes was thinking. "Hold on."

A minute or so later, Bruce called out again. "This is better, but it's still hard to see who ya are Wes."

"Good." Wes heard Leslie's voice to his left, moving closer.

"I'm going to act like I'm Jamie, approaching," she said.

A loud pop came out of nowhere. Wes saw a shadowy Leslie fall to the ground and heard her cry out. "I've been shot!" she whimpered.

"Jesus Christ, Bruce. You weren't supposed to shoot the damn gun!" Wes was now running in Leslie's direction.

"I didn't!" the deputy yelled. "Don't move. There's someone else out here."

Wes ignored the warning and was soon at Leslie's side. "Where are you hurt?" he asked, crouching by her side.

"My-my arm," she moaned. "It's burning like hell."

Wes pulled off his shirt and wrapped it around Leslie's arm, his mind racing between thoughts of getting her safely off the beach, wondering if the shooter was still out there and what danger that posed to all of them.

Janis also ignored Bruce's warning and was soon at Leslie's side, her cell phone in her hand.

"There's been a shooting on the beach. No, I don't have an address, you idiot," she screamed.

"Take it easy, Janis," the deputy said. He'd also left his position to join the others and was now huddled around Leslie. "Give me the phone, honey.

"911. This is Deputy Bruce Webster. We're on the beach, just out from a large pink house midway Oceanview Drive. Don't have an address. This is an active shooting scene. We're gonna try to get the injured party off the beach to a safe location. Send an ambulance to Oceanview near the main entrance to the beach. We'll find our way there.

"Stay low," he warned the others as he put his rifle to his shoulder and, using the scope, scanned the area where he thought the shot had come from.

"I can't see anyone," he said, "but we're not safe out here in the open."

Wes scooped up Leslie and started walking swiftly for the dunes. Janis was close behind. Bruce stood guard, still scanning with his scope. When there were no more shots, he moved quickly away from the water, following the path the others had taken.

"It's a pretty nasty wound," the EMT told Leslie, "but we'll get you to the hospital where they'll fix you up. Are you right-handed? I hope."

Leslie was trying not to cry from the pain and the sight of the blood. It felt like the back of her left arm had been blown off. But if she speculated too much about the damage, she was worried she might pass out. Better to remain in a state of ignorance and shock until the pain meds took over.

"Uh-huh," she said weakly.

Bruce and Janis had left in his sheriff's car and were enroute to the hospital. Wes was in the back of the ambulance with Leslie, prepared to ride with her unless they kicked him out.

"Don't say anything," she said, looking like she was going to cry.

"This time it wasn't your fault," Wes said. "I'm wondering who else knew we were out there? Bruce said he didn't tell anyone. Same for Janis."

Leslie shifted her position slightly on the gurney and groaned.

"We won't think about that now," he added. "The important thing is to get you fixed up."

It took about 20 minutes for the ambulance to transport Leslie to the mainland hospital. It was the same facility where she'd been treated for the gash on her head – the one inflicted when she was snooping around the mystery house where drugs were stored. It was also where the ambulance had taken John Mason.

She wondered if the hospital personnel would remember her and think she was some kind of a danger-prone nut. The thought passed when she realized they were wheeling her into an operating room and the round-faced doctor with a mask on was leaning over telling her that everything was going to be okay. She hoped he was right.

CHAPTER 28

Monday morning, January 4

The emergency room doctor told Wes late Sunday that Leslie's arm was broken by the force of the bullet, but the bone fragments had been removed and pins put in place. She should remain in the hospital for at least another day or two because she'd lost more blood than he liked. Satisfied there was nothing else he could do for Leslie, Wes had gone to her place to spend the night with Whalen.

The next morning, he checked with her neighbor, Jim, a retired accountant, who agreed to take care of the dog until Leslie recovered. Wes also lined up a caregiver who would be willing to stay with Leslie for a day or two, if needed, when she returned to the condo.

If questioned by someone at the paper about the ambulance run and shooting on the beach, he'd ask they not print it yet. There was a lot going on, and he had the feeling it was all connected. It was too big to be piecemealed into a two-paragraph police report article.

His column for Friday's paper about beachfront properties and the ongoing battle between private property owners and the public was done, giving him the freedom to deal with other issues on his mind...like the piece of paper locked in Sheriff Fleck's desk.

Wes always liked asking questions to which he knew the answer. Where was the report on the shootings of Frank Johnson and Jamie Thompson? Wes was eager to hear what the sheriff's response would be.

He put in another call to Chip Shelton and got his voicemail again. He pulled out his credit card, put in Shelton's name and phone number, paid $32.95 and had an address and a potential employer in short order. The Shelton residence was on the other side of the state, about a three-hour drive, and the employer was a company that operated on both coasts doing high-end custom metal roofing.

Wes loved and hated that no one had any privacy anymore.

Unless Leslie was coming home tomorrow, he'd make the trek east to track down Shelton. Today, he was going to pay Sheriff Fleck a visit.

The office was empty when he arrived; the TV set was blaring the weather news from a station in Miami, the coffee pot was nearly full and there were half a dozen sweet rolls on a plate.

Wes wondered how busy Sheriff Fleck would be after New Year's Eve weekend. The revelers were gone, and the snowbirds wouldn't be heading south for another couple of weeks, bringing with them colds and flu – presents from their adorable grandchildren – to infect the island's elderly population.

Wes called out the sheriff's name. Hearing nothing, he went immediately to Fleck's large desk. Only one of the drawers was unlocked – the top one, which was filled with pencils, paper clips and bumper stickers saying Support Your Local Law Enforcement.

As the deputy had described, Harry Fleck was a locked down, closed-mouth kind of guy who tried to keep everyone and everything under his control.

Remembering he hadn't had breakfast, Wes poured himself a cup of coffee and grabbed a bear claw, which was surprisingly fresh. Wes guessed that when it came to sweets, the sheriff had his standards.

He was checking his phone when the sheriff returned. Sheriff Fleck didn't appear to be all that surprised to see Wes. He grunted a hello and sat down at his desk.

"You here for the shooting reports?"

"Why yes, and some other important matters. Then you have them?" Wes was shocked that the sheriff was being so forthcoming.

"Yep," Fleck said, running his fingers through his curly reddish-brown hair. "For a couple of days. Who wants to be talking about those things on New Year's Eve? I locked 'em in my desk. Kept 'em away from prying eyes." He laughed, then coughed and laughed again.

"What do they say?"

The sheriff looked at Wes and smirked. "One said Frank Johnson died from a gunshot wound to the head. The other said that Jamie Thompson was shot in the back and likely died from blood loss."

"We already knew that. Anything else?"

"Did we know that?" the sheriff said, looking over the top of the half readers he'd put on. He coughed again, then cleared his throat. "You media people are always a lot smarter than us dumb cops."

"Uh, sorry. I should have said that's what I heard…or that was the speculation," Wes said, deciding that now was not the time to antagonize Fleck. "No idea who did the shooting?"

"None. The report didn't specifically say, but I'm guessing it was a high-powered rifle – the kind used by drug dealers and other criminals. Jamie probably had one of his cohorts with him. Shot Frank and then took him out. There's no explanation for what those whackos do – even to each other."

The sheriff got up to pour himself a coffee and choose a pastry. He sat down, took a sip and said, "Yep, unless something else breaks, this case will be marked closed. Just like the one from 20 years ago that you're looking into."

Fleck looked away from Wes, picked up the TV remote and switched from the local channel to Fox News.

Wes paused to think for a minute about what he was going to say next. He decided not to confront the sheriff about the bruises on John Mason's body.

"Did the deputy tell you about the shooting last night?"

"Filled out a report. I haven't talked to him about it yet. How's, um, Mrs. Elliott?"

"Her arm's pretty bad, but she'll be okay," Wes said, trying to gauge the sheriff's reaction. "Frankly, sheriff, I'm very concerned about her. Is she going to need 24-hour protection again?"

The sheriff adjusted his readers, looked up at the TV for a few seconds, then turned to face Wes again. "I don't think so. We've had reports of random gun noises on the north end of the island for years. Lots of coyotes up there and those crazy rich people with guns sometimes go out on their lanais and shoot into the darkness, thinking they're aiming at some dangerous animal."

"If that's the case, that's shocking," Wes said. He didn't remember seeing notations about random gunfire on the police report rosters, but it wasn't his job to check them. "I haven't heard or read anything about shootings, except for Frank and Jamie … and now Leslie. You make it sound routine."

Fleck ignored Wes's barely veiled "shock" and said, "The deputy's gonna talk to the neighbors up there today. See if they heard anything. Stuff happens. Life goes on. If Bruce thinks Mrs. Elliott needs protection, we'll arrange for it. All in all, we're a quiet community. And I'm gonna keep it that way."

Wes got up to leave. "I'll need a copy of those reports," he said, trying not to get angry at the sheriff for his cavalier attitude about Leslie's safety.

"The Xerox is over there. I won't charge you," the sheriff said, fumbling with a key in his righthand drawer and coming up with papers that he tossed to the reporter.

Wes made the copies, grudgingly thanked Fleck for his help and left, congratulating himself for not calling out the sheriff for being a jerk. He'd done that once to a politician in Indiana who was a bad actor. It didn't work to his benefit and only briefly made him feel better.

As he stepped onto the sidewalk, Wes saw DEA Agent McKechnie emerge from a Ford F-150 SSV, the vehicle often used by law enforcement.

"Agent McKechnie, can I speak with you for a few minutes?" Wes yelled out, as he walked toward the man in the tan cotton suit and dark sunglasses. "Wes Avery with *The Island Sun.*"

"Yeah, I remember you. If you wanna know about the Frank Johnson shooting, I've got nothing to say."

Wes wished McKechnie would remove his sunglasses so he could get a better look at the agent's eyes. They often spoke volumes and too many law enforcement types wore shades to effect. "I guess I thought you'd want this case solved…."

"I loved the guy like a brother, but the agency decided to have the sheriff handle this one since there were no drugs involved."

"So, why're you here?" Wes asked.

The agent's sunglasses remained directed at Wes, but McKechnie did not immediately answer the question.

"Ongoing threats in this area," he eventually mumbled. "The sheriff will answer any questions you might have." The agent gave Wes a patronizing pat on the arm and was gone.

As he watched McKechnie head into the sheriff's office, Wes pondered the idea that maybe the sheriff was concerned about Leslie's shooting after all.

Wes didn't share his law enforcement frustration with Leslie when he visited her in the hospital later that morning. Heavy bandages around her arm and chest made her look half mummified. The reporter decided against making a joke about her appearance.

She smiled at him and laughed a couple of times during their conversation, but he thought she looked tired and frankly, scared. Both Wes and Leslie knew this was no random shooting. He wasn't sure she was the target. But whoever among the four was meant to be in the gunman's sights, the message was still clear. This was another warning designed to keep the truth concealed.

Satisfied that she was being well taken care of for now, Wes returned to his office where he picked up the shooting reports on Frank and Jamie. He was wishing he had a cigarette when his cell phone rang.

"Mr. Avery?"

"Yes."

"This is Chip Shelton. You've left a bunch of messages on my phone, and I, um, feel bad that I didn't get back to you sooner. We're crazy busy.

I got a roof estimate in your neighborhood tomorrow and can meet you afterward."

Wes could hardly contain himself. "Great," he enthused. "You name the time and place, and I'll be there."

"That park in the center of the village. I mean, I'm guessin' it's still there. That it hasn't been turned into a shop. I haven't been in the village recently," Shelton said.

"It's still there and that's a perfect spot."

"I'm meeting the homeowner at 1. Is 2 o'clock okay?" Shelton asked.

"Yes, yes," Wes said, trying to subdue the giddiness in his voice. "And thanks."

He hopped up from his desk, stuck the cell phone in his pocket and walked into the little room where the receptionist sat. He'd seen her on the bench on the landing outside the front door many times, puffing away and staring out at the village below.

"Hey Helen. You got a cig I can borrow?"

He was determined this lapse wasn't going to signal the return to his two-pack a day habit. But at this moment, he wanted a cigarette more than anything – even more than a beer or a shot of Scotch. Just one.

Helen looked at him and grinned. "You want company?"

"Sure," he said, even though he didn't mean it.

They sat on the bench on the balcony that overlooked the heart of the village, talking about the mundane things that people who barely know each other chat about as the smoke curled around their heads.

"How long you been a smoker, Helen?" Wes asked when they each had two apiece and were readying to head back into the office.

"Too long," she said. "Started in high school. Forty years later, I've quit trying to stop."

"Where's the best place to buy them on the island?"

"The grocery store next door," she said. "It's the closest."

He thanked her and walked down the steps and across the asphalt road-way where he'd retrieved the dead lizard three weeks ago. Funny, he thought, how so much had happened since then and how little he still knew about the death of young Toby Mason and the shootings on the beach. He was reaching for the grocery door when his cell phone rang.

Who in the hell is Bobbie Bramlett?

It took a minute for Wes to conjure up an image of Bobbie, the attractive woman whose breast he'd accidently touched at the Tarpon Bar when he was buying booze for Deb and Scooter's Christmas Eve party. When he remembered, he smiled.

On the phone, Bobbie babbled something about it being short notice and invited him and his guest to dinner on Tuesday. "We have all this food leftover from New Year's and more fish in the freezer. And what the hell, we're not ready to quit partying yet."

He wished Leslie could come with him. Not only did Bobbie and her husband seem like fun people, he had the feeling they might have pertinent information about the Toby Mason shooting.

He didn't ask what he could bring. He'd already learned that everyone took the obligatory bottle of wine with them to social gatherings. Shine had shared that rule of island etiquette and then went on to explain that some folks took nice stuff and others took what the bartender referred to as "plonk" or cheap, low-quality wine.

He didn't want a reputation as a *plonker*, so after his interview with Chip Shelton, he'd pick up a couple of bottles of the house red at the Tarpon Bar.

The cigarettes were near the front of the grocery store. He walked by them a couple of times, exchanged a few pleasantries with the two men who worked at the meat counter and then returned to the cigarette aisle, studying the different brands. He picked up a carton of Marlboros, putting them to his nose as if examining a fine cigar. They smelled of cardboard.

He stuck the carton under his arm and headed for the checkout, picking up a bag of potato chips along the way.

Fuck it, he thought. *Chips were last year's New Year resolution.*

CHAPTER 29

Tuesday afternoon, January 5

An Uber driver returned Leslie to her condo before Wes even knew she'd been released. "I didn't want to be any trouble to you," she said when she called him about an hour before his meeting with Shelton to say she was home.

His protests about her safety after the shooting, having enough food or needing help with routine tasks were met with resolve. "I'm fine. And thanks to you, my neighbor Jim is looking after the dog so if I need anything, I'll call him. He won't mind. Have fun at your party…and, uh, call me after your interview."

Although he would never mention it to her, Wes's feelings were hurt. A part of him wanted to be the person Leslie turned to in her time of need. He was just learning about her stubborn, independent streak and wasn't sure how to deal with it.

She did have one request that he thought was odd, and that was to locate the pepper spray gun she'd lost in the bushes the night Frank was killed. She was worried a child might find it and get hurt, she said.

Or maybe she thinks she will need it for protection, Wes thought. He made a mental note to call Bruce and request police surveillance for her. *If Leslie and Sheriff Fleck won't do something about it, I will.*

Wes tucked his phone in his pants pocket, next to a notebook and pen and departed the office for the village park. He wondered what kind of person Chip Shelton would be, and if he'd be helpful or reluctant to talk about the shooting at Seaside Cottage. He was figuring helpful; he did call, after all.

He had 15 minutes before Shelton arrived. He contemplated getting coffee but decided instead to enter the park through the archway of leafy vines and take a seat on one of the concrete benches by the small fountain. He needed time to get his thoughts together…and have a smoke.

The heavy foliage in the area reduced the temperature by about 10 degrees. When a small gust of wind stirred the lush banana palm leaves behind him and the areca palms to his right, Wes wished he had a sweater.

He thought about how his frustration with the lack of progress on the Mason shooting was beginning to reflect in his actions: a certain testiness in his dealings with strangers, people at work and even Leslie on the night of the so-called reenactment. Although with her, he was careful not to give his negativity a voice.

He still had at least two people to interview besides Shelton: Miriam Capstone, the private investigator Mason hired and hadn't spoken with for 18 years, and the Parkers.

He was starting to wonder if Shelton would add to his annoyance by being a no show, when a figure with a military bearing and close-cropped black hair strode toward Wes, stuck out his hand and flashed a toothy smile. He was wearing khakis with a pronounced crease down the front and a red polo shirt with a silver logo that said Shane Roofing.

"Sorry I'm late. The homeowner didn't understand why a metal roof would be best for his house in this climate. I had some convincing to do," Shelton said, laughing.

"No problem," Wes said, standing up and returning Shelton's handshake. "Honestly, I'm surprised you're willing to talk to me. The others have been cautious."

Shelton sighed. "The people at the party were friends. I've lost touch with them over the years but that doesn't change my story. The shooting was an accident. There was too much drinking. Had everyone been sober, we wouldn't be talking about this today. I guess that's why I don't drink anymore."

He gazed over at the park fountain. Water cascaded from a large urn into a basin filled with pennies people had tossed for luck. "I also need to tell you that although my memory of what happened feels fairly clear, I did a tour of duty in Afghanistan after the incident and suffer bouts of PTSD. What I'm trying to say is that I've lost things and stuff comes and goes."

Wes held up his phone with the tape recorder icon on it. "Okay if I tape our conversation?" he asked and received a nod from Shelton. "Why don't we sit here and you tell me your story. I'll interrupt if I have questions."

Shelton began. "We'd gone fishing. Came back to the house to play cards and eat sandwiches. Later in the evening, people started showing up. Uninvited. I didn't know any of them, but Broky and Sloan did from work. I wanted to go to bed but there was too much noise for me to sleep.

"I went on the porch to have a smoke. It was wall-to-wall people. I was thinking about going to the main house and sacking out on a couch when I heard someone talking about a gun. The word was that one of the guys in the kitchen was looking for something and found it in a drawer. I went into the kitchen to tell Sloan that he needed to get rid of it. He ignored me, maybe didn't hear me. A gun and a bunch of drunks is a bad combination.

"At that point, Toby took the gun from the guy standing next to him. Not forcefully but horsin' around. And I'm thinkin', I need to get the hell out of here before that thing goes off. Then I heard a clickin' sound and turned to see Toby put the gun to his temple...cocked at a funny angle...and pull the trigger."

Shelton paused, looked down and went on. "At first nobody said anything. Then everyone else vanished, and Sloan and I were left staring at him on the kitchen floor, his head bleeding. Like it wasn't real."

He shook his head but kept talking. "I go to get Abe on the porch. He's studying to be a paramedic, and I think he can help Toby. We get to the kitchen and I call 911 and, I mean, I'm talking to the lady on the phone when the sheriff shows up. Like he must have been in the neighborhood. Toby's still breathing, and the sheriff tells us to get outta there.

"I just remember how fast the sheriff was there and how he was workin' to save Toby's life and how it must have taken the ambulance too long to get there because by the time they did he was gone. He was dead, they said."

Shelton was breathing heavily; his eyes darting back and forth as though he was watching a movie. Wes was hoping the strain of reliving the incident wasn't too hard on him. He didn't know if something like that would trigger an attack of stress disorder.

"Your friend Broky Lewis was on the porch and he said he saw Toby shoot himself...."

"Naw. I don't think he saw anything. I mean, how could he? Like I said, it was wall-to-wall people partying," Shelton said. "Man, it's hard to think about this. I've tried not to for a long time."

Wes looked at him sympathetically. "Sorry to put you through this," he said. "You mentioned that you were playing cards. The others talked about that, too. I'm not sure it's relevant, but what were you playing?"

"It was a drinking game called Asshole. Basically, someone throws down a card and you have to beat it. If there's a double thrown, you have to throw doubles. If you can't play, you have to take a drink. If there's a four played, everybody takes a drink. And you do that until all the cards are gone. And whoever's the last one to go out is called the Asshole."

"So, you guys...."

"Not just the guys. The wives were playing it, too, and the girl who came with Toby."

Wes's eyes widened. "What can you tell me about her?"

"I don't remember anything much, 'cept that she was there and seemed upset...didn't really want to drink when she lost...and then Toby told her to leave. Sorry, that's all I know. She was pretty young and not drinkin'."

"Could you guess what age?" Wes asked.

"15, maybe 16 tops," Shelton said. "She looked older in some ways, but I also remember thinkin' to myself, 'What's he doin' here with that kid?'"

Wes checked his notebook, wished he could have a cigarette and decided there was no reason he couldn't. "You want a smoke?" he asked Shelton.

"Sure," the young man said. "My wife wants me to quit but no luck so far."

"I guess there's two more things I need to ask you about," Wes said, as he offered Shelton a Marlboro and then pulled one out of the pack for himself. "Were you warned by anybody after the incident not to talk about what happened?"

"We gave depositions and there were lawyers there, but no one put any pressure on me that I can recall," Shelton said.

"And the 911 call. I read the transcript and at one point on the phone you say – and let me quote you," he said leafing through his notebook, "Oh fuck. He stopped breathing. Now, you told me that the sheriff arrived while you were still on the 911 call – right as you were ending the call, I guess – and when he arrived Toby was still breathing. So why would you tell the 911 person that he had stopped breathing?"

Shelton stared at Wes for a few minutes as though searching his brain for the answer. Suddenly, his face contorted. He gasped, then made a strange noise, like a cry of recognition.

"Oh God," he said softly. "I can't talk to you anymore. I'm sorry."

He stood up, turned and bolted out of the park, leaving a stunned Wes sitting by the fountain.

CHAPTER 30

Tuesday evening, January 5

W es made several phone calls to Shelton, not really expecting him to answer, but hoping he would. He'd gotten some good information from him, like the confirmation that a young girl was at the party and that she was upset. But he felt bad about how the discussion ended.

Leslie was also surprised by Shelton's abrupt departure. "Maybe remembering the scene was troubling to him," she said when she and Wes spoke on the phone.

"It didn't seem that way until we got to the 911 call. What he said to the operator in the transcript and the difference in what he told me seemed to shake him…like there was something associated with that call he'd been suppressing all these years. At least that's what it felt like."

Leslie was paying attention, asking the right questions, but also seemed eager to change the subject to a conversation she'd had with Janis earlier that day. The two were planning to attend Friday's art gala. They wanted Bruce and Wes to join them.

Inwardly, Wes groaned. Even as he was listening to Leslie tell him how much fun it would be, he was thinking how he hated those kinds of events. It was too noisy to carry on a decent conversation; the food and alcohol were usually sub-par and the women in attendance expected the men to dance. He shuddered at the thought.

"...free drinks, heavy appetizers and a good band. You do dance, don't you, Wes?" She rattled on, with still no apparent thought to her personal safety. "And art, including a couple of scarves by Janis, will be part of a raffle."

"You think you'll be ready to go out by Friday?" Wes asked. "I wouldn't rush it if I were you."

And expose yourself to whoever it was that took a shot at you.

"I found a black sling with gold sequins – online – to go with my dress," she said, laughing. "I'm feeling better already...although I don't know if I'm healing or if the pain pills are keeping me on a 24-hour high."

"Go easy on that stuff," he cautioned, thinking she was definitely getting a jolt from whatever she was swallowing. And it was making her reckless.

"And I'll go," he said.

Satisfied that Leslie was on the mend and feeling better physically, he ended the call and headed for the shower in preparation for dinner at Bobbie and Jeff Bramlett's house.

It was a coolish, pleasant night so he decided to walk the couple of blocks to the address Bobbie had given him. On the way he passed the sheriff's office, noticing the lights on inside and recognizing the government vehicle belonging to Agent McKechnie parked outside. He briefly wondered what special assignment the sheriff and agent were working on – he hoped it involved Leslie – and then put it out of his mind when he realized he was nearing the address Bobbie had given him.

The house was not on the water but was spectacular, nonetheless. On one of the village side streets, its towering entryway columns were finished in a golden-brown stain that matched the trim on the rest of the stone house. Luxurious tropical plants, including dozens of varieties of orchids, framed the residence.

Wes's knock on a heavy, carved door was answered by Jeff, who ushered the reporter in with a robust pat on the back and a "glad you're here."

The inside was as impressive as the outside. It felt like every inch of wall space was western art – paintings and bronzes – that Wes later learned Bobbie had been collecting since she was a teenager.

He could see that the dining room table had been set for 10. In a nearby lanai was a round table with eight place settings. *Social baptism by fire,* he thought and without Leslie to help him. He was on his own.

After depositing the wine he'd bought on a bar that spanned two-thirds of the kitchen, he took a seat on one of the dark mahogany barstools.

"What'll you have?" Bobbie's husband asked with a big grin that seemed part of his persona.

"Red wine and a little information about that shooting at Seaside Cottage before your other guests arrive," Wes said, returning Jeff's smile and trying not to sound too forward.

"I got this one," Bobbie said, as she moved from the fancy gas stove with red knobs to her husband's side and put a plate with crab dip and crackers in front of Wes.

Her hair and face were freshly scrubbed. She was wearing a brown top that clung to all the right places and a colorful, full-length skirt that reminded the reporter of the West. Her wrist sported at least half a dozen silver and turquoise bracelets. He remembered her gardenia-like perfume when she leaned closer to him.

"Like I told you that other night, the subject still comes up, especially at the Tarpon where the kid's dad is a regular. You gotta feel sorry for the old guy. I mean, how much longer does he have? And all he wants is answers."

Bobbie paused, took a sip of wine, and was starting to speak again when the floodgates opened and her guests poured in, elevating the noise level tenfold and making it almost impossible for Wes to hear. They were loading up the bar with appetizers covered in aluminum foil and various bottles of wine, some fancy and some not, just as Shine predicted.

Bobbie hurled a dozen guest names at Wes. He promptly forgot each one though he tried, really tried, to remember them. Unless he wrote them down, people's names were lost to him immediately after they were spoken.

The celebratory atmosphere kicked in as Jeff filled wine glasses, popped the caps off a couple of beers and swapped fishing stories with the men. Wes overheard the women talking about the upcoming art gala. Others were admiring Bobbie's latest art purchase from her trip to New Mexico.

The guests were friendly and grew even more so as the liquor flowed freely, and the crowd moved into a tight ball that violated all the unspoken rules of social contact.

A single woman with shoulder-length blondish hair, dimples and a hint of a southern accent, had more men gathered around her than women. But it was Wes, glued to his barstool so he could take in the scene unfolding before him, that she kept grinning at.

At precisely 8:30 Bobbie took a spoon to a wine glass to quiet the group, then encouraged everyone to grab a plate and come to the kitchen where there were trays of fresh-grilled grouper and medallions of pinkish beef tenderloin, steaming and enticing, on the island along with a potato dish, green beans and a salad.

Wes got off his barstool and discovered he could hardly walk. He tried to look and act sober as he approached the folks lining up for goodies. By their tone and the amount of laughter, he assumed most of them were in the same condition he was.

He chose the larger table in the living room so he could be near the hostess. The blond with the dimples sat down next to him, slipped her hand on his thigh as if trying to get his attention and asked: "Okay if Aah sit next to you?"

When it came to women, Wes was really only comfortable around Leslie. But he swallowed hard, smiled and said, "Of course."

Her name was Julie Thrasher, she said. Her late husband, a TV producer, died while eating a cheeseburger and having a beer at a bar in D. C. He was only 46. After his death, Julie migrated to Florida with her only child, a daughter, and had been on the island for 18 years. She wrote poetry and volunteered for the local theater group.

Wes spent time between bites nodding and saying "um, that's interesting" as she talked about her budding Broadway career that was cut short by love. He guessed her to be about his age, maybe a little older and past her stage prime but still attractive.

"You know, I'm working on an anniversary piece about the shooting that took place 20 years ago at Seaside Cottage," he said to the others at the table when the conversation lulled. "Was just talking to one of the kids who was there…."

Bobbie interrupted. "You all remember the incident? The one where a local kid was shot at a party, and the police tried to cover up the murder?"

A few heads around the table bobbed up and down; the others appeared curious.

"The kid's dad. You've all seen him at the Tarpon Bar. He just wants answers and all this time nothing," she said, shaking her head.

Wes cleared his throat. "Yes, and I've been trying to track down who all was there…and maybe talk to them."

"I heard it was a big party, with lots of underage girls and everyone was high…." the man at the far end of the table said. "They were doing drugs, shooting up heroin."

Wes could see how rumors spread on the island. He didn't believe there were "lots" of underage girls at the party. Just one of interest. And he hadn't heard about heroin from any of the three participants he'd spoken with. And, as far as he knew, Toby shot himself accidentally, believing that the old gun was empty.

"Mah daughter, Terri, knew a girl that was there," Julie said. Her drawl had become more pronounced as the evening wore on. "Aah remember her talkin' 'bout it – it seems that every one in school knew about her."

"Knew what?" Wes wanted to shake the woman so her words would come out faster.

"Why that she was pregnant, a' course! Had to leave school and go someplace else. No one knew where," she said.

"Did she ever come back here?" Bobbie asked before Wes could get the words out of his mouth.

"You know, Aah don't believe she did," Julie said.

"Her parents sent her away?" another woman at the table asked. Wes was chagrined to be surrounded by a table of busybodies, but he was getting his questions answered.

"Her daddy was furious, Aah heard," Julie said. "Wanted her to get an abortion. But she'd have none of it. Aah mean, the poor thing was barely 16 at the time."

"What about the mother?" Bobbie asked. Obviously, this was one part of the Seaside Cottage story she hadn't heard.

"Oh, she was devastated, they say. Her little girl about to be a mother and by some island boy who was in his 20s. Shameful," Julie said.

Bobbie stood up and reached for Julie's plate.

"Wait!" Wes yelled, not wanting any part of the conversation to be lost in the clatter of dishes being cleared. Everyone turned to look at him, their mouths open at this breach of post-dinner etiquette; yelling at the hostess. "Who was the girl's father?!"

Julie laughed. "Oh mah, you startled me, Wes. But Aah thought maybe you all around the table knew. He was the law…the sheriff back then and the sheriff today. Mister Harry Fleck."

Wes wanted to kiss Julie, thank Bobbie and bolt out the door. He felt like the 20-something who'd been chatting up the girl at the bar, gotten what he wanted in a locked stall in the ladies' room and couldn't wait to get out of there.

Instead, he responded with another, "Um, that's interesting" and worked his way through the piece of fresh blueberry pie with whipped crème that Bobbie sat before him.

"Thank you for a great evening," he said after finishing dessert and carrying his plate into the kitchen.

"You leaving? It's early," Bobbie said, looking disappointed.

"It's almost 11. Way past my bedtime. Gotta work tomorrow. But I really appreciate that you included me. The dinner was great and the company outstanding. You have nice friends."

"What did you think about Julie? She's single and seemed to enjoy sitting next to you," Bobbie said, giving Wes a little nudge with her elbow.

"I-I-I'm sure she is," he said, realizing after he stepped outside that what he said made no sense.

CHAPTER 31

Wednesday morning, January 6

Wes wished the body didn't need sleep to survive. His was 3 a.m. – the universal wake-up and can't-go-back-to-sleep time. His mind raced. He wanted the name of the sheriff's daughter. He wanted to speak with her. He wanted to know what she recalled that night. He wanted to know if John Mason and Harry Fleck had a grandchild in common.

He was certain the daughter was a key to whatever mystery surrounded the death of Toby Mason, and he wondered why more people hadn't mentioned her before now. Was it because they were afraid to speak about the sheriff's daughter and her condition at the time of young Toby's death? Or was this just a salacious sidebar to the shooting at the guest house at Seaside Cottage?

He tossed and turned, finally falling asleep about 4:30 a.m.

When he arrived at the newspaper shortly before 9, groggy and out-of-sorts despite two cups of coffee, he gave the others a terse hello, headed for his office and closed the door. After searching through some of the papers he'd copied, he located "Final Report" from Miriam Capstone, the private investigator Mason hired to look into his son's death.

On the cover page, she'd written:

After review of the police account, I put additional thoughts into this report intended to stimulate the state investigator. We must find out where the gun came from, and who is responsible for it. Also, the reference to the young girls near the end. I tried to get the point across without making unsubstantiated claims. In any event, the seeds were planted!

I will need another $1,300 for time and expenses.

It was signed: Best, M and the name Miriam typed underneath.

Wes turned on his computer, typed in Miriam Capstone, private investigator, and found a few quotes from her in old newspaper articles. But there was nothing recent. Wes decided she was either retired, had moved away or was dead.

He walked into Randy Long's area. "You know Miriam Capstone… private eye?" Wes asked, skipping the formalities of a hello.

"Nope. Ask Helen. She knows everybody?"

"What about the sheriff's daughter?"

"The one that was at the party the night Toby was shot?" Randy did not stop working; did not miss a beat at the layout table.

"Yeah, that one, Randy," Wes said, making no effort to hide the irritation in his voice. *The one you didn't tell me about.*

"Willow," Randy responded.

"Did you know she was pregnant. And that Toby Mason was possibly the father?"

Now, Wes had Randy's full attention. "All I know is that her daddy got her out of town shortly after the shooting and no one has seen her since. Pregnant, huh. That stirs the pot."

"Let's keep that pot on simmer for now," Wes said. "We don't know if that's true. Dinner party gossip."

Randy mumbled something about that not being the most reliable source of information and returned to his work.

Wes didn't worry about Randy keeping his mouth shut. Seems like he was aware of the girl – knew her name, in fact – and withheld that from Wes. Besides, digging up information on his own gave him a better sense of the whole story. Having pieces handed to him sometimes made him sloppy in his fact-gathering; could skew his thought process. Randy, being an old newspaperman himself, would know that.

Wes ambled toward his new smoking buddy, Helen, who said she didn't know Miriam and suggested he ask Bruce Webster, who was also supposed to know everybody.

Might as well take the bull by the horns, Wes thought, as he bounded down the stairs and headed for the sheriff's office once again. If Sheriff Fleck was there maybe he could get him to talk about his daughter. Just a casual conversation – a hint as to where she might be living now.

Deputy Webster was at his small desk in a corner when Wes walked in and reached for another cup of coffee.

"Help yourself to a donut," the deputy said. "Thought ya should know, I assigned our temps to keep an eye on Leslie until we learn more about the shooting. Seemed like the right thing to do…for her safety and our piece of mind."

"Great," Wes said, feeling a sense of relief and gratitude that the deputy was on top of the issue. "Know anything else about the incident?"

"Harry thinks it was a random shooting. But I gotta tell ya, I don't agree with him. Whoever shot Leslie knew what he was doin'. Janis and I been talkin' about it. She's got some ideas. I think she's way off base. Anyway, we're not sharin' yet."

Wes nodded and grabbed a couple of donut holes covered with powdered sugar, immediately wishing he'd picked something less messy.

"How do you guys keep from getting fat around here?"

"I don't eat that stuff," the deputy said. "You can draw your own conclusions about Harry."

Wes chuckled, scanning the credenza behind the sheriff's large desk for family photos and finding none. "Where is he?"

"At the doctor's, gettin' his cough checked out. Thought it was red tide. But that's gone now. I'm kinda worried about him."

Wes sat down in a beige office chair that was stuck in a corner by a small table and picked up a copy of *Law Enforcement Technology.* Bruce could probably answer all of his questions immediately, but he'd discovered that the deputy subscribed to the Randy Long theory of providing information:

give 'em as little as you have to. Wes would start out slow but was not leaving without Willow's contact information.

"So, we're going to that shindig at the gallery on Friday," Wes said.

Bruce sighed and shook his head. "I'd rather have my teeth pulled, but I guess we got no choice."

"I have choices," Wes said. "You don't. You are hook, line and sinker into Janis Johnson and you know it."

The deputy looked up. "And ya don't have a thing for Leslie?"

He did. But he wasn't going to tell Bruce, who would share that tidbit with Janis, who would definitely pass that information onto her new best friend.

Wes had observed that most men are pathetic when it comes to understanding and dealing with women. He was no exception, and he knew it. In Leslie's case, he'd decided after his New Year's Eve kiss was not scorned, he'd move forward but at a slow and easy pace. Leslie wasn't going anywhere. And with Frank gone there didn't seem to be any competition.

Next topic, Wes thought. "You know a private investigator named Miriam Capstone?"

The deputy scratched his head, opened the middle drawer of his desk and pulled out a piece of paper. "She used to do work in the county," he said, scanning what must have been a list of some kind. "This could be it. Not under Capstone but Buchanan. Miriam C. Buchanan. 941-555-0041."

Wes jotted the number down on the back of his hand and popped another donut hole in his mouth.

"Ya need a private investigator?" the deputy asked.

"She was hired by John Mason to look into his son's death."

"Guess she didn't do the job he wanted," the deputy mused.

"Don't know. I'm gonna talk to her, if I can locate her."

Wes got up, stretched and walked over to Harry's large desk. "The sheriff married?" he asked, keeping his back to the deputy as though he was abstractly scanning the walls behind Fleck's desk. "Don't see any family photos here."

"A long time. Wife's name is Regina. A sweet woman. Got a couple of kids. A daughter who lives out in the Midwest someplace and Harry Jr. who's a policeman in Chicago."

"Whoa, that's gotta be a tough job," Wes said, thinking about much he used to like Chicago and how now he didn't feel comfortable visiting there because of the street crime that nobody seemed interested in doing anything about. "What's the daughter do?"

"Housewife," I think. "Harry doesn't talk about her. I think they're estranged; I don't even know her name."

"Any grandkids?"

"Maybe one," the deputy said. "Why ya interested in Harry's family, Wes?"

Wes contemplated sharing his findings about the pregnant daughter with this deputy he considered a friend. But he'd also knew that Bruce had a strong loyalty to his boss. If the sheriff had any hint that Wes knew about his daughter's alleged past, the situation would surely escalate and not in Wes's favor.

"Just curious," Wes said, deciding he would have to get Willow's number from someone else but wasn't sure who. "Gotta go. See you Friday."

You'll find out soon enough my friend, he thought.

CHAPTER 32

Wednesday afternoon, January 6

Wes had called Leslie to fill her in on the latest findings and said he was on his way to meet with Miriam Capstone, now Buchanan, who lived about 15 miles away in what she described as a "remote" part of the city. Leslie insisted on going with him and was in the parking lot, waiting, when he arrived.

Her arm was itchy and still painful, but she was tired of sitting around feeling sorry for herself and annoyed, yet relieved, by the presence of a *bodyguard*. When they returned from their interview, she planned to pick up Whalen from the neighbor.

She and Janis had talked on the phone several times about the beach shooting, she told Wes as they drove through the off-island community enroute to Miriam's place. Janis had a theory that she'd been kicking around with the deputy. He was skeptical, but Janis felt that if the four of them could get together and talk about it, Bruce could be convinced. Even though Wes remembered the deputy saying just that morning that Janis's idea was "way off base."

When they'd driven about 30 minutes, he passed a greenhouse that advertised geraniums and orchids – a landmark that Miriam had mentioned – and made a sharp right onto a dirt road with no street sign. A black Ford with Leslie's protector inside dutifully followed

After passing three cinder block homes, they came to the dead end that Miriam had described as being their destination

Off to the right was another cinderblock house – this one painted gray with murals of flowers adorning one side. It was surrounded by tall casuarina trees and various Florida "weeds" that take over untended property in the summer growing season.

Yellow flowers that looked like daisies flourished along the stone walkway that led to the entrance where there was a sign posted: *Without art, the crudeness of reality would make the world unbearable.* – G. B. Shaw.

"That's the truth," Leslie said, acknowledging the hand-painted plaque. "Appropriate for someone who spent most of her life investigating the seamy side."

"Come on in," they heard a voice from the back calling to them as they approached the door. "Ignore the mess."

They wound their way through a small gallery with paintings of fish, turtles and mermaids in bright green, blue, orange and yellow lining the walls; frames and cardboard boxes littered the floor. In the back behind a plywood table and with a big grin on her face was Miriam Capstone.

"Welcome to my humble studio," she chirped. "Can I get you something to drink?"

She was a large woman with white hair piled into a messy bun atop her head, no lipstick or makeup except for a thin brown line penciled in where her eyebrows had once been. Leslie, guessing the woman was in her early seventies, thought "earth mother" but decided that was an inappropriate stereotype for a woman who must have been a tough professional and was now focused on the softer side of life.

"Nothing for me, thanks," Wes said. "Leslie?"

"I'm fine…and well, frankly, in awe of your artwork. How long have you been painting?"

"Ever since I was a child. Studied art in college and then quickly found out that it soothes the soul but doesn't put food on the table," she said. "Blood and guts are more lucrative. And that's why you two are here, isn't it? Not to buy my art but to pick my brain about murder," she said and laughed good-naturedly.

"That mermaid would go perfectly in my apartment," Leslie said, admiring a free-flowing painting of a woman with long brown hair and a shimmery tail swimming amid a school of colorful fish. "Is it...for sale?"

"You betcha. It's $250 and that includes the frame," she said. "I make 'em, the frames, myself."

Leslie reached in her purse for her checkbook and noticed that Wes was glancing around the room and tapping his foot anxiously. "Don't wait on me. Go ahead, Wes," she said.

He nodded and launched into the interview. "As I mentioned when I called, we're thinking about doing an anniversary piece on the shooting at Seaside Cottage. But a part of me also wants to give John Mason the answers he's been seeking all this time."

"Good luck with that," Miriam said, shaking her head. "John only wants one thing. That's for someone to confirm that whoever found the gun and handed it to Toby in the kitchen is guilty of a crime. And then he wants the man or woman – in their forties by now – to be thrown in jail. As far as he's concerned there's no other option. Frankly, he's wrong.

"I took this case and agreed with him at the start," she continued. "There were plenty of reasons to. The police investigation was a travesty. When they got to the scene, everyone except the two women who'd been sleeping in the main house was intoxicated. No one claimed ownership of the gun.

"The police wrote it up as a suicide, then an accident based solely on what they were told by the people still on the scene. No one was taken to the police station for further questioning. They didn't attempt to find any of the partygoers who showed up uninvited and scattered when Toby shot himself.

"The next morning the scene was cleaned up in preparation for the rental family scheduled in the following day. The police didn't even dig out the bullet until weeks after the event – and only then because Mason applied pressure.

"How does law enforcement mishandle a crime scene like that?" She picked up a brown and silver Yeti mug and took a drink. "That's another reason I quit. I found myself getting too worked up about this stuff."

She'd been standing by her painting table and now took a seat on a stool. "The case was reopened but all of the forensic evidence was gone. Witnesses all had varying versions of the incident and refused to talk without their lawyers present. There was not enough left of this case to put it together properly.

"Mason just couldn't accept that. He thought there should be charges for manslaughter at the very least. Bringing a gun into a situation where all parties were shit-faced. And I don't think he'll ever believe, deep down, that Toby shot himself."

Wes and Leslie had been captive to the woman's story. Now Leslie was eager to share what Wes had recently discovered.

"What would you say if we told you that Toby Mason had a girlfriend, barely 16, who was at the party – not when he was shot, but earlier." Leslie glanced over at Wes who had scooted to the edge of his chair. "You tell her."

"Yeah, and that maybe she told Toby that afternoon or early evening that she was pregnant, and he was upset about it," Wes said, his voice animated.

"Are you telling me the shooting was a suicide?" Miriam said. She was shaking her head and saying no repeatedly. "Based on everything I heard this was not the…."

"I'm not saying that. I'm saying that the man who arrived first on the scene, the man who told the other kids to leave him alone in the kitchen with the victim and then who directed the sloppy police work that evening was the same man who learned earlier that day – or maybe the day before – that Toby Mason had knocked up his teenage daughter."

"What the fuck!" Miriam said and rose from the stool she'd been sitting on like she'd been shot out of a cannon. "Fuckin' Harry Fleck!?"

Wes and Leslie remained quiet while Miriam Capstone made the transition from artist back to private investigator. They watched her pace back and forth muttering to herself, reviewing the details.

"He was alone with Toby. Alone," she said. "He would have had the time. No one would have guessed he would do something like that."

"Yeah, and one of the kids – the one studying to be a paramedic – said he thought the bullet had only grazed the scalp and that Toby had a good chance to live," Wes said.

"Harry must have smothered him while he lay on the floor gasping for air," Miriam said, nodding her head in confirmation of her theory. "Any father would have wanted to kill the son-of-a-bitch that got his 15-year-old pregnant. I mean the kid might have been on the right path when he died, but he had been a drug user…morphine, heroin, cocaine and ecstasy. John Mason said he got treatment. But you never know when the devil drugs will drag you back in. Harry wouldn't want his daughter hooked up with someone like that."

Miriam headed toward a brown metal cabinet at the back of her studio and began digging through files, moving from one drawer to another. "Listen to this. The sheriff's office has no reason to believe this unfortunate incident was anything more than a suicide or accident. There is no reason to believe that any criminal actions were associated with this death. Based on the investigation conducted, this case will be closed as unfounded, as the elements of a crime do not exist."

She tossed the paper on her worktable. "That's straight from the criminal investigation report by the guys who arrived after Harry. They got the basic facts but no mention of the sheriff being alone with the victim while they were waiting for the ambulance to show up."

"Or at what time he arrived on the scene," Wes said. "Was it before or after the 911 call was made?"

Leslie's eyes lit up. "We have to find out from his daughter when she told her dad about the pregnancy. If he didn't know that day, then he wouldn't have had any reason to want to kill Toby…I mean, Wes, would you murder someone who got your daughter pregnant?"

"If I was Harry Fleck, I would have relished this unexpected opportunity."

CHAPTER 33

Late Wednesday afternoon

"I'm gonna tell Bruce I need Willow Fleck's phone number, and I don't care how he gets it," Wes said as he and Leslie drove away from Miriam Capstone's residence with what the two of them decided was a plausible theory about Toby Mason's death and a new piece of artwork for Leslie's apartment.

Leslie shook her head. "Putting Bruce in the middle isn't fair. How about we check the high school and see if they have contact information for her?"

Wes appeared to be thinking. "You think she graduated? And, if she did, would they give her information to us?"

It was Leslie's turn to be contemplative. "How about I call Harry's wife, tell her that the school is having a class reunion, and I'm on the committee and need to contact the daughter."

"You mean lie?" Wes said.

Leslie looked at him and smirked. "Wes Avery, reporter. You never fudged the truth to get a story?"

"I was good at sounding empathetic when I didn't give a rat's ass about anything but the story I was going to get," he said, chuckling.

Leslie gave him a lock of mock horror. "Shameful," she said. "But, really, I'm willing to hang up on truth to get to the truth."

He shrugged. "Let's go for it."

When they were back in Leslie's condo, Wes called Randy at the newspaper who tracked down the listing in a 10-year-old island phone book.

"Good luck," he told Wes. "Hardly anyone has home phones anymore, so this probably won't work."

Leslie volunteered to do the deed and was soon chatting with Regina Fleck, who answered the phone with a hesitant hello.

"Who did you say you were?" she asked.

"Leslie Rainey. I'm on the homecoming committee."

"Rainey. Oh yes, I remember some Raineys from around North Port," she said. "Are you kin?"

"Probably. We're all related in this part of the country," Leslie said. She'd never met a person named Rainey. But the perceived relationship with someone else in the area appeared to give Leslie an opening with Regina Fleck.

"Willow and her family live in Carmel, Indiana. That's north of Indianapolis. Not sure she'll wanna see her classmates again...." Regina paused, then sighed. "Here's her number."

Leslie scribbled down the 10 digits, thanked the sheriff's wife and turned to Wes with her cat-ate-the-canary grin.

"Lightning didn't strike me," she said.

"Let's call...and put her on speaker phone."

"What are we gonna say?" Leslie asked.

"That we're looking into the death of her boyfriend 20 years ago...and would she meet with us. We can fly up there. Up and back in a day."

Leslie looked at Wes and shook her head. "Why don't we say that we're friends of John Mason's, and he's been sick and wants to meet his grandchild...after all these years."

Wes scoffed. "Like that will work."

"If she has any heart at all, she won't refuse," Leslie said. "It's almost 6. If she's got a job outside the home, she's probably fixing dinner about now."

"Six? Let me get a Scotch," Wes said.

Leslie sat down on the lanai and waited for him to return, staring out at the last remnants of sunset and thinking that if they flew to Indianapolis it would be cold, and her winter clothes were in storage. Permanently, was her plan.

She also revisited the word "flew." She hated flying and had been forced to do so twice in the last year. She wanted to be with Wes for the interview, but flying again? It made her nauseated thinking about it. Could she be enticed to do it for the reporter and his story. And to satisfy her curiosity?

When Wes returned, he brought her a glass of wine. "I miss the dog," he said. "Should we pick him up when we finish the call?"

"Not if we're leaving tomorrow."

"Oh, right," he said, watching intently as Leslie punched in numbers on her cell and put the call on speaker.

"This is Willow McDonald's phone," the male voice said.

"Is Willow there?"

"Who's calling?"

"Leslie Elliott. I just got her number from Regina."

"Um, okay. Mom, it's a friend of grandma's."

Leslie felt her heart skip a beat. Was she speaking to the young man, now close to 20, whose father died that night in Seaside Cottage? She felt a surge of emotion.

"This is Willow. Is Mom all right?"

"She's fine," Leslie said, in control again. "This call isn't about your mom, although I did speak with her. I told her I was with the school homecoming committee to get your number, but I wasn't being truthful. I, um, we, my friend Wes from the local newspaper, um, want to talk to you about the night Toby Mason died."

As Leslie waited out the silence, she contemplated what her reaction would be to a phone call like this. Why would anyone want to discuss what happened that night with the media?

"I don't want to be part of any article," Willow said. "I'm a single mom with issues of my own. What's the benefit of digging all this up again?"

"Don't you want people to know the truth?" Leslie responded. Wes was sipping his Scotch and nodding at the question.

"Why do they need to know? What right do they have? It's horrible that the rest of us had to live with it all these years…that it changed our lives forever."

"Doesn't John Mason deserve to know the truth of how his son died… and that he has a grandson?" Leslie decided that if Willow didn't hang up after this question was thrown at her, they had a chance to meet her and the boy. "He's not in the best of health."

More silence, then a terse response. "I gotta talk to my mom about this. I'll call you back." Then the phone went dead.

"We're sunk," Leslie said, looking at Wes.

"Maybe not. Remember how Bruce said that Harry Fleck never talked about his daughter. She may not suspect that he played a role in Toby's death. But she does know that she was sent out of town and, apparently, disowned by her father. This is her chance – and maybe her mother's – to get even."

"We'll see if you're right," Leslie said, getting up from her chair. "I've changed my mind. Let's go get the dog."

CHAPTER 34

Thursday afternoon, January 7

Thursday morning came and went with no word from Willow Fleck. Without corroboration from her about the timing, their efforts to help John Mason were at a standstill. Wes could still write a 20th anniversary story if he was so inclined, but there was nothing new to report or even hint at. At this point, all of his and Leslie's theories were speculation.

Whalen, obviously happy to be home, pranced through his morning walk and looked disappointed when Leslie returned him to the condo and told him she'd be spending the afternoon at the Gallery Centre.

She left the lanai door open so he could get the full effect of the breezes blowing off the Gulf and filling her place with the smell of salt air. When she pulled the screen door shut, she looked back and saw him climbing into his favorite pink lounge chair. Life was returning to normal. Except for the constant presence of her human watchdog.

Deb Rankin had her long dark hair in braids and was wearing jeans and a work shirt when Leslie entered the door to the gallery. Five or six other people, similarly dressed, were hanging the last of the decorations and scrubbing smudges off the doors of the main entrance. Outside, workers in the tent were putting the final touches on the stage for the band.

"Check it out," Deb said, directing Leslie to the back gallery where some 30 paintings were hung, each numbered, with pieces of paper covering the artist's name. "When you buy a raffle ticket, you pick out the three pieces you like the best and write them down. If your number is drawn, you go for your first choice. If that's gone, the second and so on. We are calling it Whodunnit."

"Fun idea, but why do you have to write down your choices? Can't you just pick it out when you win?"

Deb shook her head. "Oh, honey. We gotta move this along. Some of these people would take hours pickin' what they want."

"Guess you're right," Leslie said. "What's my assignment, boss? And, please, no more truth-telling sessions over wine."

"It worked, didn't it?"

"Yes. Although I barely remember what happened," Leslie said, laughing.

Deb eyed Leslie's arm, encased in a blue sling, and suggested she make sure all the names in the Whodunnit display were covered and that the pieces were straight. Leslie was alone when she first entered the area. Within minutes others joined her.

"My painting's in the bottom row, why is that?" The artist with bright red hair was not known to Leslie. Her work was an abstract oil in red, yellow and blue. "Let's move it up there," she said snatching a watercolor of a channel marker with an osprey on it off the display and putting it on a nearby table.

Leslie frowned then nodded. "I guess that would be okay unless Deb has a reason for displaying these the way she did."

"Wait a minute," she heard a voice coming from behind her. "If Martha's moving her piece, then I want mine up there on the top row, too."

Soon, all five workers who'd been helping hang decorations had stopped what they were doing and were surrounding Leslie, demanding more prominent locations for their artwork.

"I've been in this organization for 10 years and I deserve top billing!" A large man who walked with a cane was wagging his finger at Leslie.

"Stop!" Leslie was relieved to see Janis hustling her way, determination all over her face. "Clear out. This section is done. We're not changing anything," she said.

The crowd dissolved quickly, eyeing Janis and Leslie, but afraid to take on either one of them, particularly since they were presenting a united front for a change.

"They'll get over it," Janis said.

"Thanks for rescuing me. Is it always this bad?" Leslie asked.

"They all work hard and like their efforts to be appreciated. Sometimes jealousy rears its ugly head. It's human nature."

Deb arrived on the scene and put her arm around Janis. "Thanks for takin' charge. Why don't you two check on the set-up in the tent? Don't let 'em put the tables too close together. Make sure the dance floor is big enough. Scooter's looking forward to gettin' out there and showin' everyone that he's still got it."

"I don't think Wes and Bruce share his enthusiasm," Leslie said, winking at Janis.

Once inside the tent, Leslie provided updates on the Toby Mason shooting to her newest friend, detailing the theories offered by the former private investigator Miriam Capstone and the brief conversation with Harry Fleck's daughter, now living in Indiana.

"Oh my God," Janis said. "You haven't told Bruce, have you?"

"No way, and you mustn't tell him either. Not until we know more," Leslie said.

"He's been actin' funny the last couple of days. Like he has a secret. And I've been trying to convince him that the sheriff had somethin' to do with shooting on the beach. He won't hear of it."

"You think Harry shot me? Why?"

"With all this investigatin' you and Wes are doing on the Mason shooting and then with Frank and Jamie's deaths, it feels like the sheriff's rattled. Bruce hinted at that," Janis said.

"But, then, who shot Frank and Jamie?"

"A puzzle I'm still working on and getting close," Janis said. "You feel like goin' to the Tarpon and talkin' about it?"

Leslie laughed. "No way. I'm in too fragile a state to spend the afternoon drinking with you and John Mason."

The harp-like sound of the phone sent Leslie running for her purse, which she'd put on a folding chair near the stage. She recognized the area code as being from Indiana.

"Fingers crossed," she mouthed as she crossed her fingers at Janis and pushed the button to answer.

"Hi Willow. Thanks for getting back to us. Okay. Um, okay. Saturday? I can't make any promises. I don't even know if he's doing a story...or just interested in finding out what really happened to Toby. You can call either one of us. I'll text you Wes's number. Bye."

Janis's eyes widened. "Saturday. Are you going to Indiana on Saturday?"

"Even better. She's coming here and bringing her son with her. Her mother asked her to, and she's willing to talk to us while she's here. The good news is that I don't have to get on another plane," Leslie said.

"Is she gonna talk about what happened that night?"

"Not sure she'll know. But I'm betting she'll have some idea of Harry Fleck's state of mind...and if he was mad enough to kill."

CHAPTER 35

Not expecting an answer, Wes had, nonetheless, put in calls over and over to the number he had for Jessi and Sloan Parker, leaving messages each time. He just wanted to hear their take on what happened that night; not to make either of them look bad. How tough would it be for them to respond?

Unreturned phone calls were an annoying part of being a reporter. When you're working on a deadline, the people you want to speak with should be available when you need them was Wes's attitude. He hated sitting around wondering if this legislator or that lobbyist would call before it was too late, or if he'd have to say in his story that so-and-so did not respond to his inquiry.

He stood up, stretched and was heading for the newspaper's porch and a cigarette when the phone rang.

"Is this Wes Avery?"

"You got him."

"This is Benji Gehrig. I'm an attorney with Edwards and Gehrig offices in Fort Myers, Tampa and Miami. I understand, you've been trying to reach my clients, Jessi and Sloan Parker?"

"Uh-huh," Wes said. It was not the phone call he wanted.

"My clients are responsible citizens with a family and won't be responding to inquiries about an unfortunate accident that occurred 20 years ago," the attorney said.

"No surprise there," Wes said. "Perhaps when I finish writing my story, and they have a chance to look at it, they might rethink their position."

"Let me warn you that we will take seriously any accusatory conclusions you or others reach and will consider legal action...."

"Yeah, yeah," Wes said. "In regard to your clients, I won't be printing anything that isn't available in public documents or hasn't already been published. Although I will say that the Parkers' attorney informed me they had no comment on the shooting or the remarks of others that were there that night. Fair enough?"

"So, you'll be sending us a copy of your story before you print it?"

"Only if your clients agree to make themselves available for an interview," Wes said.

"Let me talk to them," Gehrig said. "You understand that they don't want this tragic incident resurfacing. What's past is past."

"For some people on this island the story has never gone away," Wes said. "And it won't, until the truth of what happened that evening is known."

"I'll get back to you," Gehrig said and hung up.

If Wes hadn't bought into the idea that Harry Fleck was in some way responsible for Toby Mason's death, he might have pursued the remote possibility that the hosts were culpable. And still could if the attorney decided to be a dick about the whole thing.

Wes walked into the bathroom and washed his hands vigorously. It was a common ritual for him after speaking with lawyers, lobbyists and politicians. He had particular disdain for all three groups. He felt like the world's woes all emanated from what he referred to as the terrible trio.

He strolled onto the porch, took a deep breath of the warmish air and thought about how much he liked living in Florida in the winter months. He sat down on the little bench reserved for smokers – really just him and Helen – and wondered if not being able to speak with the Parkers made things easier or more difficult.

If they shared their story and it didn't match what the others had told him, it would be harder to determine what was real and what wasn't. Jessi was in the main house when it happened. And if Sloan was as drunk as the other partygoers, he wouldn't remember much from that evening anyway, except whatever emotions he felt when he saw his friend put the gun next to his head and pull the trigger.

The sound from his phone brought Wes back to the present. It was Leslie, telling him they would be meeting with Harry Fleck's daughter on Saturday; not in Indiana but somewhere on the island.

"Harry isn't going to be there, is he?" Wes asked. He was glad not to travel north but wondered if interviewing the daughter on the sheriff's home turf was a good idea.

"I-I didn't ask," Leslie said. "I guess I assumed that he wouldn't be... since I get the feeling the two don't speak. She did say Saturday. I wonder if that's his day off?"

"Where are we meeting?"

"She said she'd call. When she does, we can set up a neutral location. What if she wants to bring her mother?"

"I don't think we want the mother there either. Unless it's a dealbreaker if she doesn't tag along," he said.

Wes hung up and was into his second cigarette when the phone rang again. He didn't immediately recognize the number, but the 754 area code looked familiar.

"Mr. Avery. This is Chip Shelton. Is this a good time?"

"Sure, sure," Wes said, shifting his position on the bench and pulling out his small pad in case he needed to take notes. He was surprised and happy to hear from Shelton again.

"I wanted to apologize for the other day...."

"No problem," Wes interrupted. "I figured we hit a nerve or something."

"Yeah, some nerve," Shelton said. "I'm not gonna be in your neighborhood anytime soon. Is it okay if we talk over the phone?"

"As long as you're comfortable, I'm fine with it," Wes said.

Shelton got right into it. "The night of the shooting when I saw Toby on the floor and went and got Abe, I remember I didn't immediately make the 911 call. I mean, I remember the sheriff coming through the door... well...it seemed like seconds after the shot was fired. Like he was standing outside or somethin' when it all went down. He pushed Abe aside and said he'd take care of Toby and for us to get out of the kitchen.

"Minutes passed and then the sheriff called me back in and told me to call 911. I was makin' the call and I was scared, and the operator kept askin' me questions and then the sheriff told me to tell her that Toby had stopped breathin'.

"Then he called Abe, Sloan and Broky into the kitchen and asked us if we'd seen his daughter there. We all said yes. I don't think we knew she was the sheriff's daughter. I didn't. But he said Willow, and I remembered that was the girl's name. And he told us that if we told anyone she was there he'd kill us. Kill us, man! He scared the shit out of us…and we were already half-crazy upset about Toby."

Wes knew his own eyes were wide open. *Jesus*, he said to himself and then re-focused on what Shelton was saying.

"Then the sheriff said his cousin Earl could help clean up the place after the deputies interviewed all of us. Gave Sloan his number," Shelton continued.

"We weren't to tell anybody about Willow. We weren't to tell anyone that I didn't make the 911 call until the sheriff told me to. If any of that got out, he would kill us…like I said before. In return, he'd make everything go away. I think those were his words. It would all go away."

"Where was Elisa Chaves when all this was happening?" Wes asked, remembering that she was the first to zero in on the underage girl at the party.

"She wasn't really involved. I mean, she came in and saw Toby and went outside. Same with Broky. He said he saw the shooting, which I don't think he did. When the sheriff showed up, they were both outside, along with Jessi. They stayed there until the sheriff called Broky in to warn him.

"You gotta understand that 20 years ago, the sheriff was someone you didn't mess with. So, when he warned me…said he was gonna kill us; I kept my mouth shut. Shortly after that, I was in Afghanistan and the nightmares I used to have about Toby's death got all mixed up with the stuff happenin' there. It was when you asked me about the 911 call that day in the park that it all came back to me."

Shelton let out a long sigh that sounded like a balloon deflating.

"That's some story," Wes said. "And you're sure that's what happened. I mean – and don't be offended – these memories aren't linked to your PTSD?"

"I can't be sure. But I don't think so," Shelton said.

"If I do a story about this, can I quote you?"

Shelton was silent. Wes hoped he wasn't losing him again.

"If they reopen the case, I'll testify in court to what I just told you," Shelton said. "But even though I'm not scared of him, the sheriff is still the man on that island. You wanted the truth and I gave it to you as best I could. I wouldn't want to see what I told you in an article in the newspaper."

It was Wes's turn to remain quiet as he contemplated his next move. He finally decided not to press Shelton. "Okay," he said. "I understand. I appreciate you calling me back, and I'd like to stay in touch."

"Gotta go," Shelton said.

Wes hung up and realized that it was no longer the story he was interested in; it was about finding the truth.

CHAPTER 36

The loving toast Janis Johnson made to her teenage son, Stevie, that day at the picnic table had lingered in Leslie's thoughts. She remembered Frank telling her how he got full custody after Janis abandoned Stevie while she went off with a man for a couple of days, leaving the boy with nothing to eat but peanut butter and crackers.

It seemed outlandish, but that was Frank's story and, at the time, Leslie believed him.

Later, however, she heard from Deb that the fisherman's mother, Georgia Johnson, was supposed to be looking after Stevie while Janis was away. It seems she left Stevie, then 10 or so, to go to the grocery store and was not there when Frank showed up. When Georgia returned and discovered that Frank had taken Stevie with him and left Janis a nasty note, she was afraid to tell him the truth. She was no fan of Janis. Why should she defend her?

Which story was true, Leslie wondered?

She could believe almost anything about Georgia, who she met briefly at a Gallery Centre event and found to be cold and unfriendly. At the same time, Frank could have exaggerated Janis's incompetence as a mother. Or Janis could have been going through a bad period, perhaps not totally of her own making.

Sometimes the Cracker soap operas, as Deb called them, made Leslie's head spin.

With Frank gone, Leslie had come to believe that Janis should be reunited with her son. Her starting point was Frank's attorney, Michael Land. She'd spoken with him when the fisherman first went missing several months ago.

"Miz Elliott. Of course, I remember you. So sorry to hear about Frank's passing," he said. "Are you calling about his will?"

"I'm interested in Stevie, his son. When Frank left the island, he took Stevie with him and no one, not even his mother, knows where he is. A teenage boy who's lost his father should be reunited with his mother, if even on a part-time basis."

Leslie could hear Land rustling papers in the background and a mumbled "hold on." After a few minutes, he returned to the conversation.

"Frank made no mention of custody for a minor child in his will, but I agree with you….as long as she's fit it's always best for the child to be with his mother. Do you have an address for the boy and his grandmother?"

"I assumed you did."

"Unfortunately, no. Frank and I were scheduled to meet the day after he was shot, to tie up loose ends. He told me his plans were uncertain, but he wanted to make sure that Stevie and his grandmother were taken care of, and if anything happened to him his ex-wife would receive some money."

"She wasn't really his ex-wife…I mean they weren't divorced."

"I thought you knew," Land said. "It had been a couple of years and neither one pressed the issue, but their divorce was finalized a month ago. I told Frank when he called to schedule our meeting – the day he was shot."

Leslie did a quick review of the day's events. Frank never told her that he was, at long last, a free man. Maybe that's why he wanted to speak with Janis. Tears formed in her eyes as she once more faced the reality that Frank had a long list of crucial details about himself that he hadn't shared with her.

"Miz Elliott?"

"Sorry, Mr. Land. I was trying to remember if Frank…well, never mind. Any suggestions on how I can locate Stevie? And should I hire you now to be Janis's attorney in a custody fight?"

Land cleared his throat. "That request will have to come from Mrs. Johnson. But I am also trying to locate the family to share the information from Frank's will. If I hear anything, I'll let you know."

Leslie gave Janis's phone number to Land, thanked him for his help and said she would be in touch, her thoughts turning to Miriam Capstone. Maybe the retired private investigator would be willing to put down her paint brushes and take on one more case.

A quick text to Janis resulted in a photo of Stevie and thoughts Janis had about where the boy might be living with his grandmother.

"THANK YOU!" Janus texted when it became clear that Leslie was going to try to help her regain custody of her son.

"Check with Bruce," Leslie responded.

"My Bruce? If he knew where Stevie was, he would tell me."

"Not necessarily. Loyal to Frank."

"You're probably right," Janis texted, adding a red-faced emoji that appeared to be swearing.

"We'll find him," Leslie responded.

The early evening air was cooling, prompting Leslie to wander over to the lanai to close the sliding door. Whalen, stretched out on his favorite chair, lifted his head to look up at her, then sighed and resumed his nap. As the dock lights nearby popped on in response to the darkening skies, she stood there, staring at the water and thinking about the secrets Frank had kept from her.

What is wrong with me? Always falling for the wrong guys. First, my uptight, controlling husband, Scott. My married boss Brad, who said he was leaving his wife but turned out to be a womanizer of the worst kind who chased me away from my job at the utility. Then Frank. Lots of chemistry but too much baggage. And it turns out, not too trustworthy.

Why can't I fall for a really nice, stable guy who's fun to be with and makes me laugh, who shares my sense of adventure but knows when to put on the brakes and who really cares about me? Why is someone like that so hard to find?

The phone rang. It was Wes Avery.

"Just checking on you," he said. "Got any dinner plans?"

She hesitated, unsure if she really wanted company.

"While you're thinking about it, I got a call from Chip Shelton. He remembered everything that happened that night. If we can get the sheriff's daughter to speak to his state of mind, we can nail the bastard," Wes said.

"Really?" Leslie responded. "Did you say pizza…topped with juicy details?"

CHAPTER 37

Friday morning, January 8

Miriam Capstone returned Leslie's call late Thursday evening and agreed to help find Stevie Johnson and wrest him from the clutches of his grandmother, Georgia. Leslie had texted the boy's photo to the private investigator, along with the few pieces of information she had from Janis. She was confident Miriam would find him.

Now, helping Deb with the last touches for the gala, Leslie's thoughts returned to the discussion she had with Wes about Chip Shelton's memories of the sheriff's actions on the night Toby Mason died. It was a stunning revelation. But like so many things in life, there were no easy answers and proof was elusive.

Wes said he'd reached the same conclusion but was still convinced they would eventually have the answers they were seeking.

As she straightened the artwork for the third time in the Whodunnit section, she thought about Frank and Jamie and the shot on the darkened beach that shattered a part of her humerus and earned her a surveillance team.

She touched her arm, still encased in the cast and sling. She'd gotten used to the lingering discomfort. But she wasn't sure how much longer she could stand having her arm strapped to her body. It definitely cramped her lifestyle. And made walking the dog on a leash difficult and hurty.

"Hey, good morning." Janis swept into the gallery carrying a large bouquet of white daisies and chrysanthemums and flashing a dazzling smile at Deb and Leslie. "Where do these go?"

"Put them on that table, honey." Deb said. "Good to see ya lookin' so happy."

"I am happy, Deb. Thanks to my friend here." She patted Leslie on her good arm. "I got some coffee outside on our picnic table. Join me?"

"You two go ahead," Deb said. "We're almost done here."

The two women sat down at the table where they'd bonded over a bottle of wine and the transgressions of their former husband and boyfriend. Janis took a big gulp of coffee, removed the pink sweater tied around her waist and slipped it over her head.

"I was awake all night," she said. "Excited about Stevie. And then I got to thinkin' again about the shooter – the one that killed Frank and the one that shot you in the arm. Bruce has been discounting my theories, but I'm pretty sure I've finally hit on the right one. I can't keep it from you any longer."

Leslie's felt her adrenaline kick in. "And?"

"Let's assume the two incidents are connected. If some druggie shot Frank and Jamie, he'd be long gone, not patrolling the beach and waiting for us to show. It has to be someone from around here. Someone we know. That's why you and I are going trunk diving."

"Trunk diving? Like dumpster diving?"

"All of my suspects' cars are parked out by the sheriff's office this morning. I saw them on my way here. We'll be checking their trunks for weapons," Janis said.

"You're still thinking it was Harry Fleck or one of his guys? Why would any of them want to kill Frank?"

"If my suspicions are correct, I'll be able to answer that soon," Janis said, draining her cup.

Leslie was on her feet and ready to go. "How do you propose to get into their trunks?"

Janis, who was also getting up from the table, held up an odd-looking device. "I have Bruce's magic key. He confiscated it from a crook breaking into cars by the fire department. Imagine, stealing stuff from our first responders." She shook her head and frowned.

In what Leslie considered would be one of her gutsier moves, she and Janis hopped on the Gallery Centre's red golf cart, making sure they weren't seen by Leslie's bodyguard, and headed for the street where the sheriff and others in law enforcement routinely parked their cars.

Bruce had told Janis that the sheriff, Agent McKechnie, a couple of his men, the deputy and temps were having a meeting to "get things under control...whatever that meant." Bruce was irritated that the sheriff had ordered sandwiches and drinks and assigned him as errand boy to pick them up. That meant a two- to three-hour meeting, at which the sheriff would spend most of the time pontificating about the state of law enforcement and nothing would get done.

"Like Congress," Bruce had said.

The sheriff's office was on one of the village's busier side streets, with a bakery, hardware store, restaurant and construction business. Today the area was alive with golf carts and a steady stream of people and their pets wondering about with no real purpose and acting like they had the right-of-way.

With so much activity in the area, the women were convinced no one would notice them investigating the trunks of parked police cars. Janis had urged Leslie to "just look natural."

"Let's start with the sheriff's vehicle. It's this one," she said, pointing to the familiar white SUV with green and yellow trim.

She pressed the button on the device Bruce had loaned her and the trunk lumbered open, accompanied by a loud beep. There was a 12-pack of toilet paper, several neatly folded blankets, a jacket, a couple of lanterns, a spare tire and jack, a first aid kit and a fire extinguisher. No weapons.

"I guess that's a good thing," Leslie said. "He must keep his guns locked up. Wonder why he has that big thing of toilet paper?"

"Because he's full of it," Janis said, chuckling while Leslie rolled her eyes.

They went through the next three vehicles, all belonging to the sheriff's office, and found similar items. One had a stack of girlie magazines, prompting Janis to check the license plate. "Good thing for Bruce this isn't his truck," she said.

The next vehicle was a Ford 150 SSV. It wasn't part of the sheriff's fleet but had the look of law enforcement about it. Leslie glanced inside and noticed the cupholders each contained a large drink from McDonalds.

"This must be the guys from Miami...the ones that were watching my condo that night," Leslie said.

They were walking toward the trunk when Janis put her hand out to stop Leslie. "Shit. They're coming this way. The meeting can't be over. Bruce said it would last until way past lunch."

She grabbed Leslie's good arm and steered her to a row of fiscus bushes that divided the street from a nearby golf cart path. Standing behind the landscaping cover, they watched as Agent McKechnie and two others got into the vehicle, backed out in a hurry and drove away.

"Damn," Janis said. "The last one and now he's gone."

"That's okay. I don't think those guys had anything to do with the shooting," Leslie said, remembering the story Frank told her about his former partner and good friend.

Frank Johnson and Don McKechnie were cops in a small community in north Florida. One evening they were investigating a drug deal when it deteriorated into a shootout. A teenager, riding his bike home after playing video games with his buddies, was killed in the crossfire. When the investigation was done, it was determined that the bullet that ended the boy's life came from Frank's gun.

Despite pleas from McKechnie that he'd done nothing wrong – that it was just a horrible accident – Frank traded in his police work for odd jobs on a yacht anchored in Tampa. When his boss sailed to the island, Frank jumped ship. He worked and saved enough money for a down payment on his boat, the Dreamcatcher, and went into business for himself. Several years later, he married Janis and Stevie was born.

"Don loved Frank and the feeling was mutual," Janis said. "He was the one that convinced Frank to start workin' undercover. Said if Frank could keep one kid from gettin' involved in drugs and possibly overdosing, it would make up for the shooting years ago.

"Then there was the reward money the feds were willing to give Frank for the drugs he recovered. It was big bucks, and Frank always needed money, I guess for Stevie and me," Janis said. "Especially for me, I was never satisfied. And look what came of that."

She turned from Leslie, looking off into the distance and wiping her eyes with the back of her hands.

"So, like I said, McKechnie and his guys didn't have anything to do with it. If we're looking for suspects, that leaves Harry Fleck," Leslie said.

"Come, listen to my theory. The one Bruce says is bogus." Janis walked over to the bench by the post office and sat down, with Leslie following her lead.

"I don't think McKechnie would let Frank meet Jamie without back-up. After the time was set, I believe Don took his weapon, whatever that might be, and headed for the sand dunes near the fallen tree. He was going to protect his friend.

"As you pointed out, it was a dark night. Frank was wearing a hoodie – a cover-up that McKechnie wouldn't have recognized – and had a goatee just like Jamie. Even with a good night scope, it was tough to see a person's face clearly.

"You said that when Frank left, he had his gun in his waistband. He wouldn't have kept it there if he thought there was any threat from Jamie. But he could have been uncertain, maybe had his hand on it when McKechnie fixed his scope on him."

Leslie sat up straight and pivoted to face Janis. "You're saying that when McKechnie spotted the gun and thought his buddy, Frank, was in danger, he took the shot...not realizing it was the wrong man."

Janis's head was bobbing up and down in agreement. "Then he pointed his scope on Jamie and realized it wasn't Frank...and that he'd killed his friend. That's when he shot Jamie."

"And in the back because Jamie, who saw Frank go down, was running away!" Leslie was breathless in the excitement of the moment.

"You got it!" Janis said so loudly that passersby cast suspicious glances at the women. "If you're a DEA agent, you can't just shoot someone for no reason. It's murder. And McKechnie knew it.

She continued. "Bruce doesn't remember telling McKechnie about our plans to reenact the scene. But over those damn donuts and coffee they're always eating in the sheriff's office, it was bound to slip out. McKechnie took that shot to scare us off. I don't think he cared who he hit as long as he didn't kill one of us."

"Bingo," Leslie enthused. "And if we find McKechnie's weapon and match the bullets with the funny name and same markings...."

"Yeah," Janis interrupted.

Both women had been so focused on the mechanisms of the crime, it suddenly felt to Leslie they'd forgotten the human element. Two men lost their lives; one a criminal and the other not exactly a saint but still a father. She found herself weeping silently for Frank's loss and for the release she felt at hearing a solution that, at long last, had the potential to be right. She hoped for everyone's sake that it was.

CHAPTER 38

Leslie and Janis waited around for another 40 minutes. When Agent McKechnie didn't return, they drove the golf cart back to the Gallery Centre, hugged each other and departed for their separate residences to get ready for the gala.

Back at the condo, Leslie climbed the stairs and fumbled for the keys in her purse. She didn't like locking her door. She didn't worry about it her first few months on the island; she was told that everyone left their doors unlocked. But with the events of the last couple of months and reports in *The Sun* of golf cart thefts, she had become more cautious.

Whalen, still lacking the skills needed for a proper watchdog, was waiting on the other side of the screen door, wiggling and whimpering.

"Gosh, buddy, I wasn't gone that long," Leslie said as she pushed open the screen. Free at last, Whalen exploded forth, nearly knocking her off-balance as he scurried down the steps to the nearby bushes.

Realizing that she, too, had to pee, she dropped her purse in the hallway and trotted toward the bathroom. Taking her shorts off with one arm wasn't near the challenge of getting them back on and then fumbling with the zipper.

When she emerged from the bathroom, she expected Whalen to be waiting patiently for her by the screen door. Except that he wasn't.

She stepped outside and spotted him in the bushes between her condo and the next building – where she'd tried to hide from the criminal Jamie Thompson. The dog had discovered something, was tossing it in the air, catching it and then shaking his head vigorously.

"What have you got, Whalen?" Knowing him, she thought it could be the corpse of some long-dead animal, like a possum or armadillo. When she called his name, he took off running, racing around the parking lot as though being chased by other dogs determined to snatch his prize.

Leslie's security guard remained in his vehicle, apparently assuming that the situation posed no risk to the person he was supposed to be protecting.

"You come back here!" Leslie commanded to no avail. She made her way down the steps toward the frolicking animal, determined to give him a good scolding and call Harry, the island's popular dog trainer on Monday.

Leslie's yelling and the presence of the dog had drawn the attention of the cranky neighbor she thought of as *old Mr. Morgan*. He was inching his way toward the trash bins housed on the other side of the parking lot in a white structure made of fencing.

What appeared to be a very old fishing hat was askew on his head. He had on the same red plaid shirt Leslie had noticed him wearing last week...and maybe the week before. He sent a scowl her direction, shifted his trash bags from one hand to the other and muttered something she couldn't understand.

"Sorry for the noise," she called out to Mr. Morgan. She acknowledged the security guard, then returned her attention to Whalen. "You bad dog; you drop whatever that is. Drop it!"

Whalen, sensing that play time had come to an end, jerked his head upward, opened his mouth and tossed the dark object high into the air. When it landed, it hit the asphalt pavement with a thud.

"Oh my god, the pepper spray!" Leslie said with a startled cry.

The force of the gun smashing against the ground, combined with the weapon's condition after being outside for a prolonged period of time and then being tossed around by a dog, was enough to trigger the now faulty release mechanism. Leslie watched in horror as the pellets ejected and headed in the direction of Mr. Morgan.

"Watch out!" she yelled.

Recognizing that he could be in peril, the old man tossed the trash bags he was carrying into the air and dove for cover behind a white golf cart. When the pellets hit the side of the trash container, the putrid smoke exploded into a cloud that quickly covered a third of the parking lot and was drifting toward his hiding place.

"On dear," Leslie muttered as she covered her mouth and nose with her hand and made her way over to where she could see Mr. Morgan's feet sticking out from behind the cart. The security guard was also at her side.

It felt like a modern-day reenactment of the scene in which the witch is buried under Dorothy's house in the *Wizard of Oz*. But unlike the wicked hag, Mr. Morgan was alive and madder than a wet hen. When he saw her, he pulled himself into a sitting position and glared. "You crazy bitch. I'm gonna sue you for firing a weapon at me."

"I'm so sorry," Leslie said, trying to stifle a giggle at the sight of the cantankerous man whose hat was even further askew but still affixed to his head. She was pretty sure he was okay but asked with genuine concern. "You aren't hurt, are you?"

"This used to be a quiet neighborhood until you moved in," he growled at her and glared at her bodyguard.

He was right, she thought. "I'll clean up your trash and will be happy to compensate you for any pain I caused. Should I call an ambulance?"

"Hell, no. Just get away from me."

He stood up, dusted himself off and turned his back to Leslie, strolling toward his condo as though nothing had happened.

She scurried back to her apartment, picked up several trash bags, while admonishing Whalen for a being a "bad dog," and returned to the parking lot to pick up Mr. Morgan's garbage and put it in one of the large plastic containers. When she glanced in the direction of the security guard who had returned to his car, she could see him looking at her and shaking his head.

Darn it, Wes. You said you would take care of that gun. I could have hurt poor old Mr. Morgan. Just for that you WILL dance with me tonight at the gala.

Leslie had scoured her closet and found a gold lame dress from her "winter" wardrobe. It was one she'd worn years ago to the opening of the Indianapolis Symphony but was still in good condition. Combined with her black sling, with gold sparkles, and dangly earrings, she thought she'd fit in nicely with the mood of the evening.

She chose kitten shoes because she couldn't remember how tall Wes was. At five-foot-seven and with three-inch heels on, she often ended up looking down on her dancing partners.

Wes arrived appearing ill-at-ease in a blue blazer, a pin-striped shirt with open collar and white linen pants. His tan loafers were either new or highly polished, Leslie observed as he stepped inside.

"I feel like a dandy," he grumbled as she handed him a wrap she thought she might need later.

"You look dandy, too," she said, grinning. "I mean, really Wes, you are properly dressed for a tropical gala. Did you get part of your outfit at the island bargain shop?"

"All of it except for the shoes," he said and they both starting giggling and then broke into full-throated laughter.

"It's all for a good cause; student scholarships," Leslie said. "And you know, the blue blazer is a staple in every male closet on this island."

"That's what I was told," he said, remembering that when he bought it, he figured it belonged to someone who was now dead. "Are we off for an evening of fun and frivolity?"

Leslie winked. "Let's see what the night has in store for us."

The band Deb hired from Bradenton for the gala was playing *Walk of Life* by Dire Straits when Leslie and Wes strolled into the large tent outside the Gallery Centre.

The tables had white cloths with blue and white flowers and glittery gold masks as centerpieces – a continuation of the Whodunnit theme, Leslie guessed. Twinkling lights were strung around the tent and the stage where the band played.

Leslie found herself snapping her fingers and bouncing up and down to the music as they headed for Table #4. Her feet wanted to dance but her partner was looking around the tent, for the bar.

When she got his attention, she raised her eyebrows and tilted her head toward the dance floor, which was only half-filled. "Now's a good time. I won't be jostled," she said, looking at her arm.

Wes sighed and followed her toward the wooden boards laid over the grass. A while back, the two of them had watched the movie *Hitch*, taking particular note of the scene where Will Smith is teaching Kevin James how to be a cool dancer. Leslie commented at the time that "just moving back and forth" was a safe step for a man. She hoped Wes remembered that. And it appeared that he did. She thought he handled himself admirably, although she couldn't tell if he was having a good time.

When they stepped off the floor, Janis and Bruce were waiting for them at the table, along with two other couples Leslie didn't know but were introduced as friends of Janis.

"Excuse us," Janis said before Leslie could sit down, "but I need you to come with me. Deb wants our help. You boys get drinks. And don't be afraid to ask any of the single ladies to dance."

Leslie was surprised but went along willingly. "Don't be afraid to ask the other women to dance...are you kidding me?" she said when they were outside.

Janis ignored Leslie's remark and was now pulling her toward the golf cart parked by the side of the Gallery Centre.

"What the hell? I'm not riding in that thing. My hair will get mussed," Leslie groused.

"Forget about your hair. Agent McKechnie's vehicle is parked over by the sheriff's office. I noticed it when Bruce and I drove by. We're checking his trunk," Janis said.

"What?! Do you even have that thingy we were using this afternoon?"

Janis reached in her small beaded handbag and held up the device Bruce had loaned her. "Ta-da!"

Leslie was reluctant, but she could sense that Janis was determined. Leslie had seen her new friend in action before and decided that Janis's reckless streak was even greater than her own.

The sheriff's vehicle and McKechnie's were parked next to each other but not adjacent to the office. Most of the parking spaces near there had been taken by patrons at the corner restaurant. Leslie decided that was a good thing; the DEA Agent wouldn't be able to look out the window and see his vehicle being broken into.

"You stand watch," Janis said as they approached the Ford SSV. She pressed the opening device, heard a beep and watched as the trunk popped open. Janis was soon fully into the vehicle moving around blankets that must have been put there to hid the trunk's contents. "Here it is," she whispered. "It's in a gun safe, and it has a scope!"

Leslie watched Janis back out of the trunk, dragging the weapon and then hoisting it out of the vehicle like she knew what she was doing. "Com'n," she said as she slammed the trunk and carried the gun to the golf cart, placing it on the back seat.

Leslie's mouth dropped open. "You're stealing a gun that belongs to a DEA Agent. Are you nuts?"

Janis had turned on the cart's lights and was waving her hand to encourage Leslie to climb onboard. "What did you think I was going to do? I'm borrowing it. To run a few tests at Mike's shooting range. Don will never miss it."

"Until he does, and we go to jail," Leslie said, glancing around to make sure that her security detail had not tailed her from the gala.

CHAPTER 39

Saturday morning, January 9

It was mid-morning before Wes listened to the two voicemails he received while at the gala where he'd been one of the winners of a Whodunnit painting. It was a mixed-media piece with colorful handmade paper, seeds and feathers displayed in a white frame. He would have kept it for his apartment, but Leslie was oohing and aahing over it, so he gave it to her right before she told him about the theft of the DEA rifle and scope.

He was sure that revelation had prompted him to drink too much and left him with a hangover. He regretted his lapse in judgment when it came to alcohol. He was interviewing Willow Fleck...whatever her last name was... from Indiana this afternoon, although he didn't know a time. He wanted to be in good form.

The first voicemail was from Willow, telling him she was on the island and that she and her mother were deciding the best place to talk, without her father. She would call back on Saturday before lunch. Good news, he thought.

The second message was from Benji Gehrig, attorney-at-law, saying that under no circumstances were Jessi and Sloan Parker willing to speak with the media. And legal blah, blah, blah. Sue you, blah, blah, blah. Don't try to reach them again, blah, blah, blah. Wes hung up before Gehrig finished his recorded rant, his headache crying out for aspirin and hot coffee. A simple *they're not interested* would have sufficed.

He decided to walk from his apartment to the bakery as penance for last night's debauchery and discovered that Leslie had dragged him out on the dance floor one too many times. Who knew that swaying from side to side and snapping your fingers occasionally worked so many muscles? He foresaw two more aspirin in his future.

The mysterious gun with the scope had stayed in the golf cart throughout the gala and then, he assumed, gone home with Bruce and Janis. Wes would have liked to have been a mosquito on the deputy's arm when Janis stuck the weapon in the car and told Bruce to pay no attention to it.

At least she gave Bruce warning as to the whereabouts of the stolen property before Harry Fleck exploded that morning and was still raging about the missing rifle when Wes passed him and Bruce on the street enroute to the bakery.

"Morning sheriff, deputy," Wes said, wishing he had a hat to tip in a genteel manner.

They both mumbled a hello, after which the sheriff returned to his commentary from the spot that Wes assumed had once contained Agent McKechnie's vehicle. "The fucker was right here. I want to know how someone opened the trunk and stole the damn gun…."

Wes glanced over his shoulder as he entered the bakery and saw Bruce, hands on his hips, alternately shaking, then nodding his hand. Unable to resist, Wes signaled a big thumbs up in Bruce's direction. He was sure he saw the deputy crack a slight smile before focusing again on the sheriff's diatribe.

Wes was working on his second cup of coffee when the phone rang and, to his delight, had an Indiana area code. "Willow?" he answered. "Do we have a plan?"

Yes, they were meeting at 2 o'clock in an old garage on Fifth Street that had been converted to a man cave and belonged to a friend of her mother's. He could spend as much time with her as he wanted. But, more important, she said, she wanted her son to meet his paternal grandfather, John Mason.

Wes panicked. It was close to 11 and a Saturday morning. The pale-faced man was known to arrive for his first drink at the Tarpon around 10 on the weekend and be out of it by 11:30 at the latest. Willow wanted her son, Brian Tobias McDonald, to meet his grandfather late afternoon and, she hoped, have dinner with him.

Inwardly, Wes was screaming, *gotta go, gotta go*. "I'm sure we can work that out, and I know that Mr. Mason will be thrilled and honored to be with Brian."

Wes took off in a dead run for the bar, passing the sheriff who was climbing into his vehicle, past the post office and finally through the wooden screen door to the bar.

"Stop!" he yelled as Shine was preparing to put a drink in front of Mason.

"How...many...is...that?" he managed to say, sucking in air between words and regretting the day he took up smoking again.

"No. 2," Shine said, as Mason turned to scowl at Wes and then whirled around to try to wrest the glass out of the bartender's hand.

"Gimme that," he growled.

"We...gotta...talk," Wes said, sitting down beside Mason and still trying to catch his breath. "Give me...a...minute."

He looked around to see if anyone else was there. A man at the end of the bar was scanning the bottles of wine. A few waitresses serving customers in the dining room were running back and forth with drink orders. Other than that, it was just Mason, Wes and Shine.

"Listen buddy," he said, his wind returning. "The night your son was killed, well, he'd learned that day that he was going to be a father." Wes felt his throat tightening with emotion.

The pale-faced man was silent, his hollow eyes riveted on Wes.

"And you have a grandson. He's 20. Born five months after Toby died." Wes's voice was cracking, and as he struggled to speak, he noticed tears streaming down the pale-faced man's sunken cheeks.

"He's here, and he wants to meet you and have dinner with you," Wes said, putting his hand on Mason's shoulder. Mason was weeping openly. Shine was wiping his eyes with a bar rag.

"How did you find….?"

"It was Harry Fleck's wife. She helped us." *Unwittingly*, Wes thought.

"You don't say. God bless her," he said, his shoulders shaking.

"Don't you think you should go home, tidy up the place a bit in case Brian – that's his name, Brian Tobias McDonald – wants to see where you live?"

Mason was off his barstool and embracing Wes; his frail body clinging to the reporter for almost a minute.

"Thank you," he said as he broke free and headed for the door, with no seeming thought to the vodka he was leaving behind.

Shine smiled at Wes and wiped his eyes again as he poured Mason's vodka down the sink. "Damn, man, it's too early for this sentimental stuff," he said then laughed. "I thought when I first met you, now this is a good guy. I'm never wrong about those things. Never wrong."

He extended his hand. When Wes grabbed it, Shine patted him on the arm. "Can I get you something on the house?"

"Later, thanks," he said. "I've still got a lot of work to do today."

Wes and Leslie were at the Fifth Street location shortly before the expected arrival of Willow McDonald and her mother, Regina Fleck. He assumed Brian wouldn't be joining them for this part of their conversation, but he couldn't be sure.

"This was a garage?" Leslie said, eyeing the structure that had a metal roof, white siding and flowering hibiscus bushes around it. A Chicago brick pathway led to a large home nearby.

When the car arrived and Willow and Regina got out, absent Brian, Wes could see that the young woman looked more like her father than her mother. She had his coloring, that curly reddish-brown hair, but not the extra weight Harry carried around his middle. She was lean like a runner or, at the very least, someone who didn't focus on three squares a day.

Regina Fleck was also slender and had a hard face that softened when she smiled. Wes assumed that since she was married to the sheriff, that didn't happen too often. Her eyes looked a little puffy. Wes wondered if she had been crying...maybe with joy at seeing her family. Mason cried when he learned he had a grandson.

The four entered the former garage, now air-conditioned and with a large screen TV and walls lined with bookcases, a desk, leather couch and two matching chairs, a small refrigerator and, in the corner, a bathroom. The large room had a dampish odor, but that was Florida.

He wished he could meet the owners, who obviously relished solitude, contemplative thinking and the literary endeavors of a host of writers, ranging from the classics to contemporary authors. He assumed because of the TV that someone liked sports. He could be happy here even if the place didn't have a full kitchen.

The Fleck women sat down on the couch. Wes and Leslie took the leather chairs; Wes noticing that Willow had reached over and was holding her mother's hand.

"What do you want to know?" she asked.

"Can we start with your relationship with Toby Mason?"

Wes watched Willow scoot closer to her mother. "We met shortly after my 15th birthday. Dad bought me a deep-sea fishing trip and Toby was working as a crew member. He was so cute and attentive. I went home that night and couldn't get him out of my mind. I figured he was a couple of years older than I was and maybe still in high school. But I didn't remember seeing him before.

"About a week later, I was leaving school, walking, and he drove past me in a beat-up truck. I nearly peed my pants. The rush I felt at seeing him was so intense I could hardly breathe. He pulled over to the curb, offered me a ride home and halfway there asked if I wanted to go to the beach instead. I wasn't going to say no.

She looked at her mother, who patted her hand.

"He had a blanket in the back of his truck and a cooler. We sat out there, talking. He was drinking beer but didn't offer me one because he knew I wasn't 21. That made me like him even more. Like he was respectful and everything.

"He talked about the books he was reading. He loved art and would paint something for me, which he did. I still have it. He was sweet and fun and had a beautiful soul.

"This went on for a couple of months – kinda on the sly – and then one day he asked me how old I was. I told him. Just 15. I could see that upset him. When he told me he was 21, I cried. He took me home, and I didn't see him for a couple of weeks.

"Then, one day, there he was in that truck again. He said he couldn't stand not being with me. We were soulmates. But we had to keep our relationship secret. I hadn't told anybody about us, not even my girlfriends. I knew in my heart that he was too old for me, but I didn't care.

"We started having sex…." Her mother looked down and wiped her eyes. Willow kept talking.

"The first time in the shack that belonged to the fishing captain he worked for. And he was so gentle. Right away I wanted more of him. We were having sex two or three times a week and doing a little weed. Nothing serious. Then the captain came by one afternoon late and discovered us in there. It took a little while to find another place, but Toby did. He said he couldn't live without me."

Leslie cleared her throat. "Was he working all this time?"

"Yes, fishing shifts and helping his dad occasionally. And he was also going to community college part time and thinking about getting a new car. We talked about getting married. That wasn't going to happen until I was 18 and out of school, and we both knew it."

"You said you were having sex a lot, were you taking precautions?"

"We were," Willow said. "He always had something with him. Except for the time he didn't. That was just once, and I told him it was okay because I just finished my period. I lied."

Willow looked at her mother whose face had remained loving and supportive throughout her daughter's story. "I never believed anybody who said it could happen like that. But it did. And Brian is proof."

"When did you find out you were pregnant?" Leslie asked.

Wes, who'd been feeling uncomfortable listening to Willow's story, was glad Leslie was with him, seeking answers to questions he would have asked but preferred not to.

"A couple of days before the party I bought a home pregnancy test. I'd missed a couple of periods but was in denial. I almost passed out when I saw the results. When you have a dad like mine, the last thing you want to be when you are 15 is pregnant."

It was Regina's turn to speak. "She came to me that very day. Told me the whole story. I couldn't believe it. We hugged. She was crying and saying that she loved Toby and wanted to have his baby. My God, you're only 15. I remember saying that to her, at the same time thinking about what Harry would do.

"We told him the day before the party," she continued. "I've never seen my husband so angry. I thought he was going to have a stroke. He demanded to know the name of the father. We had to tell him it was Toby Mason. He knew him and was yelling something about statutory rape and how he would arrest him…."

"Did he threaten to kill Toby?" Wes asked.

"No," Regina said.

"Yes," Willow said, still clinging to her mother's hand. "He did, Mom. You know he did. He said I'm gonna kill that fucker."

"Dad went lookin' for Toby that night but never spotted him. I think he was with his father or something because I didn't hear from him until the next day. He said there was going to be a party at Seaside Cottage, and he wanted me to come.

"I met him there early, took him out on the beach and told him I was pregnant. He seemed happy at first and then I could tell it started to weigh on me. I was almost 16 – and he was just 22.

"A baby was a big deal. He asked if I planned to get an abortion, and I told him no. He seemed okay with that. I mean, he told me not to drink when they were playing that stupid card game. When it was about 10, he told me to go home so I wouldn't get in trouble with my folks.

"Dad had been looking for me, figuring I was out with Toby, I guess. When I was walking home, I saw his car coming down the road and hid behind the bushes. I got home, went to bed and didn't see him until the next morning.

"He looked awful when he came down. Like he hadn't slept. That's when he told me that Toby had been shot, and that I was leaving town and going to my aunt's in Indiana until 'the brat was born,' and he'd decide what we were going to do with it.

"When I packed my bags, I knew I was never coming back. And wouldn't have if it wasn't for your call and then my discussion with Mom. After talking to her, I decided that I wanted my son to meet both of his grandfathers. Especially Toby's dad."

"Why's that so important now?" Leslie asked.

"Mr. Avery told me that Mr. Mason wasn't in the best of health, and then mom told me about Dad," she said.

"What about your Dad?" Wes asked.

"I guess you wouldn't know," Regina said, her lip quivering. "Harry has a terminal illness. The doctor gave him less than a month to live."

CHAPTER 40

Saturday afternoon, January 11

Brian McDonald had that Midwestern quality that Wes always liked: friendly, open, willing to meet strangers and hear what they had to say. He had a firm handshake and stood up straight, making him appear a little taller than his 5-foot-10 frame.

Wes was introduced to the young man, even as the reporter was reeling from the news that Harry Fleck was essentially a dead man walking. How this was going to affect Wes's plans for a story that would reveal all to the community and give Toby Mason the justice he deserved was still a question mark.

It felt like God was going to mete out Harry Fleck's punishment, and John Mason would have what he'd been seeking all these years…and more. Maybe that was enough. At any rate, none of it was Brian's issue.

The young man was in the front seat of Wes's SUV; his mother and Leslie in the back, and they were on their way to John Mason's residence, with Wes hoping that everything was going to be fine when they arrived.

Brian was expressing wonderment at everything he saw. "Wow this is cool. Look at those palm trees. What's that big lizard called? How old is my grandfather and has he lived here a long time?"

He seemed younger than his 20 years and that was okay with Wes. Naivete was an admirable quality these days when so many kids had become so worldly so young, thanks to social media. Innocence was something to be held onto and treasured. It appeared to Wes that Willow had given her son a sheltered upbringing.

As he drove, Wes prayed that the pale-faced man hadn't gone home and decided to have a celebratory nip before cleaning up himself and his residence. If he was drunk when his grandson showed up, Wes would be done with Johnny Boy. Forever.

The first thing Wes noticed when he pulled his vehicle in front of Mason's house was that the old Volvo had been moved to a less noticeable position at the side of the house. The sign about drugs was gone, and the front door was open, perhaps to air out the premise.

"John, we're here," he yelled as he rapped on the siding beside the front door.

"Be right there," was the response.

Within seconds, Wes could hear John Mason striding across the living room. When he appeared at the door, he was wearing a camp shirt with khaki slacks and clean white sneakers. His hair was neatly combed and his face close shaven. He smelled of Old Spice, but the fragrance – Wes wondered how old it was – was not overpowering.

Mason looked expectedly at Wes, then Leslie and then settled on Brian who was standing at the rear of the group. The old and worried face looked better than usual, but it suddenly contorted as if he would burst into tears. Mason caught himself and directed a broad smile the young man's direction.

"You look so much like your dad," he said, stepping forward and wrapping his arms around Brian, who returned the hug.

Leslie and Willow had tears running down their cheeks; they exchanged little smiles and followed the men into the house.

Mason ushered the group into a living room that practically sparkled; even the windows were spotless. The newspapers and boxes were gone. Most of the dusty knickknacks had been removed. How Mason had been able to clean everything so quickly was a question the old man answered without being asked.

"My neighbor came over and helped me when she heard I was meeting my grandson for the first time," he said, beaming. "That's what folks are like on this island, Brian."

There were lemonade and cookies on the coffee table and not a bottle of alcohol to be seen.

"We don't want to interfere with your family reunion," Wes said after a few minutes. "Leslie and I have a couple of errands to run. You call me and I'll pick up Brian and his mom when you're ready."

"Aren't you going to stay for dinner?" Mason asked. "My neighbor has fixed some dish with chicken. Says it's her specialty."

"Sounds good but no, thanks. You take your time and enjoy yourselves," Wes said.

As he and Leslie were leaving, he noticed that Mason had gotten up from the chair he was sitting in and was heading for the shelf that held the photograph of a 14-year-old Toby Mason, proudly showing off the fish he'd caught.

ᴇᴏ ᴄᴇ

"What do we do now?" Leslie asked as she and Wes drove away.

"I thought we'd go back to your condo, have a glass of wine and wait around for the sunset and the call from Willow," Wes said.

"Think bigger picture," Leslie said, eyeing Wes with a strange expression on her face. "We learned today that Harry Fleck, who is dying by the way, was tracking Toby Mason and in the mood to kill him because the guy had gotten his underage daughter pregnant.

"That's for starters. We also know that Janis was taking Agent McKechnie's rifle – with powerful scope – to the shooting range to fire and capture one or two of the bullets. We planned on returning the weapon to its rightful place before anyone noticed it was missing. But that's not going to happen. So, what do we do now?"

Wes wanted to think about his options in regard to the Toby Mason shooting. Maybe even discuss the situation with *The Sun's* publisher, Sara Fortune. He remembered telling his former boss that sometimes facts get in the way of a good story. He wished today's reporters had that attitude – that willingness to search for the truth instead of publishing anything they were told and by sources with an agenda.

His problem was that he didn't have absolute proof that Harry Fleck smothered Toby Mason even though he had a strong motive to want him dead. The autopsy, which was conducted twice, and the subsequent coroner's report said the young man died of a self-inflicted gunshot wound to the head. The photographs taken that night told a similar tale.

If Fleck was dying, as his wife said, why throw gasoline on embers that were only kept alive in the mind of some in the community? Newcomers didn't know about the shooting. If Wes told Randy Long his theory, maybe the newspaper's layout man could spread the word among the insiders who had long grumbled about a lack of justice for Toby. With Fleck gone, there wouldn't be much else to say; no need for vengeance.

He was also convinced that Fleck had beaten up Mason, sending him to the hospital to keep him quiet; just as he'd threatened the kids 20 years ago. But the pale-faced man didn't appear to want a legal reckoning. And now that he had a grandson that was almost the perfect likeness of his dead son, didn't need to. His journey – his search for the truth – had ended happily and with a chance to start over.

"I don't know," was Wes's honest answer to Leslie's question. "Bruce is gonna have to help us."

The deputy was behind the sheriff's large desk, busily typing on a computer when Leslie and Wes arrived. He looked frazzled and out-of-sorts.

"Ya know, Harry's got cancer," he said when Leslie took a seat by the desk and Wes stopped at the coffee pot for what he assumed would be stale caffeine. "I guessed it weeks ago but didn't say anything."

"Yes, we heard that today from Regina," Leslie said.

"He confirmed it for me this morning when we were tryin' to figure out what happened to the agent's gun. One of us knew about the stolen weapon and didn't like lyin' to his boss," he said.

Bruce got up from the desk and started pacing. Wes took a sip of the coffee, grimaced and sat the cup down.

"I feel like we're all part of a conspiracy and could go to jail. I don't like it, I'm tellin' you I don't like it," he said turning to Wes and Leslie with a strained look on his face. "What the hell am I supposed to do? The whole thing is a fucked-up mess."

"I'm no legal scholar," Wes said, "but I do think Agent McKechnie is culpable in the shooting death of Frank and Jamie. Maybe involuntary manslaughter in Frank's case; murder when he shot Jamie in the back. And there's the wounding of Leslie. Do you think the sheriff suspects?"

The deputy nodded. "Those guys have known each other for years, and Frank and McKechnie was as tight as a duck's arse. You gotta understand that law enforcement people stick up for each other. And it was a mistake that McKechnie's gonna pay for the rest of his life…one way or the other."

The hush that followed the deputy's comments was broken by Janis, who sailed into the office holding a plastic bag with several bullets in it. "Hey, baby, I got it. Fired that puppy and Matt collected the bullets for me. Now we just have to get the rifle back in McKechnie's vehicle somehow…what's the matter?" She looked first at Bruce, then at Wes and finally Leslie.

"He already knows its missing," the deputy said.

Janis plopped down in the chair next to Leslie and scratched her head. "Guess we have to come up with a Plan B. Any thoughts?"

Nobody responded so Janis got up and was now the one pacing. "We gotta confront 'em. Get the other agents or some DEA bigwigs here and ask 'em – the sheriff and McKechnie – straight out."

Leslie was nodding vigorously and saying "yes" under her breath.

"They'll deny it," the deputy said.

"Then we show 'em the bullets, which means we hang onto McKechnie's rifle," Janis said. "I wore plastic gloves when I shot it so my fingerprints won't be on it – and his will."

Wes marveled at Janis's good instincts; a match for Leslie's when it came to figuring things out.

"Damnit. I'll make the call. On Monday," Bruce said. "But we gotta leave Harry out of this. It's the least we can do for him."

There were so many things he wanted to say in response, but Wes kept his mouth shut.

It was nearly 7 when Willow called to say that she needed to be picked up. Brian was staying with his grandfather, and they were going fishing in a borrowed boat with a captain the next morning.

"It looks like everyone had a good time," Wes said when he walked in the door of Mason's house and was greeted by the sound of laughter.

"This is a fine boy. His mother raised him right," Mason said, patting his grandson on the back. "He's going to spend the night here. Wants to stick around and help me out. He's interested in the antique business. Can you believe that?"

Wes reflected on the happy thought that Shine was losing his best customer and would be pleased about that, even as he might miss the company of the old Johnny Boy. He also noticed there was a pink glow on the cheeks of the former pale-faced man.

When she'd kissed her son goodbye and thanked his grandfather for a "wonderful afternoon," Willow and Wes headed for the front door with Mason tagging along. "I can't thank you both enough," he said. "You've given me a reason to live."

Back at Wes's car, they discovered Leslie sitting there with an odd look on her face. "Call your mother," she said, handing Willow the phone. "Best do it outside the car. Over there. You'll get better reception."

Wes waited until Willow was out of earshot before turning to Leslie with a questioning look on his face.

"It's Harry Fleck," she said. "He's dead."

"What?! So soon?" Wes mentally added another person to the growing body count on the island. "What happened?"

Leslie told him that when Regina got home, she found a note from her husband saying that he couldn't go through the ordeal of dying for another month. He wanted to go out on his own terms. She'd find him at the back of the small lake behind their house – on the bench. Now that Willow was back home, he hoped that she and Brian would stay and make a life in Florida so Regina wouldn't be alone.

"She didn't notify anyone right away because she wanted to leave Harry out there alone in a peaceful spot for a while, and she didn't want to spoil Brian's reunion with his other grandfather," Leslie said. "There was also a note for Bruce, but Regina didn't open it."

Wes was shaking his head and wondering what would happen next. He hoped the note would give Bruce clarity on how to handle the McKechnie situation, but he couldn't be sure that Harry would make it easy on his deputy.

Willow returned to the car dry-eyed. "I'm not going to tell Brian just yet. He didn't know either of his grandfathers, and now he has one he's delighted to be with. That's enough. Can you take me home? My mother needs me."

CHAPTER 41

Sunday morning, January 10

There was a black wreath on the door of the sheriff's office. Inside, the deputy was surrounded by five or six uniformed men from the law enforcement community, none of whom Wes recognized.

For all of Sheriff's Fleck's faults, he was someone the people of the village had respected for more than 20 years. Not everything he did was worthy of praise, but he was considered by his peers and those who didn't know him all that well to have a good record and be a dedicated civil servant.

As he stood listening to the men around him reminisce, Wes made his decision. Harry Fleck's reputation would not go down the toilet based on a 20-year-old crime that he may have committed in the heat of passion and that couldn't be proven anyway. No sense in having a one-day story ruin more lives and vilify a man who wasn't completely evil.

What amazed him was that Fleck's fellow policemen were lauding the way the sheriff chose to end his life; not with a whimper but a bang from his personal gun, a Ruger Max-9 he'd purchased for himself for Christmas. It may have been the first time he fired the weapon, which in itself was poetic, the others said.

I guess you have to do what you have to do, Wes thought. He was reasonably sure he would die hooked up to tubes, in a sterile hospital room and in the company of a nursing assistant who'd arrived to clean up his bed pan. Such was life. Or in this case, death.

Although he was in the center of the group of men, Deputy Webster seemed detached from the others. Wes observed a white envelope in his pocket and the expression of someone who didn't quite know what was happening.

"What did the letter say…if you want to share it with me?" Wes said, sidling up to the deputy and addressing him quietly.

The deputy reached into his pocket and pulled out the envelope, handing it to Wes.

To Deputy Bruce C. Webster

From Sheriff Harry Fleck

As you now know, I have taken my own life in the manner befitting someone of my status. I didn't want to waste away for another month or so, making everyone around me suffer. I'm okay with this, deputy. You should be, too.

I planned on asking DEA Agent Don McKechnie to be my replacement. Not because you don't have it in you to be sheriff, but because you need a little more experience and backbone. I thought Don could help, but I came to realize that certain circumstances made that impossible.

I sent a letter to the county officials suggesting that you be my replacement. I also alerted them to the role Don played in the deaths of Frank Johnson and Jamie Thompson and in the assault on the beach. Since he is a federal agent, county will need to notify the DEA what happened. I expect him to be under arrest by the time you read this.

I would have taken these actions against Don sooner – after he confessed to me – but he's a good man and the shootings were a mistake that could have happened to anyone. Still, after reviewing the situation, I concluded that a killer shouldn't be shielded just because he is a law enforcement officer. It taints the good ones when that happens.

I assume you have knowledge of what happened to the rifle in the back of his vehicle and are having the bullets tested to see if they match those found in the body of Jamie Thompson. I am not stupid, Bruce. And you do not have a poker face. That information will be helpful in building a case against McKechnie should he decide to plead not guilty to any charges. Don't lose the damn bullets.

Thanks for your service. Good luck. It will be tough on you at first, but you'll get the hang of it. Try not to spend too much time with that Elliott woman and her reporter friend. They are nothing but trouble. The back-up remote for the TV is in the drawer under the coffee pot.

Your former boss and friend,

Harry Fleck

The deputy sighed. "Kind of funny how he mentioned the remote. He'd get mad at me because he could never find it after my shift. So, he bought a spare. That was Harry, always keeping things buttoned-up and in-line."

He pulled his khaki handkerchief from his back pocket, rubbed his eyes and blew his nose. The fact that the deputy could shed a few tears for the man he'd worked with for so many years – flawed as he was – was a good thing, Wes thought.

When Don McKechnie was handcuffed and taken from his office, he didn't protest but wept silently. His tears were not just for himself and his bleak future as a murderer but for his beloved friend Frank Johnson, the brother-in-arms he had killed.

As he walked out of the building that housed the DEA, flanked by two grim-looking fellow agents who'd worked with him for more than a decade, he relived that night, wishing he was the one who hadn't survived.

The bastard wants to meet Frank alone. That's not happening. I know the spot; I'll find my way there, take cover behind a dune. Damn this darkness. Glad I've got my night scope. If Jamie makes the wrong move, I'm taking him out, and answering for it later if I have to. He's a drug dealer. No one cares about wasting a drug dealer. Frank'll back me up.

Yeah, here's a good spot. Just gotta lay down here, use this piece of driftwood to position the gun. There, that works. Now I can scan the area. Shit. Jamie's already there. Son-of-a-bitch. He's got his gun in his waistband so maybe he's not looking for trouble. I can see him fairly clearly. The hoodie. The beard. The laser range finder says I'm 300 yards away. Easy shot, especially since the air is cool.

Where's Frank? Come on, buddy, let's get this over with. You take him down, and I'll show myself and back you up. Your girlfriend will be safe, and this mess will be over.

I'm just gonna put my crosshairs right on your ugly face, Jamie. Move around a bit. Fuck, he's reaching for the gun…and looking the other direction. Frank's coming and won't be able to see him. I gotta take the shot. Gotta take the shot.

Bingo! He's down. Now where's Frank? Gotta be close by. Moving my scope, moving my scope. There he is, running the other way? Why is he running away? Oh no. God. No. It's not Frank. It's Jamie. I killed Frank. Pull the trigger, asshole. Pull the trigger, motherfucker. He can't get away. Pop! My God, Frank, I swear I didn't know it was you. My brother. I'm sorry.

CHAPTER 42

Wednesday, January 13

B ecause Willow was eager to return to Indiana to pack up and put her house on the market, Regina Fleck opted to have the sheriff's funeral at the Catholic Church on Wednesday morning. The good Father, revered by people of all faiths on the island, agreed to say kind words about his departed friend who, truth be told, was a bit of a lapsed Catholic.

Leslie had received a phone call as Wes was waiting on her to finish getting ready for the funeral. She'd told him she would be awhile and apologized, saying she would drive herself to the service.

His curiosity was piqued. He was a little concerned that she was already involved in another nefarious activity without putting this one to bed. She'd tell him soon enough, he thought. Like him, Leslie was not good at keeping secrets.

The interior of the historic church – dark and with statues of religious figures throughout – was too small for the crowd that wanted to pay their final respects to the sheriff. The number of folding chairs needed in the church courtyard grew quickly, with Wes and Bruce and several other men busily adding more as the service drew near.

When Leslie and then Janis arrived, their seats were toward the back of the gathering and, unfortunately, not in the shade of the giant Royal Palm trees that flanked the sacred structure.

Because of the sun, Wes thought it a good thing that Leslie was wearing a big straw hat. Then he took a second, admiring glance and decided she looked way too amazing to be attending a funeral for a man she didn't particularly like.

Besides the hat, she had on a black sleeveless sheath, a large black and white polka dot belt that cinched her waist and spectator pumps. He knew little of fashion but thought spectator pumps had gone out of style a couple of decades ago. On Leslie they looked like a fashion statement with new life breathed into it.

Janis was also decked out – that was the term that came to Wes's mind – in a navy V-neck dress with spaghetti straps and a 12-inch border of white daisies around the hemline. Circling her neck was a three-strand beaded necklace. Wes thought she still looked too good for Bruce but deferred to the old saying that love is blind.

The rituals lasted about 20 minutes, followed by a eulogy from Harry Fleck Jr. His message, though delivered with little outward emotion, was a nice tribute to the father he seldom saw.

During the service, Leslie kept looking over her shoulder. When the last hymn was playing and the family was filing out of the church, Leslie got out of her seat and rushed for the entry gate.

"What's with her?" Bruce asked, leaning past Janis.

"Best not to ask, Bruce. Now that you're about to be sworn in as sheriff, I'm pretty sure you won't want to know. Follow the advice Harry gave you about us."

All three laughed, then stood up to acknowledge the members of the Fleck family as they walked into the courtyard and headed for the street. A reception was to be held at the island hotel afterward. Wes remembered how the secretary at his former newspaper would go to funerals and bring back cake for the late shift. He wondered if funeral cake was still a thing.

Out of the corner of his eye, he could see Janis leaning forward and staring at a smallish figure, head down, walking, then skipping her way.

"Oh my God! Stevie! My Stevie!" she shrieked. She pushed past Wes and the remaining mourners to throw her arms around a boy, about 13, with unruly brown hair and a t-shirt that said *I paused my game to be here*. He'd emerged into the nearly empty courtyard with Leslie and the private investigator Miriam Capstone behind him.

"Sorry to make such a dramatic entrance," Miriam said to Wes when she reached his side. "His grandmother was a pain in the butt. I wasn't sure she was gonna let me take him. But I had a paper from Frank's lawyer so what could she do? He and I hightailed it here. Leslie didn't say this address was for a funeral, or I would've dressed better."

Wes grabbed her hand and pumped it vigorously. "Why did you get out of the private eye business? You're so good."

"You won't think so when Leslie gets my bill," she chuckled. "Oh, it won't be that bad. He was easy to find, and he's a nice kid."

Both Leslie and Janis had surrounded the boy, with Janis running her fingers through his hair and leaning over now and then to plant a kiss on his cheek. He was almost as tall as his mother, and Wes thought he looked like his father, Frank. He wondered what Leslie would think about the resemblance.

"Oh, baby, I'm so glad to have you home. Mommy loves you so much," Janis said. She looked over at Leslie and smiled warmly. "You are something else. I know now why Frank loved you."

Leslie returned the smile. Wes saw her mouth the words: *Did he?*

Bruce stepped into the little circle and reached out to shake Stevie's hand. The boy looked at him and threw his arms around the deputy's waist, giving him a lingering hug. Wes felt himself choking up. He marveled at how emotional he'd felt these past two days.

"I think we got the makings of a family," Bruce finally said, his face reddening.

Janis looked at him and then at her son. "Did that sound like a proposal to you, Stevie?"

"Uh-huh," the boy said.

Wes turned from the happy threesome to see Leslie rubbing her arms as the sun snuck behind gathering gray clouds, the wind picked up and a few raindrops could be felt.

"Chilly? This will help." He slipped his blue blazer over her shoulders.

Leslie smiled and used her good arm to pull the coat tighter. "Isn't it amazing how we were able to tie everything up in a neat little package? We make a good team."

Wes shifted from one foot to the other and hesitated, unsure if he should respond or let her comment go. He finally spoke. "I don't want to burst your bubble, but I was rereading Toby's autopsy report again last night. Not sure why. And it stated plainly that the concussion from the gun cracked his skull and sent fragments into his brain. If Harry smothered him, as we believe he did, he was murdering someone who wasn't going to survive anyway."

He could tell Leslie was surprised by his comment. "I don't know what to say. Wes. I mean, Harry was guilty on so many levels," she said.

He continued. "I agree. But also, we never figured out where the gun came from, why Toby picked it up and shot himself, why Harry was able to get by with sloppy police work and intimidating the partygoers and Mason all those years," Wes said. "I'd say our package has plenty of loose paper and not enough string."

Leslie sighed, a hurt look on her face. "At least we solved Frank's and Jamie's murders…and my wounding."

Wes cocked his head to one side and prepared to deliver what he assumed would be more bad news to his friend. "Did we? Janis got the gun and tested the bullets. But it was Harry that told the officials about McKechnie. You and I didn't have much, if anything, to do with that. Except that you paid a physical price for our little reenactment and had to put up with a bodyguard for several days."

"You sure know how to make a girl feel inadequate." Leslie gave Wes a scowl and then squared her shoulders. "But you can't argue this. If we hadn't nosed around, none of this would have been resolved."

"No, I can't." He turned to watch Janis, Bruce and Stevie head for the parking lot, and then refocused on Leslie. "And you did help reunite Stevie and his mother. So, because you were willing to step into the fray and pay a price with your injured arm, I have a proposal for you."

"You do? What might that be," she said, a quizzical smile on her face – one that said she wasn't angry about Wes's comments.

"Remember when you went with Jamie to Key West and visited Hemingway's house? I've always wanted to do that," he said.

"You're not a drug dealer, you don't appear to have criminal friends and you don't have a private plane. I guess I can handle another trip to Key West," Leslie responded. "As long as we drive."

Wes laughed. "It will do us good to get away for a couple of days. And since everyone thinks you're the one that usually starts trouble, we can be sure nothing bad will happen while we're gone."

In the distance, the bells from the First United Church clanged, then stopped, then sounded again before falling silent.

"What was that? I haven't heard those bells since I've been on this island," Leslie said, remembering that Pastor Billy Cordray had announced that the next time the church bells rang would be to celebrate "glorious news."

"Beat's me. And we're not going to find out," Wes said, guiding Leslie toward her car as the wind and rain picked up. "Not until we return from Key West."

When Leslie was behind the wheel and Wes was standing outside the car, getting wet as he waited chivalrously for her to find the keys in her over-sized purse, he noticed she had stopped looking and was dabbing at her eyes with a tissue. Was she crying? He wondered why after all that had happened, she was suddenly so emotional.

"There's one more thing we have to do before we leave," she finally said, her voice cracking. "I've been thinking about it all morning. And it's the right thing to do, Wes. Even though it breaks my heart."

The reporter stared at her for a minute, then in painful realization took out his own handkerchief and wiped his eyes. "Whalen has to go back to Stevie. Frank would have wanted that," he said, softly.

She nodded, looked at Wes with tears filling her eyes again, and drove off.

ABOUT THE AUTHOR

S usan Hanafee is an award-winning former journalist whose career as a reporter for *The Indianapolis Star* spanned three decades. She formerly headed corporate communications for IPALCO Enterprises and Cummins Inc. She resides in southwest Florida.

Hanafee's blogs can be found on www.susanhanafee.com. Her previously published books include *Red, Black and Global: The Transformation of Cummins* (a corporate history); *Rachael's Island Adventures* (a collection of children's stories); *Never Name an Iguana* and *Rutabagas for Ten* (essays and observations on life); *Leslie's Voice*, a novel, in which her heroine Leslie Elliott is introduced, and the sequel, *Scavenger Tides*, a mystery.